Chef Chronicle

by Jim Ruch

Chef Chronicle

Guild Multimedia
pajovajim@gmail.com
chefchronicle.com

To my parents.
My father for giving me my first copy of Larousse Gastronomique with the inscription:
"Make sure you get the words right." and my mother for telling me
"Your final coat (of varnish) is only as good as all the coats beneath."

Acknowledgments

I'd like to first thank some of my non-living heroes. Not only for their great bodies of work tangible and not, but also for their grit, humility, sarcasm, and above all for carrying on through seemingly insurmountable difficulties to leave us their inspiring legacies: Michelangelo di Lodovico Buonarroti Simoni, Leonardo di ser Piero da Vinci, Meriwether Lewis, and Jerome John Garcia. I also need to thank all the historians who've taken the time to document these and other legacies.

I've been very fortunate in my career as a chef to have worked with some great chefs, captains, crew, and owners. I forged a long road up this mountain witnessing craters, washouts, and some fine overlooks. Thanks for your confidence, standing by me and telling me when I needed to get my act together.

Special thanks to Phyllis Peterson, my longtime friend. For believing in me from way back; supporting my music and with the stellar graphics and design, then and for this project. Patience and understanding are the marks of true mastery.

• • •

Table of Contents

Preface

The setting for this story came to mind riding home in a New York taxi. I was working midtown as a cook at a famous old Irish restaurant. I'd just gone to seven performances of the Jerry Band at the Lunt Fontaine. The Theatre had opened in 1910, and I was overwhelmed by the architecture and beautiful woodwork. Having studied classic food, I regarded cooking as an art form. The Theatre seemed a perfect setting for a restaurant.

Rome

The restaurant is located near The Pantheon. It occupies a renovated three-story building that dates back to the thirteenth century. There's no sign outside and only a few people in Rome know it exists. Fewer dine there.

Three blocks away a man dressed as a bricklayer unlocks a small metal door. The dusty cobalt blue work coat makes him invisible. He's been coming into Rome without anyone noticing for years.

Down a long stone staircase, he enters an aqueduct illuminated by lanterns and dancing shadows. In a carpeted recess a small wash basin and towel are set out. Hanging on the wall is a garment bag holding a lightweight, black silk suit. He sends a text to his old friend Lorenzo upstairs to let him know he's arrived. A small modern elevator carries him up five flights to the third-floor dining room.

Conversation stops and the four men at the table stand as he enters the room. He's clean-shaven, tanned, and fit. Seventy years of clean living and a simple diet have served him well.

Lorenzo Orsini steps forward. He's thin, elderly, and also elegantly tailored. Although he's been a cardinal for nine years, he rarely wore the traditional attire outside Vatican City. This is highly irregular, but being a Freemason in the Roman Catholic Church meant he didn't play by the rules to begin with. Offering an introduction in English he opens, "Papa, buona sera. This is Mike Ambrose. The gentleman who knows Licio."

The guest of honor looks around the table and quotes Caesar Augustus in Vulgar Latin, "There's a stranger in our sandbox. Are we hosting a burial?" He raises his eyebrows.

Across the table are Roberto Salvi, a banker, and Angelo Vilotti, Vatican Secretary of State. Mirth is in the eye of the beholder.

The man in black commands the room. He looks at their guest's features and clothing and holds out his hand, "Michele." His voice is like rich dark gravy. He uses the elegant Italian pronunciation, *mi-KEH-leh*. "Is this true? Our chef Licio was recording our dinner conversations for more than ten years?" He smiles faintly.

Mike addresses him as instructed, but surprises Lorenzo by speaking Italian, "It is Papa. There are menus catalogued by both date and dinner guests. From Rome to Sao Paulo. The conversations are transcribed in screenplay format. It's a work of art, and what meals they must have been!" This is spoken in a lilting dialect. As he finishes, he holds his arms out to the table.

The room is oddly silent. Mike Ambrose, thirty-seven-year-old freelance journalist, stands a burly five-nine. His eyes are animated like a child's, belying a fox's intellect. Lorenzo is intrigued by Mike.

Papa continues to look directly at Mike as they all settle into their seats, "So you've seen this *work of art*. And are there any names you recognize in this *chronicle*?"

Mike returns his attention. He'd been watching the young nun pouring wine. "I've seen parts of it. But I don't have any idea who or what it's about," he lies, looking at his glass. Mike begins to realize these men are likely the main players from the recordings and it gives him an uncomfortable chill. He knows exactly what the conversations represent. "He told me about it in passing one day. He's got all kinds of interesting stories."

"I still don't believe it," says Salvi.

Mike reaches for his glass of wine and scans the table. The theme "Last Supper" resonates. There's no escape and these cats are ready to pounce. He looks at the menu card but doesn't pick it up. Everything seems very real.

Papa picks up his menu card and smiles. Speaking to Lorenzo in the informal Latin he asks, "Gianario De'Veneto? I see quenelles, and I know he loves quail. The broth is always like velvet, tell me again how he clarifies the broth?"

Lorenzo smiles as he looks at the menu card. "Yes, Gianario is in the kitchen. He clarifies his broth with smashed olive branches bound with quail's egg whites and young onion shoots. His aunt lives on a big farm in east Lazio. He's got her feeding the birds mineral water now. Good for the bones he says. He's keeping her very busy." Lorenzo raises his eyebrows.

Mike remains still, wondering what's next. Papa smiles as his old friend continues. "Tonight, an amber broth with the quenelles roasted dark. *The Hunt Dinner.*" He pauses and smiles nostalgically.

• • •

The dining room is spacious. It has a high ceiling and windows covering an entire wall. There is a large bookcase opposite and dark walnut paneling throughout the room. The draperies are pulled back to display the views. Over a stretch of rooftops, the hills of western Lazio disappear into a hazy Roman summer sunset. The table is grand; laid simply for five but dwarfed by the space.

Three young nuns are serving the meal. They're from a convent on Spain's Costa Brava and are known to sing for their guests after dinner. They speak only Spanish and do not understand Italian, English, or Latin.

Looking over the rim of his glass, Mike makes eye contact with the young woman pouring wine. Her skin has the tone of fine butter. The simple coif of coarsely woven silk frames her face. She has shining dark chocolate brown hair and eyes the shade of hazelnut. He marvels at the complete beauty of what he knows to be pure Spanish genes.

• • •

Lorenzo continues in Latin, "When I spoke to Gianario last week to set tonight's menu, I asked him, as I always do, if he's heard from Licio. He tells me he's received this package from Licio, copies of menus they'd prepared together with a list of guests and dates."

"What a coincidence. Have you seen the package?" Papa asks.

Lorenzo pauses. "Yes. It's here. We'll look at it later. I still can't believe it," he says. "It's pure genius."

"Licio was always a purist," He says and picks up his spoon, turning it over in his hand. Admiring the polish, he adds, "He's learned from the best." He looks at Lorenzo and smiles. "But I think he may have beaten you at your own game."

"Thank you. And I can only wonder what our friend Mike really knows," Lorenzo puts down his glass. He frowns, both fists on the edge of the table. Speaking softly, continuing in Latin he says, "I've always known it was wrong what we've done to his father, commissioning his sculptures for so cheap and reselling them as Ancient Roman works for such profit. I also know Ligurians don't forget such things." He leans back. "I should have known if Licio found out, he would never forget."

"Don't forget it was a very profitable enterprise. It funded your, what did you call it? With the Paraguayans?" Papa says.

Lorenzo nodded. "Yes, the *incursion*." He smiles. "That went very well, all considering."

"It did. And it was a brilliant orchestration with a noble cause." Papa makes a humbug gesture. "We need to talk to Licio. Find out where he stands, he can't want for anything. He's got plenty of money."

Papa unfolds his napkin and continues in Latin to the man across from him. "Roberto, Banco Ambrosso is crashing. What do you think, less than a month?"

Roberto Salvi is Italian. He speaks only rudimentary Latin and understands nothing of the rapid Vulgar style spoken by Lorenzo and Papa. He's a short balding man, aged beyond his years. Like the others, his suit is also very expensive but not in the classic style. Lorenzo always thought Salvi's manner garish at best. Salvi is smoking a cigarette and seems to be perspiring. He is chairman of the failing Banco Ambrosso. The fall-out from this financial collapse will impact the Milan stock exchange and the Vatican Bank. It will destroy numerous political and banking careers and a handful of people will die because of it. The realization that he will likely go to prison is beginning to take its toll. As per protocol, he responds to Papa in Latin, "Six to seven weeks." he says.

"Yes," Papa says. He turns to Lorenzo, "I'm more interested in our new friend here. What does he know?"

"I've a complete background on him. Tomorrow we'll know more. I have a very close eye on him." Lorenzo taps his cheekbone.

"And do you think Licio knows I'm not dead?"

"No. I am positive he doesn't, nor does anyone else, I'd know about it. It's only Angelo and myself who know. With the mustache, sunglasses, and hairpiece I can hardly recognize you. Besides you were only in office for thirty-three days and we've eliminated nearly all the public images of you. And also, those who didn't believe you are dead." Lorenzo glanced down at Papa's hand. "Deus Meus Albi. You're wearing your ring." Lorenzo says abruptly, gently putting his hand over the ring. Papa looked at Lorenzo with eyes slightly widened and slowly put his hands in his lap, removed the ring, and put it in his pocket without anyone noticing.

Chef Giancarlo comes out to plate the consommé of quail on a side table.

The three quenelles are chestnut brown. They're crispy and served in a large shallow bowl, waist deep in consommé. The small egg-shaped morsels are made of quail, onion, thyme, quail's egg yolk, and cream. The small, skinned birds had been braised in stock, their meat picked off the bones and pounded in a mortar and pestle. The broth is a rich amber color, and Mike can clearly see the red and gold motif on the bottom of the bowl.

The fine white and black habits of Catalonia flutter as the nuns seem to float to the table. Their bare fingertips have polished the candelabra and other silver giving it the sheen of liquid mercury. The thick linen tablecloth is starched and pressed with a proud crease running down the center.

Papa tastes the broth and speaks to Mike in English. "Please, tell us what you know of our friend Licio. I'm also interested to know what your plan is." He takes another spoonful of broth and puts down the spoon. Without sitting back, he looks at Mike and adds, "If you don't mind."

Steam drifts up as Mike looks at each pair of eyes around the table. He clears his throat and begins the story as the men start the consommé.

"Well, Licio Gella is living in the United States under the assumed name of Jack Stanley. I'll refer to him as Jack since that's how I know him. He and his parents emigrated to Boston from Italy when he was five or so. His father was a sculptor, coming from a long line of *cavatore*. His father's family has owned and operated marble quarries in the Apuan Alps outside Carrara, for five generations. They were wealthy but Jack grew up very simply. After his parents married, his mother continued working at her father's stables where she'd grown up raising horses. A few years after Jack was born, they moved to Boston with three other families and opened a sculpture studio. His mother managed the studio and also cooked for the other sculptors and their families. They all lived together in a sort of commune there in Boston's North End."

Salvi and Vilotti are both turned in their chairs facing Mike and smoking. All are looking at him and silent. It is very interesting to Lorenzo that Mike would know these details of Jack's childhood.

Mike drinks some of his wine and continues. "Both of Jack's parents' families were established and well known around Carrara. The wedding must've been a spectacle. The fifties were a wild time there with the marble industry booming. 'More statues than people and the people were mostly sculptors and quarrymen.' Those are Jack's words." Mike smiles, looks around and takes another long sip of his wine.

Lorenzo coughs and Mike continues, "Eight or nine years after moving to Boston, Jack was sent back to Italy to work as a cook at a large estate. I suppose you all know the rest of the story."

"No, no, please, continue," says Lorenzo, holding out his hand.

Before becoming Vatican Secretary of State, Angelo Vilotti had managed the estate in Italy where Jack had come to live when he was fourteen. Vilotti knew Jack's father personally and was aware of, and appalled by, the sculpture scam that Lorenzo ran. Vilotti and Lorenzo were some of Jack's closest acquaintances from his years living in Italy.

Mike continues, "After a number of years, he began working exclusively for a group of men based in Rome who operated a kind of private restaurant. He created, prepared, and executed hundreds of meals over a period of fifteen years or so. Usually parties of three to eight, members of his core clientele and two or three guests. He also traveled with them." What Mike didn't know was that he was in the very restaurant where Jack started working those twenty-odd years ago.

Mike drinks more. Over the clink of silver and fine porcelain the gentlemen start eating as Mike speaks more directly to Papa. "At some point, he began recording the dinner conversations so he could hear what they were saying about his performances on the lute before dinner. During his last few years there were a few recording devices on the table, another in the men's room, and one by the phone. This made it easier to distinguish the speakers and to hear individual conversations. It's a very interesting piece of work." The men are all looking at him. Salvi's mouth is slightly open. Vilotti puts down his spoon and lights another cigarette.

"Nine years ago, he quit without notice and left Rome," Mike looks bored, picks up his wineglass and takes a high final sip. "Disappearing, it seems."

"For some reason, he changed his name. And now he's operating a restaurant called Jack's Café. It's really nice, built into an old theater. And the food is great. I heard something about a boat, but…"

The girls are clearing the first course. The room is silent and Papa interrupts, "Thank you for sharing this with us Mike. We look forward to hearing more from you."

Lorenzo takes Mike by the arm, and they stand. Mike looks down at his untouched consommé and says, "The soup looks wonderful, and the wine was lovely." Lorenzo leads him across the room. "Thank you all very much." He turns from pensive eyes and walks out the door.

"Dinner will be brought to you," Lorenzo assures him quietly as they reach the stairs. "I'll see you tomorrow before you leave." Lorenzo gives a few quick orders in Italian to various people in the kitchen. A man in a tuxedo shows Mike downstairs to the kitchen where he meets the brown-eyed girl who's been pouring his wine. He's given another glass of wine, and they begin speaking Spanish. To his surprise and delight, she accompanies him to the limousine and on to a villa forty minutes outside of Rome.

Lorenzo walks back into the dining room to the window and watches the limo drive away. He turns back to the table. "They're gone."

Conversation erupts in Italian. Vilotti is watching Salvi closely. He never trusted him and could see that he was beginning to crack. Lorenzo mused privately that Salvi would be indicted within the next few days. And that he would be offered immunity for his testimony which he would most likely give.

Salvi lights another cigarette and suggests blandly that they should simply make Jack "the end of the road."

Vilotti realizes instantly that Salvi has reached the tipping point and must not go any further. A brief glance to the others confirms they're thinking exactly the same thing. Papa was quite fond of Jack and would not allow anything as drastic as having Jack killed. Lorenzo and Jack had been very close, having worked together through some of their greatest years. They had a mutual respect for each other's planning and tactical finesse. While their means and objectives were on different levels, many of their late-night conversations revealed similarities in their tradecrafts.

Salvi was asking where Jack had his restaurant. Lorenzo immediately responded that it was somewhere in southern Mississippi. Vilotti said that he thought it was in the town of St. Judas. Salvi wrote this down in his small Morocco bound notepad and put out his cigarette, "I need to go." He says unceremoniously and gets up to walk to the door. Lorenzo follows and insists he use one of their drivers which Salvi accepts.

They were getting used to Salvi's strange behavior of late. Papa shook his head slowly. Salvi was a relative newcomer to their circle, having been introduced by

Lorenzo thirteen years ago. No one ever really trusted him, but he was malleable and had served a purpose. Now the remaining three men in the room knew exactly what had to happen; get rid of Salvi before he got to Jack. Lorenzo, always one step ahead, put a plan into motion he's had ready for weeks.

Three days later Roberto Salvi's body is found hanging from a small bridge over the Tiber on the outskirts of Rome. The suicide note wrapped around a brick in his pocket describes the collapse of Banco Ambrosso as having brought him to a breaking point.

• • •

Mike and the young nun he's come to know as Alejandra speak Spanish in the limo, on the terrace and into the bedroom. There is a feast waiting for them there, and afterward they're both satisfied. Mike is surprised and thrilled by her appetite. She's very alluring and quite persuasive. As instructed by Lorenzo, she sets about getting Mike to tell her everything he knows about Jack. Mike tells her exactly what Jack wants them to know.

CHAPTER ONE

The Writer

Three weeks earlier, Samson Missouri.

It was early evening on a hot Wednesday in June. Jack's Café was cool inside and smelled like great food. Phil, the dining room's captain, was checking the settings for a party of seven that were friends of Remus the piano player.

Remus was at the keyboard punching out handfuls of chords and Helmut the piano tuner was on a small stepstool leaning over the great sound box. Occasionally Remus would stop and hammer on a single note. He'd tilt his head and the argument would follow.

"Why can't you have your piano tuned like a *normal* man?!" Helmut shouted with his shrill German accent.

Remus always replied calmly, "Helmut, the piano's got to be tuned to the room."

"With the treble strings *sharp* because you don't play them so hard!" Helmut would sneer. He was secretly proud of the piano's incredible sound inside the theatre.

Phil listened as he scanned the table settings, looking for a fork out of line or a crease off kilter. He often wondered about parallels between the arts of music and cooking. Creating beauty always seemed to be some kind of struggle. They certainly argued in the kitchen.

The phone at the podium lit up. It was the reservation line that didn't ring, and no one ever answered it.

It was quarter to six, tables were set, and Jack was at the bar talking with Pamela the bartender.

"Jack's Café." Phil paused, listening. "You want to speak to Jack? Who's calling?"

Phil covered the mouthpiece. Helmut was shouting again. The man had to be going deaf. The dishwasher banged a pot in tempo with the low E booming through the auditorium. The string came up to tune and completely filled the room. Remus stopped.

"Damn you!" shouted Helmut. Two more raps on the pot echoed Helmut's words. It was all very loud.

Jack's conversation with Pamela broke as they both looked back toward the kitchen. Phil laughed to himself. The alpha chaos moment. He walked over to Jack and handed him the phone.

"Call for you," Phil said with a wooden face.

Jack looked at the handset. It wasn't on hold. "Phil *what* the...?" Jack never took calls on the dining room phone.

"A friend from Aspen." Phil shrugged. He was in the mood to cause trouble.

"Hi, this is Jack." He looked at Phil and Pamela who lingered to listen. "Mike Ambrose... Yes, I remember, we met last summer. You're a writer... Sure, the party with the girl in the elf shoes." Jack looked over at Phil and raised an eyebrow. "You're writing a food column for the St. Louis Trib and your agent wants a story on small town restaurants...?" Phil and Pamela both laughed out loud.

• • •

Jack was in the kitchen before noon the next day looking inside the fridges around the grill station. Jimmy Mac, the grill man was usually first in the kitchen and was surprised to see Jack. Jimmy had been working at the restaurant since it opened seven years ago and was responsible for most of the kitchen's design.

Jimmy grew up in the Ozark Mountains. His family came from Derbyshire, England around the turn of the century and had discovered one of the largest lead deposits in the country. Before meeting Jack, he ran the grill station at St Louis' top steakhouse, the Clayton 6. Jimmy was also a crack diesel mechanic. He regularly worked on some of the largest mining rigs in the state.

All this interested Jack. But it was Jimmy's understanding of food and cooking that led Jack to forgive him for his most disturbing trait; Jimmy loved to argue.

"What the fuck?" Jimmy was standing next to the grill. He was wearing a Guns N' Roses T-shirt, long blue jean cutoffs and work boots. He put his box of knives on the grill.

"What the fuck what?" Jack stood up from the fridge.

"What the fuck you lookin' at?" Jimmy was picking at one of his fingernails.

Jack was a bit taller than Jimmy. "Looks good in there."

"I know it looks good in there."

"You know I don't like the plastic wrap on the steaks."

"Man, we're over this. Those are my steaks, and I'll wrap them however the fuck I want."

This was in fact true. They had a unique "arrangement" where Jimmy bought the meats from Jack and had leeway on the menu pricing. He took his cut from the nightly take based on sales from the grill. The plastic wrap was one of many arguments they had from the beginning; Jimmy preferred to wet age the steaks after they were cut, Jack preferred to let them sit dry.

"I know, I know. Listen I got a guy coming by tonight."

"What guy?" Jimmy crossed his arms.

"Just a guy, a writer."

"A writer. What kind of writer?

"I'm hungry. I'm making an omlette. You want one?"

"No man I don't want an omlette," But go ahead, this better be good Jimmy thought. He knew Jack well enough that his coming in to cook breakfast meant he had something important to talk about.

"You know my friend Vilotti from Italy. He's been here a few times."

"Yeah, chain-smoking Dracula-looking guy. Ambassador to the Vatican or something. Which I don't believe."

"Vatican Secretary of State."

"Woooo-hoo! Man, where do you come up with this shit? That guy dresses like a farmer from the nineteenth century."

Jack laughed as he tossed the garlic and onions and poured the eggs and cream into the hot pan. "I know." He turned to face Jimmy and shrugged, "It's just how these guys travel when they don't want to be noticed." Jack was still smiling, Jimmy really was funny, he could spin a twisted angle on anything.

"Go on." Jimmy was unpacking his tools.

"Okay. Seriously, I don't want you talking about this with anybody." Jack plated the omlette. "How 'bout a Bloody Mary?"

"Sure man." Jimmy knew this was serious now. Jack had a lot of cool stories, and Jimmy had a funny feeling about this.

They headed out to the dining area. Jimmy started making the drinks while Jack sat at the bar opposite. "Anybody else know about this?" Jimmy asked.

"Remus and Phil. Sarah doesn't know a thing."

"Pamela?"

"Some of it. But nobody knows what I'm about to tell you."

"Cool." Jimmy put the drinks on the bar and Jack tasted his.

"Hoowow, how much horseradish you put in this?"

"About two tablespoons, lots of lemon. Spicy and sour, no salt."

"Tom yum."

"Hah. Nice call. Yea." Jimmy raised his glass.

"So Vilotti called me last night. He's put the writer onto me." Jack began to eat.

"I'm sure Vilotti knows how to spin a web. I'm glad you weren't messing with the Japanese before you came here, we'd have Ninjas coming down from the skylights on zip lines."

"Yeah. So far so good," Jack looks up to the ceiling. "Anyway, this guy, Mike's his name, thinks he's coming here to write a book. Probably going to hang around for a few weeks asking questions. All he knows is he's here to write a book, he doesn't know Vilotti put him here. And I'm going to give him some information that's going to make it back to Rome."

Jimmy took a big sip and coughed. "Wow that is hot. Okay, it's still pretty vague. Did you think this up?" He grabbed a small plate and a fork from the bar back. "Here give me some of that." He cut into Jack's omelet and took a little more than half of what was left.

"So, my father was a sculptor, you know that. And he did a lot of commissioned work for the people I ended up working for in Italy. They pursued him when we moved to Boston, and they paid him well. To do these classical religious themes. My folks didn't need the money, I think he felt it was noble work. My mother always wanted him to do more original work. I have a small warehouse in Boston with all his modern pieces. It's amazing stuff, I'll show it to you someday."

"I'd like to see that."

There is a moment of silence and Jack continues. "So, I find out they'd been taking his sculptures and aging them to pass off as Ancient Roman. Fuck, do you believe it!" Jack was gesticulating and Jimmy was watching him.

"They'd rub the marble with cheese, burn it in hay, and bury 'em. Then they'd sell the pieces to private collectors as Ancient Roman at outrageous profit!"

"Fuck that! Vilotti told you all this? When?!" Jimmy shouted to match.

Jack really enjoyed Jimmy's humor, and he sometimes had to make an effort to be serious. "Yes! I was like nineteen at the time, and I wanted to kill somebody. Vilotti thought it was horrible too. But he gave me an idea how to force them to make amends."

"That must've taken some restraint. How long's it been?"

"Yeah well, I think my mother knew all along. So, I waited. My folks were happy, it was a great time there in Boston, they probably had their best years after I left. Besides if he'd found out, I'm sure he would've done something crazy and that would've been the end of all of it."

"So Vilotti gave you a way to… what did you say, force them to make amends… that's great."

"It's complicated. See, the group I used to work for were businessmen, bankers and politicians, right? All with connections to the Vatican in one way or another."

"This is starting to sound shady. And dangerous."

"Don't worry you're not gonna have a problem."

"Hey, bring it on. Let's nail the fuckers!"

Jack laughed, "Yeah. So Vilotti set me up with these miniature recording devices and I put 'em around the dining room at this private restaurant where I worked. Which is funny because they built the place so they could meet privately and usually in secret. There's an entrance from an aqueduct below the street that leads to a building three blocks away. And for servers they brought in nuns from Spain who couldn't understand anything besides Spanish."

"Oh man I love it."

"I did this for over fifteen years."

"Don't tell me. Is this about the Banco Ambrosso Scandal?"

"You heard about that?" Jack was surprised.

"Man, you know I've been doing work at the Sarzana mine expansion, it's a big Italian multinational and all the guys are Italian. It's all they've been talking about the last few weeks. And man, I heard about this restaurant."

"Hmm, I wonder about that. It's not getting much coverage here in the states."

"Nothing at all, I looked it up. It was these guys from Milan. I heard it from… So, you got all the info on this. Hah. My god, it's a major investigation. They're speculating about how it happened leading up to this, and who's involved. They're saying the Vatican was involved in funding the overthrow in Paraguay and that they used the mob to launder money. Too friggin' wild."

"Wheels within wheels. You wouldn't believe the elaborate schemes. You wouldn't believe what the sculpture sales funded. I got everything. From the beginning. Only thing is they don't know I have it."

"And you're just going to let them know what you got. I see where this is going, '*Hey where's Jack? I don't know, he just disappeared.*' Case closed." Jimmy lit a cigarette.

"I don't think they're that stupid."

"That stupid? Dude, if I was facing jail time because of information you had, I'd go all Jimmy Hoffa on your ass."

"Remind me never to mess with you."

"I'm having another drink. You want one?"

"No. I gotta go." Jack stood up and picked up the plates.

"But give this guy Mike a hard time tonight. I know they're paying him a lot so I'm sure he'll stick around."

"No prob boss, should be fun." Jimmy turned around to make his drink.

"Okay, I'll see you later."

"Yup. I'll be here."

• • •

At 6:05 p.m. that evening, Jack came into the kitchen with Mike Ambrose in tow. Wearing Jack's chef jacket, toque, and kerchief, Mike looked like the man who'd shrunk in his suit. The outfit was tailored Egyptian cotton measured for Jack's six-foot plus frame. The crew was dumbfounded. Jack rarely wore these beautiful clothes. The sight of this strange man wearing them was absurd. They stared in silence as Jack introduced.

He spoke to everyone. "Okay, this is Mike Ambrose. He's a writer and he'll be spending the evening with us here in the kitchen. *Behind* the line."

This had never been done before. They knew he was coming but the two behind the line looked at each other as if to say, "Where's he going to stand?"

14

"Hah," Jimmy laughed out loud as he scraped the grill. Sarah, at the center station, was wiping the cutting board as if marking her territory.

"Jimmy, what's so funny?" Jack called over to the grill.

"I love the outfit. Who's your tailor, Mike?" Jimmy shouted across to the pickup area.

"Looks good, hey?" Mike adjusted his collar and hat, seemingly unaware of how droopy he looked.

"Okay Mike, you'll start down at the grill with Jimmy." Jack pushed the toque to the side like a beret. "There, that's how a Frenchman wears a hat."

Jack winked at Sarah, who shook her head with a trace of smile.

"Man, it's hot back here," Mike said. He stretched his hands toward the grill like it was a campfire.

"Jack, Mike needs something to drink." Jimmy was sharpening his slicing knife menacingly.

"Mike, what would you like? Soda, beer, or how about some of our house red wine? It's a Bardolino."

"I'll try the house red. That sounds great. Thanks."

At each station was an ice bucket with large bottles of mineral water. Jimmy and Sarah each drank two to three bottles a night.

Jack returned with the wine and continued, "For the benefit of our guest down at the grill station I'll do a breakdown of tonight's reservations. Sarah maybe you could put together one of the roast pheasant specials and we can see what he thinks."

Jack did this regularly and everyone knew it. All the same, Mike appeared to be feeling more important by the minute. Jack summarized the reservations, reading them aloud like a lawyer giving opening arguments. "We got twenty-eight before seven and at seven-thirty another twenty-five. At eight, twenty-four more and we're slammed. By ten-thirty we have one sixteen. The big jam's around nine."

The restaurant was consistently booked solid two and three nights a week.

"Sounds like you know what you're doing, Jack," Mike said as he raised his glass.

"Well, we're only as good as our last show. Let's hope we don't drop the ball tonight. Sarah, how's the pheasant? Let's plate one up."

"Coming right up, Jack." Sarah looked sharply at him.

"Thanks Sarah. We get the pheasants from a friend of mine in Tennessee. His ranch is a few thousand acres. It's one of the largest properties in the state. It's a beautiful place."

Jack looked over at Jimmy, who was facing the grill. He went on. "He sent me twenty-six a few days ago and I hope to sell most of them tonight." Jack was watching Sarah as she worked.

"How is it prepared, Jack?" Mike was working his way into the wine.

"I'm glad you asked. You see it's a wild bird, Lots of flying, blood circulation. Mostly dark, so the flavor's a bit strong. We hang 'em in a cool room downstairs for a few days. This lets the flesh concentrate and mellows the character," Jack explained, "I thought juniper berries and coriander seed would stand up to season it. Sarah, you agree?"

"Yes, Jack, I think that works well," Sarah stopped to face him. The recipe had been evolving over the past few years and was a source of many heated discussions between them. The pheasant's availability was inconsistent, but it was one of the most popular dishes and changed only slightly, month to month. Sarah sliced between the thigh and drumstick with a large knife and was about to chop off the claw when Jack held his hand above the counter, motioning for her to leave it on. The claws were given to the dishwasher who took them home to make "Ozark soup." From the beginning, Jack had wanted to serve it with the claw on. After arguing with nearly everyone about it, he finally gave up and they served it with the claw off.

Jack went on. "We sear it in a hot carbon steel pan with olive oil until it's dark golden brown. Then we let it rest. When we're ready to plate, Sarah puts it in the oven to finish. Sarah, how do you make the sauce?"

"Maybe I should start from the beginning," she suggested blandly.

"By all means." Jack was enjoying this and poured himself a glass from Mike's carafe. There were no reservations for another half an hour and Paulo, the dishwasher, was leaning against his machine with a soda. Pamela and Remus were standing inside the backstage curtain. Everyone was curious about how the evening would unfold.

"Jack insists we get the birds whole with the head and feathers on," Sarah started. "This way we can tell they're fresh. They also stand up better to the aging this way." She glanced at Jack, who was now standing with Pamela and Remus. They were all happily content. Jack gave a slight nod.

"Paulo plucks the feathers, and I burn off whatever's leftover with my blowtorch. They're always covered in bugs. After that, I rinse and scrub them with a soft brush and then pat the skin dry with a clean towel. Lately the stock's been made with the necks, mushroom stems, and roasted carrots so it's mostly sweet and deep. I use a *remouillage* of Jimmy's for the cooking liquid and simmer it gently for an hour or so." She turned around to stir one of the pots and adjusted the flame.

"I split the birds in half and brush them with olive oil. Then they're rubbed with ground juniper berries, coriander seed, black pepper, and salt. I work it in hard, inside and out and then put them in the refrigerator overnight. In the beginning we were toasting the seeds whole before grinding them and adding a little brown sugar to the rub." She looked hard at Jack. "These days we're grinding the seeds raw and using roasted shallots in the sauce to keep the sweetness up."

She reached around with a rag in her hand and pulled a pan from the oven. "Tonight, we're serving it with brown rice I cooked with sauteed onions and celery, a few bay leaves, white wine and pheasant stock." She grabbed a small pot from the stovetop. "I also have a mixture of Tuscan white beans cooked with a little smoked bacon and garlic. This goes on top of the rice."

Sarah took a drink of water and looked around. Everyone was watching and no one spoke. She stood directly in a shaft of light. Jack's eyes were on the plate as he walked over to the pick-up area opposite Sarah. Everyone was watching Sarah's hands. Just shy of six-feet tall, Sarah Monet had a powerful athletic beauty. The economy of movement as she turned around, bent over, and opened the oven was like a fluid, effortless dance. She held the spoon like a large pencil, an extension of her arm. The knife was balanced in her hand and seemed to guide itself between the bones. Jack remembered Phil's recent comment about filming the workstations with the strong overhead stage lights.

She continued. "As Jack said, we sear the half-bird in a hot pan with some olive oil. After that I toss the oil and add roasted shallots to the drippings and deglaze with a little white wine and some stock. Then the bird sits in the pan to rest. When Jack gives the order to fire, I put the pan in the oven to finish cooking and let the sauce come together. Depending on the guest, I may mount the sauce with a bit of butter or sour cream. Jack's a little weird about changing preparations to suit some of our guests' preferences. Here it is."

Sarah had been plating as she talked. The pan went back on a burner, and the sauce came to bubble. After drizzling the glaze onto the plate, she tossed the pan into a metal pail on the floor. She added a sprig of rosemary and a swipe of lemon zest and then wiped the rim. Giving the plate a push with a spin across to the pick-up area, it ended up facing Jack just as it had been facing her.

"Absolutely beautiful. Brava, Sarah!" Jack started to clap and everyone joined in. "Mike, let me know what you think. I'll get some more wine." Jack picked up the plate and handed it over to Mike. "Jimmy, get Mike some silverware and a napkin, would you?"

"Sure boss." Jimmy said.

Mike pulled the plate closer and then looked up and smiled as everyone watched him.

Jack took the carafe and followed Remus and Pamela out to the bar.

"That was great," Pamela laughed as she filled the small carafe.

"Mike Ambrose. He handled that well. I think he just might fit in. Let's see how he deals with Jimmy." Jack had a strange twinkle in his eye.

Phil had watched most of the kitchen demo but stepped out to answer his phone. He came to the bar holding the house phone and said to Jack with a straight face, "Jack, listen… I have someone on the phone. He says he's a friend and it's important."

The three at the bar laughed.

"Very funny. You may regret this," Jack pointed at Phil. "It's all good, I like the guy. Let's see what he thinks of the claw we left on the bird." Jack picked up the carafe and Remus walked over to the piano and sat down.

"Jack, that guy called again about the piano," Remus said, facing the keyboard. He let out a short twinkling scale with his right hand.

"Really. Okay," Jack said, looking at the carafe and then to Remus.

The call about the piano was a signal. Vilotti in Rome was letting him know he needed to watch out.

"Mike how's the pheasant?" Jack boomed as he came back into the kitchen.

Mike had the claw in his hand and was chewing on the drumstick. His plate was clean. He put down the food and wiped his mouth before answering, "Jack, I've never *tasted* food like this. It's like the flavors are in color. It's so real. I don't know how to explain it. Simply beautiful." He gave Sarah a sideways glance.

"Good, I'm glad you enjoyed it. Problem is I still can't decide whether to serve it with the claw on or off. What do you think?" Jack put down the carafe and stood opposite Mike.

"I think you should serve the claw on. It's wild and adds a renaissance touch." Mike held up the leg like a goblet.

"*Great!* We serve the claw ON tonight!" Jack raised his glass and spoke to the entire kitchen as if to say, '*Finally, somebody agrees with me on this.*'

The moment subsided with everyone reeling from the rush of new energy in the kitchen. Jack headed out to the bar. Phil scratched his neck and smiled at his copy of the reservations. Looking up, he made eye contact with Remus. They almost laughed aloud watching Mike ask Jimmy about what was in his fridge. Jimmy had just folded his rag. It was in his left hand on his hip. He picked up the tongs and pointed, "Pull out that tray and I'll show you some steaks." Noticing Phil and Remus watching, he gave them an upward nod with a wink. "Come on Mike, we don't have all night."

Sarah came around to the pick-up area opposite the grill and was wiping down the stainless, detailing the station before service. She was watching Mike's interaction with Jimmy. "Mike, have you ever worked as a cook before?" Sarah asked.

"I've done some kitchen work. Why?"

"You know, we're real busy here." It was clear Sarah was in charge. Jack was the boss, but Sarah ran the kitchen. She kept a running inventory in her head and knew every bit of food in the kitchen. Where it was, how much of it there was, and when more was coming.

"I'm getting that feeling." Mike was playing up the doughboy chef. "I'd love to see your pantry," he said, looking squarely at Sarah.

Sarah smiled and blinked. "That may be possible later. Hey, if you know how to cook why don't you step up to the plate and flip some steaks. Jimmy doesn't mind, do you Jimmy?" She pushed a large stack of plates toward them.

Mike was weighing one of the carbon steel fry pans like a tennis racket and rounded to Jimmy who was shaking his head, "Not at all." Jimmy gave his tongs a pistol-spin and handed them to Mike, who was about to speak to Sarah when Jack came back into the kitchen.

"The governor's brother's here. Party of ten," Jack said to Phil. "Let's get the big table up." Phil looked over to Paulo, who nodded and headed downstairs to get the table.

Jack went on. "He's with his brother and friends. They just walked in. No call. They're at the bar. Make sure that table's set nice."

Phil closed his eyes and shook his head, still grinning, "Right. I'll give Pamela a hand. Did he bring the dancer?"

"No, he's with a different girl. She looks quiet. We may get off easy tonight." Jack was looking over at the grill. "Jimmy, you cut those rib eyes yet?"

"Nope. I got nine whole racks downstairs. I'll probably cut into three tonight." Jimmy enjoyed cutting the steaks to order. Two out of three people eating at Jack's ordered some type of steak from the grill.

"You want some fat ones for the Gov?" Jimmy called out.

"You know how they like it, big and rare. Trim the tail off and char the hell out of 'em." Jack often wondered how many steaks Jimmy had cut at the restaurant.

"St. Louis black and blues," Jimmy said. His steaks were legendary, and it was a well-deserved reputation.

"Right, someone mentioned that. Wait for the order, there may be six or seven. Sarah, let's send out some antipasti. How's those marinated porcinis?" Jack stepped toward the cold station.

"Nice. They're like silk. I have about two pounds," Sarah looked across to Jimmy who reached into a fridge and produced a stone crock with a clamp lid. He opened it, slid it over to Jack, and handed him a spoon.

Jack gave the mushrooms a stir. Lifting the crock, he inhaled deeply and said, "Good. The smoked garlic added a nice tone. Took a while, right?" He threw a questioning glance at Sarah. She and Jack had these conversations often, dueling over the preparations. Sarah disagreed with the smoked garlic, saying it was too dark and would overpower the porcinis. Jack told her to let them sit for a week or so. "It'll sweeten up. Those mushrooms are strong," he'd said. Still, she'd added less garlic than he'd asked.

"Week and a half," Sarah said as she dipped in for a mushroom and gave a lovely smile with raised eyebrows. "Not bad at all."

Jimmy was laughing to himself. Sarah headed back around to her station and Jack peeked under the shelf saying, "What's so funny, Jimmy?"

"Good thing you're serving it. She would've eaten all of them!" said Jimmy. Sarah gave him an elbow in the back as she passed behind.

"Make sure you put more *garlic* next time," Jack said, and Sarah and Jimmy laughed out loud. "Okay, strain the porcinis and add some parsley and lemon. And put some good oil and flaky salt on top. Jimmy, I want you to baste those big rib eyes with the leftover mushroom juice. And save one for me."

Jack leaned in to speak to Jimmy. "If we haven't eaten all the Ragusano, that Sicilian cheese, cut some up into a dice, same size as the porcini chunks. Sarah, make some of those nice olives you've been doing, just browned in a pan with thyme and onion, and throw in some hot chilis and extra oil. After you finish the olives strain the oil and toss the cheese with it."

He turned to Phil. "Put some toothpicks on the table." Phil nodded.

They waited for Jack to stop speaking. He looked at each of them as they turned and headed back to work. This could be a loud place, but no one interrupted Jack when he issued tasks in the kitchen. In the beginning, Jack occasionally had to prove he was boss. And he could be loud if that's what it took to make his point. Early on he discovered the dishwasher was stealing whole strip steaks by putting them in the trash and picking them out later that night. Jimmy had immediately noticed the inventory was off and it only went on for a few days. He and Jack waited by the dumpster and caught him one night. Jack personally threw him into the dumpster and Jimmy locked the lids. They let him out the following afternoon and the kid never came back for his check.

Everything revolved around the food, and everyone took it seriously. For Phil, it was fascinating to the point of entertainment to watch Jack put dishes and menus together on the fly.

"Yo, Mike! Bring me two whole racks from the walk-in downstairs. Bottom shelf. We'll cut some steaks." Jimmy pointed to the stairs with the tongs.

"Put him to work, Jimmy!" Jack called on his way out of the kitchen.

• • •

Vic Sindano, the governor's brother was Jack's personal banker. His visits were notorious. Well-dressed gentlemen, a few ladies, and always a late night. Like most of the Café's regulars, they came here for the food and to party. And Remus' music always went late. These meals were some of the greatest the Café put out. With Remus' party in from Chicago, it was a particularly special evening.

At the end of the night, Vic made his rounds and tipped each member of the restaurant's crew one thousand dollars. He knew everyone by name. From the beginning, Jack had refused to give him a bill. He would dramatize, arms extended. "Vic, please, it's nothing. I told you, your money's no good to me. I'm just glad you came." And Jack would hear no more of it. His only suggestion was to find another restaurant where he could have the same meal and whatever it cost, divide that equally among the crew as a tip. These evenings were full throttle VIP treatment. And the crew always partied late afterward.

Later that night, after Sarah's tour of the refrigeration and dry goods storage, Mike wandered out to the dining area. Jack was at the end of the bar. His suit jacket was draped over the back of a barstool, and his shirtsleeves were rolled up. He was telling a funny, animated story to Pamela, who was across from him. She stood behind the bar with her hands on the counter, shoulders high, listening to him like a schoolgirl. A beautiful woman and a beautiful smile; her lips were perfect. She had shining auburn hair and dark hazel eyes. Her skin tone was a Mediterranean sun-kissed bronze with more than a few freckles. She was one of the most wildly attractive women Mike had ever seen in person.

There was no one else around. Mike paused at the edge of the backstage curtain to take in the scene; two interesting people obviously comfortable with each other, sitting in this incredible setting of The Theatre. He felt fortunate witnessing this and having had the evening's experience.

He walked out to the bar, careful not to interrupt. "Jack, thank you. You have an incredible operation here."

"Good. I'm glad you like it, Mike. Take a seat." Jack motioned to a barstool. "You want a drink?" Mike scanned the bar and noticed the Scotch selection.

"Sure. I'd love a single malt. Neat, please." He eyed Jack's glass. "Whatever you recommend."

Jack lifted his glass. "Pamela, would you please?" Jack turned to Mike. "It's a Balvenie. I like the ten-year."

Mike saw the bottle and nodded. "Founder's Reserve. They've been making it since the distillery began."

Pamela set down one of the heavy crystal glasses and poured for Mike. Jack finished his and pushed the glass closer to Pamela.

"Interesting you know of Balvenie. Pamela and I just visited the town where it's made," Jack said.

Mike waited until Pamela finished pouring Jack's drink and raised his glass. "Jack, here's to your awesome Café."

"Thanks." Jack nodded. "So, is this research, or are facts about small Scotch producers a hobby of yours?"

"Actually, I spent three weeks writing in Baniffshire last year. I stayed at the home of one of the maltmen from Balvenie."

Jack frowned as he looked over at Pamela, who had turned and was looking for something in a drawer.

"Mike, you weren't there writing a *story*, were you?"

Pamela held a manuscript with a large paperclip. She placed it on the bar and, shaking her head, said to Jack, "I don't believe it."

Jack held it up and said, "This you? Mickey Aberkeene?"

Mike took a drink and then nodded before responding, a rasp of whisky in his voice. "I was told to use a pseudonym. Where on earth did you get it?"

Jack slapped the papers onto the bar. "That is *too much*! I've made copies of this for everyone I know. You know I think it was Vic who gave it to me."

Phil stepped out and waved on his way toward the door. "Good night."

"Phil, hold on! You're not going to believe this!" Jack was nearly roaring.

Pamela picked up the bottle and Phil nodded as he approached the bar. Phil took his drink and looked at Pamela. "Thanks. What's up?" Phil asked.

Jack was flipping through the pages. "Remember this story about the distillery in Scotland?"

Phil took a drink looking down at the pages in Jack's hands. "Yeah, the girl who was sleeping with all the workers. Erotic, but you end up with a detailed under-standing of Scotch whisky making." Phil looked over at Mike who had his nose in his glass. "You said you'd always wanted to meet the guy who wrote it." He pointed to Mike, then looked at Jack and Pamela with raised eyebrows. "Don't tell me."

"Yeah. Meet Mickey Aberkeene. We just found out." Jack was laughing to himself.

Phil put his hand on Mike's shoulder and said, "Mike, that's quite a piece of work. Everyone loved it. Jack always said he wanted this person to write a story about the Café."

Mike looked at Jack. "Actually, Jack, that's what I came here to talk to you about."

Jack looked up. Still smiling, he said with a chuckle, "I'm sorry, Mike, but we can't have people screwing in the back of the restaurant. Besides I think that story's been told before. Right?" Jack laughed.

"No, no, Jack. What I have in mind is completely different." He looked around. Pamela had her arms crossed, Phil was drinking with one hand in his pocket, and Jack was giving Mike his full stare. It was as if they all were saying, *Go ahead. This better be good.*"

Mike hated making a pitch. Presenting it to the key players all at once made it even worse.

He continued without missing a beat. "Well, first of all it would be laid out as a series of interviews. The focus would be on the food and the cooks. No sex. Of course it wouldn't be difficult to fit in, but…" Mike looked at Pamela, then to Jack, who was shaking his head. Mike smiled. "I'm joking, Jack. But really, there's something special here. This restaurant has quite a reputation. I want to paint a picture of it from the inside."

Jack peered over his glasses. "You know this restaurant is home to all of us who work here. I couldn't allow our livelihood to be misrepresented. But I like your idea, and I like your style. Have you mentioned this to Sarah or Jimmy?" He laid the manuscript onto the bar.

"No, I haven't mentioned it to anyone."

"Good. Thanks for that. See, I don't believe in censorship, but I do have to be careful about what kinds of things are written about the restaurant. Not just for me, but because we've all invested a lot of time and goodwill working here. Phil, what do you think?"

"Jack, it's a great restaurant. I think the story should be told from the inside. But I agree, you have to be careful. No spin, no slant. A restaurant is a very personal thing to its crew."

"Nice. Pamela, how do you feel about all this?" Jack looked at Pamela and took a sip of his drink.

"Mike, I just loved your story, 'The Maltman's Daughter,'" Pamela had a sexy smile. "But how did he feel about your portraying his daughter that way?"

"Actually, the Maltman I stayed with was seventy-six and his daughter was fifty-two. Not twenty-two. Honestly, they both loved it. If you remember, the Maltman in the story was the big burly handsome guy and his daughter was the fox. After everyone at the distillery read it, those two were rock stars. Fact is, I've always been interested in Scotch whisky and wanted to learn more about it. It's strange how these gigs come about. Someone was actually searching for a description of Scotch Whiskey in a prose version. Hah! So, I helped out around the distillery from March thru June. I tasted all different kinds of Scotch at different stages..." Mike couldn't help smiling as he finished his drink. "It was really fun. I was there with a girl I'd met in Italy. I'd just published my book on winemaking and had a bunch of cash. We were traveling when I got the call. She ended up coming along and stayed until she had to go back to Italy."

All attention was on Mike. Jack stood up and said, "Mike, that's great. Let me speak to Sarah and Jimmy and we'll talk tomorrow. Come by around noon. How's that?"

"Sure, Jack, and thanks again for tonight."

"Okay. Good night you all." Jack waved and left.

"Night, Jack." Phil and Mike responded.

Pamela returned the bottle to the shelf. "Okay, boys, I'll see you." She held out her hand to Mike. "Nice to meet you, Mike."

"Yes, Pamela, it was nice meeting you." He took her hand and looked in her eye. She gave him a wink and turned to leave.

Phil took Jack's seat. "Mike, why the two-sided story? I mean the whisky tech could have been in a trade journal. Whenever a question came up about Scotch production we referred to it. Jack has stood here and read parts of it aloud to people and I can't tell you how many copies of it we've made. But the story of the girl and the workers is so erotic. What made you combine the two? I'm trying to imagine where it would be published."

Mike laughed. "Yeah, that's just *it!* I don't think it's *been* published. The client was in contact with my agent as I was writing it and suggested a romance, and that I should make it sordid. Freelance writing gigs are always different. Most of the work I do is just research that someone wants. And a lot of the clients are very private. I never found out what happened with it. I wonder how Jack ended up with a copy."

"Well, it's brilliant. Intertwining the girl's escapades and the history of whisky production. How did all that come about?"

"Between you and me, the notion of the girl came from an experience I had when I was living in Tuscany writing a book about artisan winemaking. Hah! And this was a contract job that came with a detailed outline, easy. I hooked up with the cooper's daughter. You know the cooper is the one who makes the barrels. The real deal went down in his workshop. Sometimes the anvil was still warm…"

Phil got up to pour another round of drinks. After finishing his story, Mike asked Phil how he became involved in the restaurant.

Phil scratched his sideburn and looked into the mirror behind the bar. "It's funny. You know I haven't thought about it for years. Jack came to see me at my office. I was selling real estate here in town…"

CHAPTER TWO

The Theatre

27

The door on Prospect Street is unremarkable. Formerly the artists' entrance to The Prospect Theatre, a small brass plaque below the doorbell states its new identity: *Jack's Café.*

The building is square and nearly three stories high. From the outside it lacks character. A fire in 1957 destroyed the high-ceilinged lobby, a supreme example of Deco opulence, and the rear third of the original auditorium. The damaged area was gutted, bricked out, and eventually became a wholesale flower market. The train station two blocks away closed three years after the fire.

In its glory, The Theatre kindled raw spirits of the twenties and harbored survivors of the thirties. After closing in the late sixies its history was completely forgotten to all but a few. Then Jack Stanley came along and bought it.

During its conversion to a restaurant, The Theatre's remaining banked seating area became two tiers of marble café tables accompanied by the original chairs. Guests are struck not only by the simple grandeur of The Theatre but also a severe irony. Spectacle and spectator interchange roles as life presents an eerie imitation of itself. Terraces on a surreal vineyard are seen from tables on the stage. Looking down at the stage the guests witness a performance of café society. *Live at Jack's.*

Seven years earlier, Samson Missouri.

Early morning bedsheets can make some of the loudest noises. She's still asleep. Your wallet, keys, and phone are on the bedside table and you *do not* want to wake her. The makeup's a bit faded, but it's still there from the night before. She is a knockout. A sleeping pout; eyelashes intertwined, and the eyebrows are pinched and slightly raised. "What is she dreaming about?" Phil pondered this age-old mystery thinking Michelangelo could not have carved and polished a more lovely vision. He called her Miss Kelley.

Driving home as daylight arrived, Phil thought about his present situation and how he'd always wanted to get into real estate. His desires were based on dreams of meeting people, making deals, and surviving on his smile and ability to read people. At age thirty-nine, his aspirations were facing a paradigm shift. Maybe that's why Miss Kelley lost interest. They'd been dating since he opened the real estate office, when he was on top of the world. Now it was routine, a sale every few months, a rental here and there, and an occasional appraisal. That was about it for the real estate business in Samson Missouri, population 14,075. But he was his own boss, happy enough, and he owned his house outright. Phil genuinely liked almost everyone and was comfortable here where he grew up. Small as the town of Samson was, he had a handful of good friends and a few interesting hobbies that kept him busy. He practiced photography with an old, large-format camera that had been at The Theatre since it was built. He also ran a custom-designed sound system for Remus' piano at Evangeline's, the local blues bar. Life really was good.

What he didn't know was that his life was about to make a dramatic change. Phil's subconscious must've been working overtime because he kept going over and over the day he met Jack Stanley a week ago.

• • •

"You're looking for three to five thousand square feet of commercially-zoned space with plenty of electricity. Here in town." Even though Phil owned Leica Realty he was the only person who worked in the office. Jack had walked in off the street.

"More or less," the man said.

Right away Phil thought Jack a unique individual. Wearing a strange pair of old and shined brown leather boots, his fingernails were clean, but his hair was a bit long. He wore a pair of blue jeans and a dark sweatshirt. A biker? He'd said his name was Jack Stanley. Phil wondered if that was his real name as he did the property search on his laptop. "Multi-use you say?"

Jack nodded patiently. He crossed his arms, wondering how long it would take Phil to bring up The Theatre.

Phil stopped typing and realized there was only one place in town that fit the description, The Theatre. He'd stopped there this morning to have coffee with his friend Remus, the caretaker. He also knew the owner lived out of town. Sitting back in his chair he said, "I can show you the Prospect Theatre. But it's just an old theater and part of it burned down in the fifties. I don't know if it would interest you. It's got a big stage and a small auditorium, some large rooms downstairs, and lots of woodwork. The whole place is made of wood on the inside." Phil wasn't sure how he would respond.

"Sounds interesting. Might be perfect. When can we see it?" Jack sat back and put his hands on his thighs, ready to stand up.

Phil slowly sat forward. He'd listed it for seven years and shown it maybe twelve times. He loved bringing people by, just to see their response as his old friend gave the tour. But there had never been an offer. He and Remus joked about what kind of person would finally buy the place and Jack did not fit the profile. "We can see it now if you like."

"Great." Jack stood up.

Phil got up and looked out the window at The Theatre across the street. There was a blue sports car parked in front. They walked out the front door and paused in front of the car. "Wow. Is that yours?"

"You wanna drive?" Jack asked.

"Yeah! What is it?" Phil was amazed by the blue paint.

"It's a sixty-five AC Cobra 427 and it kicks ass. Really. Be careful." Jack handed him the keys.

Phil smiled. "Thanks."

The motor roared to life. The interior was simple and smelled of leather. The car was old and in beautiful condition. The dash and steering wheel had the look of antique furniture. The seats were wrinkled like a fisherman's face and there was no top. Sitting in the driver's seat, Phil had the feeling the car was all wheels and engine. He put his hand on the shift knob as he settled into his seat and buckled the seatbelt. He found neutral and gave the engine a punch. "You know, I think I should show you The Tannery. It's in Chicago. We can make it in about seven hours." Phil kept a straight face as he worked the shift lever and pedals.

Jack lit a strange-looking cigar. "Hah! We could make Chicago in less than *five* if we needed to."

Phil eased the car out and drove to the corner. "Nice car, Phil!" a woman called from a storefront, and Phil waved. As they drove around the block, Phil waved at three other people before coming back to the exact spot they started from.

"Here we are." He pointed across the street. He kept a straight face and didn't make eye contact as he shut off the car.

"You're kidding!" Jack smiled genuinely, appraising Phil.

Phil nodded, handing back the keys to Jack. "You asked if I wanted to drive."

"That I did." Jack was looking closely at the brickwork on the corner of the building. Phil gave a brief history of The Theatre as they walked around the side of the building.

Remus Brown was The Theatre's caretaker and had been a close friend of Phil's for many years. Remus' mother had worked at The Theatre when it was operating. The story went that he'd been born downstairs during one of Billie Holiday's performances at The Theatre. Remus spent his childhood there and most of that time he was at or near the piano. The Theatre closed when Remus was nine and a year later his mother passed away. Remus stayed on as caretaker of the building and had lovingly maintained the interior for most of his adult life. The brass and woodwork were polished, and the floors were always swept. He played the old piano on stage every day. Phil considered Remus his best friend and admired many things about him: he was always in good spirits, he never complained, and he went to church every Sunday. Remus knew just about everyone in town.

Phil knocked twice on the side door and then opened it. "Remus!" He shouted into the auditorium. His voice echoed through the interior and Jack heard the faint resonance of a piano.

Footsteps came across the stage and a man arrived at the door. He was wearing a heavy tan woodworking apron with a white button-down shirt underneath. There was a rag in his hand and a light odor of turpentine in the air. Remus had great teeth. "Hey, Phil."

"Hey. This is Jack Stanley. He wants to see The Theatre."

"Okay. Hi Jack. Come on in." Remus held out his hand.

"Thanks Remus, nice to meet you." They shook hands and walked inside. Jack looked across the stage at the piano. Seeing it almost made him shudder.

"That's quite a piano," Jack said. It had been over a year since he'd seen it last. The finish gleamed and the piano was big, bigger than he'd remembered. The three legs were nearly a foot in diameter each. The sound box holding the strings was more than nine feet long. It was actually larger than a full concert-size grand and there were no pedals. Still, it held a modest spot on the large stage.

"It must be very loud. It looks like a Cristofori?" Jack walked to the piano and bent over to look underneath. He tapped his ring on one of the legs. Yes, it was hollow, but not empty. "Nice legs."

Remus looked at him strangely. In all his years playing piano, he'd come across very few who knew of the Cristofori, Tuscan forerunner of the grand piano. "Yes, it is. Only this one was built in Germany in 1936 to the original specs from Florence. The body's solid ebony. And it's loud." Remus hit a three-note chord near the bass end. The piano thundered throughout the auditorium.

"It's strange though. It was delivered here about six months ago. A gift from someone who said they saw me playing at the Drake up in Chicago. But there was no name or return address. I did a bunch of research on it, but haven't found out anything."

Jack did not move, listening closely.

"Well, I can tell you about that some other time," Remus said, waving his hand. Jack couldn't wait.

"The finish is lovely." Jack took a closer look. "French polish?"

"That's right." Remus smiled.

"Beautiful," said Jack as he bent close to look at the surface of the top.

"Yes, it is," Remus replied slowly and smiled. thinking this man quite peculiar.

Remus launched into a nine-minute monologue as they walked across the stage, through the wings and finally up into the auditorium to look down at the stage. Jack was silent during the tour and finally said, "I like it all. When can I meet the owner?"

Phil would later swear that Remus' short graying afro stood straight up. They were both speechless.

Jack picked up on the moment and said, "Hey, I'm starved. You two like to have lunch with me?"

Phil recommended they walk to Heidle's Tavern, a German deli-café two blocks away. It was agreed and they went to see the dressing rooms downstairs. Jack noted the condition and craftsmanship of the woodwork. The entire interior of The Theatre was covered in polished hardwood.

They entered Heidle's Tavern and crossed to the rear seating area. The wood of the walls and tables had a style and finish similar to that of The Theatre. The black and white tile floors were old, worn, and swept. The tables were covered with red checkered tablecloth and there was a clean smell of hickory smoke, sausage, and beer.

Heidle came over to greet Phil and Remus, then looked at their guest as Phil introduced. "Heidle, this is Jack Stanley. We were just showing him The Theatre."

"Hello Jack." Heidle was hardy and hale and spoke with a thick German accent. He had silver-gray hair down to his shoulders and a neatly trimmed salt and pepper beard. His large brown eyes gazed out from beneath dark eyebrows. Wearing a plaid flannel shirt and a clean white apron, he seemed the wizardly master of his space. He had a large smile, meaty hands, and radiated the proud energy of a seasoned host. "Wonderful! What a lovely building The Theatre. Remus has done such a fine job with the woodwork." They shook hands.

"Yes, it certainly is a lovely building," Jack said, as he looked over at Remus.

Phil added, "Remus did the finish on the interior woodwork of The Theatre."

"Remus, really? And you said nothing when I mentioned the woodwork," Jack said. He looked at the woodwork of the seating area as Heidle waved an arm in that direction.

"He did all *this*, too!" said Heidle.

Jack smiled at Heidle and turned to Remus. "Remus that's amazing. You're an artisan. And truly modest."

Remus smiled. "Why thank you, Jack."

Jack had liverwurst and mustard on a Kaiser with a side of vinegary potato salad and the fermented cabbage with caraway seed. Phil and Remus both had sausages and spätzle. Heidle had just tapped a cask of Marsenbeir from the spring. He insisted they each have a glass and there was no argument.

The Theatre wasn't mentioned during lunch. Jack asked a lot of questions and got a fairly detailed history of the town from Remus. Phil, who'd also grown up in town, told his story as well. Jack found it interesting that Phil and Remus knew nearly everyone that came into The Tavern.

They ordered coffee and Jack lit another of his strange-looking cigars as he addressed them both. "Okay listen, this is what I'd like to do with The Theatre, and I want to know what you guys think."

Jack spoke in startling detail about his plan to build a restaurant in The Theatre. Except for the seating rows, there would be no structural changes. This seemed to please Remus. The kitchen would occupy the space directly behind the backstage curtain and the bar would be located at stage right. The dressing rooms downstairs would be used for dry goods, refrigeration, and wine storage. Remus' personal quarters would remain in the VIP dressing room if he'd like to stay and play piano on salary.

Remus simply replied, "I have no problem with that arrangement."

Jack turned to Phil, with a signpost that would alter the course of his life. "Phil, if this happens, I could use someone like you to help me run the place. You're good with people, you know the town, and you know how to talk. As far as the restaurant business goes, it's simple and I can teach you all that. You interested?"

Remus would later swear he saw Phil's hair stand straight up as they made eye contact. Phil replied, "Sure, Jack, that sounds great."

"Remus, I know where to find you. Phil, where can I reach you after hours?" asked Jack.

Phil and Remus looked at each other with the words *Evangeline's Blues Bar* written across their faces.

• • •

The following Monday morning was a windy rain, and Remus woke to his daily 6:12 a.m. alarm. It was a ninety-ton steel rooster called the *12 Bar Special* out of St. Louis. Remus' brother was the train's master, and he blew the whistle loud and long every time he roared past The Prospect Theatre. The evening was Evangeline's and Remus was at the piano. He'd been playing St. Louis blues at the small club since it opened twelve years ago. Phil managed the house sound system that he'd designed and installed. With a series of microphones and unique electric pickups, Remus' voice and piano were mixed and played through a custom built 7.1 surround-sound system. The eighty-eight piano keys were separated into eight separate audio channels that made his playing seem to dance around the room.

On his nightly break, Remus would have a sweet sherry wine and a cigar. His limit was one, maybe two on a Friday, and he never stayed late. For years, Remus had been a fixture at the bar. He didn't dress fancy, but his suit was always pressed and his shoes and pocket watch were shined. No one knew exactly how old Remus was, but his voice rang clear as a bell, and his stories and songs lit up anyone within earshot.

Remus' private joy was sitting and talking with Pamela the bartender. She had beautiful eyes, great teeth, and outfits that drove everyone wild. The white vinyl pants, leather minis, and space-age body suits she wore flattered a dancer's figure. Her wit is sharp as a tack and her sense of humor cracked like a whip. She could tastefully defuse any come-on. Pamela would tap dance once or twice a night, occasionally on the bar, and also sang, accompanied by Remus at the piano.

Remus was presently *"Rustling up some fine young woman-folk"* when Phil walked in. The girls moved on and Remus said to Phil, "Chin up, Phil, that guy's gonna call about The Theatre, just you watch."

Phil sipped his Scotch and smiled at his friend. "Remus, how come you always know what I'm thinking?"

Remus returned a big smile and said, "Phil, you and me been friends for how — damn, look who it is!" He was looking over Phil's shoulder.

Jack Stanley walked into Evangeline's. He was wearing a navy-blue sweatshirt, Red Sox ball cap, jeans, and the boots. There was an aloof manner of ease as he approached the bar. Phil and Remus watched Pamela double-take when she looked at him. Neither of them had ever seen her do that before.

Phil leaned over to Remus and said, "You see what I see?"

Jack had Pamela in conversation for what must have been three minutes. With a rare shyness, her eyes sparkled as she polished the glasses.

"Yeah, I always wonder what that girl look like when she smitten," said Remus.

Jack noticed the boys and came over. "Hey, I know you two."

Phil and Remus both raised their glasses. "Evening, Jack."

Pamela was cleaning Remus' ashtray as Jack lit a cigar and said to them, "I just bought The Prospect Theatre."

Pamela, Phil, and Remus stared at him and said in unison, "You *what*?"

"I thought you'd say that. You guys still in?" Jack puffed on the cigar as he laughed.

Pamela looked at Jack and then the other two as she squinted and said, "This is the guy you've been talking about?" Her eyes returned to Jack with a twinkle. "Hmmm." She turned to serve the rest of the bar.

Jack looked at them with a questioning eyebrow. Phil and Remus both shrugged and took a drink. Evangeline's was never the same.

• • •

Remus fumbled with his keys to The Theatre as Jack, Phil, and Pamela stood on the sidewalk. It was nearly 2 a.m. and Jack was telling a story about eating live sea urchin roe on a side street in Paris. The streets were shining wet from the evening's shower and Remus reflected on the five glasses of sherry and three cigars he'd had. He was in fine spirits, and everyone was in the mood for coffee. Their footsteps echoed as they entered the dark space. Arriving at center stage, no one said a word.

Jack looked up and turned to Remus. "Remus, do the stage lights work?"

"Sure, Jack. Come on. I'll show you." They walked off stage and Phil smiled at Pamela. She poked him in the stomach.

Behind the side curtain at stage left were the lighting controls. "These are the stage lights left and stage right. And these here are the center, front and rear." Remus was proudly displaying the seventy-year-old machinery. The Theatre seemed to inhale as the lights came up full and Remus' eyes were bright.

"My friend Morris is an electrician. He helps me look after things." The controls' action was smooth and the brass gleamed. The light filtered around the curtain and trickled over them.

Jack smiled at the scene. "Nice. Turn it up full."

Remus ran his hand over the controls. "I'm glad you like it." A stranger listening would not have known exactly who owned The Theatre.

They heard the echoes of voices and walked out to join them. The on-stage light was beyond daylight. They each gazed out from the stage as if surveying some uncharted land. Remus removed his jacket and said, "I'll make us some coffee."

The rest of the evening passed in ease. The overhead spotlights cast a pure white light and cut crisp shadows on their faces. Phil commented on the design and carpentry of the interior, Pamela described how she felt the chairs and windows should be dressed, and Remus sat on the edge of the stage telling his favorite stories. Jack asked lots of questions.

• • •

At 5:35 a.m., Remus let everyone out and closed the door with a smile. By the time he hit the bed he'd barely removed his pocket watch and shoes. He didn't hear the train's morning whistle.

At 11:30 a.m., Remus was ironing a shirt and had coffee going on the stove. He wore a white tank top and boxers, with black socks and shoes. He was lighting a cigar when he heard a knock at the door upstairs.

"Good morning, Remus," Jack smiled.

"Morning, Jack." The sunlight blazed in and Remus squinted.

"Remus, we need a doorbell."

"Okay, come on in. What's in the bag Dad?" He saw the white bag with grease spots and knew it was from Rosie's Bakery.

"Strawberry jelly roll." Jack handed him the bag as they walked across the stage. Remus peeked inside.

"Hey, my favorite! How'd you know?"

"Rosie told me."

"A little bit of Rosie's jelly roll in the morning do me just fine." Remus beamed and they shared a quick laugh.

Jack gazed out into The Theatre. "Remus, these windows are beautiful. I didn't realize how much light would come in."

Jack looked up at the large windows on either side of the auditorium. He recalled Pamela's comment last night that the windows should have deep red damask draperies and that they should match the seats and barstools. Probably her lipstick, too. The girl had style.

Remus looked up as well. "It changes through the day. Late afternoon comes in the other side." He pointed upward. "Come on downstairs. You want some coffee?"

"Sure."

Entering Remus' suite, Jack was hit by the aromas of coffee, cigar and the man's personal scent. Not to mention the fact that Remus was standing in his underwear. "Don't mind me, Remus. I'm just going to have a look around." Jack headed out as Remus set up the coffee.

"You want cream, no sugar. Right, Jack?" Remus called.

"Yes, please, Remus. Do you mind if I grab those blueprints?"

"They're all yours. In the small room under the stairs."

• • •

For weeks, Jack's office was center stage. A folding chair, an ancient cosmetics table and a thirty-foot telephone line. The stage was covered with a chaotic jumble of chairs, tables, mirrors, boxes of old makeup, and two large garment racks full of vintage costumes. Backstage and the downstairs dressing rooms were empty, and the main stage had a dust problem. Jack was on the phone with John Tenyon, owner of the De Soto Woodshop.

He was holding the phone's base, walking with the long cord following him around the stage. He bent down to inspect the edge of the stage.

"Not too much right now. I have five rooms worth of old wooden furniture to be cleaned, and all the floors need to be refinished. I think it's about three-thousand square feet."

John was intrigued by the call. He could always tell a big job in the making, but this sounded interesting. "Let me get a pencil. Who's speaking?"

"Jack Stanley."

"Jack Stanley. Good Lord! You bought The Theatre! I've been meaning to get over there. What are you doing with the place?" There was concern in John's voice.

"Why don't you come by John? We should talk. Phil told me about your shop and your connection to The Theatre."

"Yeah sure. Phil and Remus are old friends of mine."

John's grandfather had set up The De Soto Woodshop shortly after being contracted to design and build The Prospect Theatre in 1926. He and his brothers came from Heidelberg, Germany in 1917 and had established themselves in the St. Louis area as premier architects and cabinetmakers.

"When can you make it over?"

"Give me twenty minutes."

"Great. Looking forward to it."

It was raining and windy. John arrived in green overalls and work boots, carrying two large photo albums in a heavy clear plastic bag. Jack got up to greet him at the door.

"John, I'm Jack, nice to meet you." Jack noticed the photo albums.

"Hi, Jack. Great to meet you, too." John shook Jack's hand and looked around at the paneling and up at the coffered ceiling as he came inside. "I haven't been in here for some time."

"Come on in. Would you like some coffee?"

"That sounds great."

They crossed to center stage and John took the albums out of the plastic, placing them on Jack's table. "Jack, you should take these. They're my grandfather's photos of The Theatre as it was being built."

Jack ran his hand over the leather binding and opened the album to a page. Then he looked at a few more. All eight by ten black and white photos, in startling detail. The building was filled with tools, workers, and lumber, shown in various stages of construction. The four men in the photos seemed to be brothers.

"John, this is incredible!" Jack turned a few more pages. There were hundreds of photographs. "This will take some time. Thank you, but I think they really belong to you."

"My pleasure, Jack. The building has quite a history. You'll see pictures of the camera in the mirror of some of the dressing room shots. It's an original Deardroff V-eight from 1913. The negatives are eight by ten-inch glass plates."

Jack pondered this, thinking he'd like to see the camera and negatives. "You still have the camera?"

"I do. Phil does a lot of work with it. Every once in a while, he buys a few hundred plates. He's done a lot of photography here. The light coming in those windows can be pretty dramatic."

Phil came out on stage and John gave him a wave. "Hey Phil."

"Hey John."

"So, your grandfather designed and built The Theatre?" Jack went on.

"Yes. And there's quite a story that goes along with it, including his journals. I'll bring them by another time."

"I'd really like that. It sounds interesting."

John nodded. "Sure. What are you planning to do here? I heard a restaurant." John's brow furrowed.

"That's right. We're taking it slow, though. I'd like your thoughts on a few things."

John looked around The Theatre and then down at the stage. "Here it is. He always put his trademark into the flooring. It took my grandfather over a year to collect all the planking for the stage. See it's a technique called book matching." John looked around and positioned himself at center stage, pointing up at one side of the auditorium.

"If you look at all the raised wall panels you can see that they're each of a single board that was split and opened like a book. That way they're symmetrical. They do the same with stringed instruments. With the stage, he started at the center and built outward with each split plank. You'll see the center plank is double wide. On boat decking this would be the king plank."

John continued as he stepped off the stage and backed up the center aisle. "From here you can really tell. It's like a great mirror image on the floor. It also served as a reference for the performers as to where they stood in relation to center stage." John bent down and looked closely at the wood. "These are particularly long, wide and thick planks of Iroko. They'd make a great boat. It'll be beautiful when it's refinished."

Jack was now looking down at the stage in amazement. "I did not notice this." Phil walked out on stage and had overheard the description. He too was looking down at the stage and listened as if John were telling a crackling tale.

John walked to the edge of the stage and turned around. Pointing to the walls of the auditorium he continued, "Now if you look, you'll see that the five panels on the left of the auditorium mirror those on the right. This makes the auditorium structurally symmetrical as well. The Theatre was known for its acoustics. It's really a giant hardwood sound box."

Phil and Jack both looked from side to side as John's voice radiated from the walls. Jack walked down and held out his hand. "John, you come from a family of master artisans." The two men shook hands.

"Thanks, Jack. I'm glad you appreciate it." John was clearly and justly proud.

John turned to Phil. "Where's Remus? The place looks great!" It was true. The woodwork was brightly polished.

At that moment, Remus walked out. "Hey, this place is still famous for its acoustics."

"Remus, how you been?" asked John.

"I'm just fine, John. Thanks. It's been too long."

"Yes, it has. The woodwork is looking fine as ever." They shook hands.

"Can't let the spirits down. I guess you heard we have a new owner." Over the years John and Remus had discussed projects they felt were needed in The Theatre, but both knew there was no maintenance budget.

"Looks like some long overdue projects will finally get done. The stage is going to look spectacular!" John exclaimed.

The phone rang and Jack excused himself. Walking to the phone he had the comfortable feeling that The Theatre did not belong solely to him.

"Pamela. Good morning," Jack said as he sat down at his table. Phil had joined John and Remus, and at the mention of Pamela's name John said, "God, I bumped into her recently. She's so beautiful. Every time I see her. How is she?"

Remus shook his head with a grin. "She's just fine. A special vintage getting better with age."

"So, what's going on here? What does Jack want to do?" John was earnest.

Phil looked over at Jack, who was in conversation facing the other direction. "Come on downstairs. I'll show you the drawings." They turned and headed to the wide stairway leading down to the old dressing rooms.

John frowned. "Drawings, oh no..."

Phil smiled. "Don't worry, it's nothing drastic, nothing structural."

John was preoccupied with the word "drawings." How could he possibly want to change the design of the building?

The trio arrived in the large back room where there was an old round table covered with a set of construction plans. John immediately looked to the bottom left corner and ran his fingers over his grandfather's name. He looked closely at the precise work and spoke softly. "I thought these had been lost. They look like they were drafted yesterday."

"I found them a few weeks ago. They were in that box." Remus pointed to a large flat hardwood box with brass hardware and a leather handle. "It was in a strange place. There's a void behind the stairs. I wonder what else is stashed around here."

"Maybe a skeleton or two," cracked Phil.

"Yeah, with a beer stein in his hand," Remus said.

"Oh man. And a garter belt in the other," said John. They all laughed and looked around.

Phil walked to a side table and picked up a small drawing. He handed it to John. "Here's what Jack wants to do."

John looked at the drawing and for a moment was silent. "Jack drew this?" He smiled and chuckled. John was a big man, built like a bearded medieval woodsman. "It's creative. I like it. Looks like he thinks the seating platforms on the incline should be wood."

"He wants it to be traditional." Phil pointed to part of the drawing. "Continue the style of the paneling."

"I can appreciate that. But you could never really replicate those patterns." John pointed to the drawing. "First of all, it'll definitely be a different wood. And it's probably impossible to find router bits to copy the raised panels. I think we should make a form and pour concrete. Then cover it with carpet."

"*Concrete*! I never thought I'd hear that!" Jack boomed as he entered the room. He craned his neck and looked at the drawing. "Wouldn't that be too heavy?"

"Not at all. It won't take much to grade the three new rows and it'll be solid as a rock."

Jack looked at Phil and Remus as they shrugged affirmatively with eyebrows raised. Jack returned to John and said, "Fine. We'll do it with concrete."

And so, the building of Jack's Café began.

CHAPTER THREE

The Boat

When John and Jack first started talking about the construction and redesign of The Theatre into a restaurant, the bar area became a priority. John casually mentioned that he had a bar in storage, but that it might be too big. He gave Jack the rough dimensions and the next morning Jack had paced it out on the stage. *A little big but not impossible,* he thought to himself. *It'll have to go all the way into the kitchen.*

Later that day, John came in and showed Jack a Polaroid shot of the bar. "What do you think?"

"Wow. I *love* it!" Jack smiled at John. "The two wood tones are beautiful together."

"I know, aren't they? It needs a little cleaning, but it's really a special piece. The bar top is full-length planks of longleaf yellow pine, and the corner carvings and vertical panels are walnut. It's funny. I've always wondered how it would look on the stage. You want to see it?"

"Sure, any time you want to go."

"It's out in De Soto at the shed. You'll like the boatyard. It's about a half-hour drive. I'm free now if you are.

"Great. We can take my car. How about if you drive?"

"Okay."

Outside The Theatre they were both silent looking down at the gravel as they crossed the parking area to Jack's car. Jack pulled out his keys and stopped before getting into the passenger side. "It's perfect. The pine is light like some of the Iroko on the stage and the walnut matches the panels in the auditorium."

John smiled and nodded. "I know. I've thought the same thing. You want to know something funny? My grandfather bought it, and it's been in storage ever since. Must be over a hundred years old. It's from a Missouri River steamboat that was called the Lady Prospect that crashed and sunk in 1896."

"That's too much." Jack tossed the keys to John and they settled into the car. "Any connection to The Prospect Theatre? Did your grandfather work on boats?"

"Yes, he did. As far as the connection, that's a good question. You'd need to look into who contracted The Theatre to be built. The riverboat era was pretty much over by the turn of the century, and The Theatre was built in '26. But there was a lot going on around town at that time. And they did projects all over the region. It was the railroad station that put this town on the map. Once the railroads took over the freight business, the riverboats couldn't turn a profit. All the local newspapers going back to the turn of the century are on microfilm at the library. This was a busy little town back then. Might have been the same owner, now that you mention it. My grandfather did some work on steamboat interiors."

John knew the roads and drove a bit faster than anyone else. Jack enjoyed this and lit a cigar. There was very little talk on the way to the boatyard.

• • •

Jack made it clear he enjoyed being a passenger in the Cobra. He never complained about anyone's driving, and anyone got to drive the car if Jack was going. Its wheelbase was just over seven feet and the V8 was just under seven liters. The 550-horsepower roadster was a man-eater.

Remus never drove the Cobra in town, but at Jack's insistence would occasionally take it to Chicago. "It's a great stretch of highway," Jack said to him, encouraging him to take it anytime. He gave Remus his pair of English driving goggles and said to leave the top down. "And be sure to make up a good story about the car when you get to Chicago."

Remus rolled into the Loop reflecting the soul of the city, a pure statement of casual yet slick.

During Remus' first trip with the car, he had a photo taken of it with his two brothers and a friend. It's a full shot of the Cobra from above and slightly forward parked on a side street in South Chicago. The men in the photo have similar graying afros and great white teeth. One of the men is wearing a white fedora and Remus is wearing the goggles. The woman draped across the Cobra's sloping hood is wearing a long ivory-colored dress with a bow on the side of her head. The deep red lipstick matches the bow, a fine accent to her skin's café au lait tone. Phil had printed it desaturated and toned for a vintage feel but left her lipstick and bow in living color. It hangs just above the handrail at the bottom of the stairs. Remus signed the photo, "Thanks, Jack," and gave it to him framed, after he got back. A few days later, Phil suggested they start a photo gallery on the stairwell with prints of The Theatre's construction.

. . .

Jack had heard about John's "shed" out in De Soto, but he'd never been there. It was up the river and the property covered about nine acres. What awaited Jack was beyond anything he'd ever seen. Along the river was a dock with three boats. Phil lived here on his forty-foot wooden fishing boat, the *Pajova*, which he'd recently bought from John with his commission from the sale of The Theatre. He'd also sold his house; with so many memories of Miss Kelley filling the place, he just didn't want to look at the walls.

Jack was silent as he got out of the car and surveyed the property. There were three large sheds. On the left was the wood shop. Stretching perpendicular to the river, it was nearly fifty feet wide and open, lean-to style, on the long side. Rollers with a heavy canvas tarp hung along the top to close off the opening in bad weather. At one end was a large table saw and long worktable. Behind were shelves of hardwood stock and scraps. At the other end was a drill press, different metal-working tools, and a small table with an anvil and vice.

Across from the shop was a smaller closed shed that looked more like a barn. Between these two buildings leading down to the river, was a system of rails. This was a launching ramp between the river and a three-story open structure facing the river. Inside the shed was a huge unpainted wooden boat hull nearly one-hundred-twenty feet long. Jack was thunderstruck, absolutely amazed.

"John, are you building this?" Jack motioned to the big boat.

"Yeah. It's been about five years. I did the woodwork. Couple of guys helped me. There's a lot of electrical work to do now, and the plumbing and tanks, of course." He shrugged. "We've been taking our time with the hull and structural bulkheads. It's an ox. Everyone calls it 'The Ark.' My work's mostly done. I may sell it or keep pecking away at it. Come on, I'll show you."

John was used to the effect the boat had on folks seeing it for the first time. But for Jack, pieces of a life-long puzzle started falling into place.

They climbed onto a scaffold and were able to look down into the boat. There was no deck closing it in. It was one of the strangest sights Jack had ever seen. It looked like a football-shaped house with no roof — a giant piece of furniture made entirely of wood. There were three sections. The center was the largest, with its floor at least three feet lower than the areas at either end.

John heard the phone ring, and he started back down the ladder. "Jack, I have to go over to the office and take a call."

Jack nodded and turned back to the boat and climbed in. After a few minutes walking through the boat's interior, he heard John call and climbed out of the boat.

"There's all the stools." John pointed to a large, heavy-duty shelving unit in a corner of the shed. "I think there's eighteen. They weigh a ton. And that's the bar over there." John pointed.

"God, it's massive. Bigger than I'd pictured." Jack said. "I paced it out on the stage, and it seems like it'll go. Do you have a tape measure?" He bent down and looked at the foot rail. "It needs some cleaning."

John watched closely as Jack walked around inspecting the edges. "What are we looking at to clean it up and get it into The Theatre?"

John scratched his beard and was honest. "Well, I'll tell you, really it didn't cost me anything. But to get it to the level of what's going on inside The Theatre would take eighty or ninety hours of labor. The guys doing the finish on the floors and stage have been out of work for a while. Give them a few weeks after they finish up at The Theatre and they'll be ready to do it cheap. I could offer them a set price and I'm sure they'll take it. I'd say four, five grand tops, and it's yours."

"Done and clean. Nice?"

"Sure, Jack. It'll be nice."

"Clean?"

John nodded. "It'll be clean."

They walked around it and Jack pointed out some of the nicks and gouges and where some of the fastenings had come loose.

"All right," Jack said. "But don't spend too much time on the scratches. I like the feel. Just tighten up the loose planks. Put in some new screws and maybe a little epoxy. And don't take it all the way down to bare wood. Leave the original finish and put four or five coats over that. What do you think?"

"Yeah, that's how I'd do it. It'll go nicely with the rest of the interior. I'll use a heavy-duty Dutch marine varnish, Epifanes. That's what I'm putting on the boat."

"I like it." Jack was looking across the yard to the boat. "Can we have another look at the boat?"

John chuckled. "Sure Jack." He didn't know much about this guy, but he was beginning to like him. Jack had a strange sense of composition, and he could clearly piece things together on the fly.

• • •

After first seeing the boat, the entire plan began to come together in his mind over a period of three or four days. A few weeks later, he sat down with John and made an offer. But first he had to tell John the whole plan and the whole story.

It was a cold rain that night and had just stopped snowing, something they hadn't seen in a year and a half. Jack invited John for dinner, and they were eating pan-fried golden trout in a spicy cornmeal batter over stewed okra and tomatoes. It was one of John's favorites.

The day before, John had mentioned that his brother Don had shown up unannounced with a cooler full of fish he'd just caught down in the Ozarks where he lived. John asked if they could do dinner the following evening, and by the way, could his brother stop by later to see the place? Don rarely came into town and hadn't seen The Theatre in years. Jack said he'd be happy to show him around and could he put aside three or four of the big ones for tomorrow's dinner. Don showed up an hour later.

He was the spitting image of John, beard and all, though more than a bit unkempt and probably thirty pounds lighter. He lived in the Ozark Mountains in a cabin up a rugged holler close to the river's spring. Don was eight years older than John with brown hair, brown eyes, and a beard that was mostly grey. Jack enjoyed hearing of his home and lifestyle and kept him talking for nearly three hours.

They drank most of a bottle of Scotch. Don enjoyed Jack's company and promised to be back soon with more fish. Jack said that would be great and Don stopped by often over the years. He was always by himself wearing his best clothes looking as rugged as the Ozarks themselves. Don got on well with Jimmy, and Jack made sure Don never paid for a thing.

Jack, John, and Remus ate dinner the following night in Remus' suite. They talked about how The Theatre had been built; the construction techniques, materials, and how radically transportation had evolved since the steamboat. All this fascinated Jack. The fact that John grew up building and working on boats was even more interesting. A third bottle of wine was open, another seven-year-old Barbaresco. They were drinking out of short water glasses. Jack eventually told them most of his background and how he went to Italy so many years ago.

"John, how do you feel about The Theatre? I mean have you ever wanted to own it?" Jack asked.

"Hah. You know Jack, it's like a set of china that's been in the family forever, only somebody else has possession of it now and it's gathering dust. And I can't even go in and clean it. Remus, don't get me wrong. You've been taking care of this place better than anyone could've ever dreamed and everybody's fortunate for that, but can you imagine how bad I've wanted to come in here and work on it? It's just that I could never afford it. I'd give nearly anything for it."

"Okay, here's an idea. Remember we talked about how the boat would look if the interior was finished similar to the interior of The Theatre?"

John laughed heartily. "Yeah, I been thinking about it ever since. That would be quite a boat. I especially like your vision of a huge, cavernous central salon without any lower level with cabins." He paused, Jack was grinning slightly as he watched John become serious and add, "You know, I have the perfect staircase in storage. What do you have in mind, Jack?"

"What if you were to finish the boat like that with the big main salon, but use all the paneling from inside The Theatre. When it's finished, I'll trade you The Theatre, minus all the paneling, for the boat?"

John sat still for just a moment then picked up his wine. "You're serious, aren't you?"

"I am." Jack shrugged.

"What are you going to do with it?" John held onto his wine.

"I want to take it to Italy. And run a restaurant out of it." Jack looked from John to Remus. It was hard for them to tell if he was serious. His eyebrows were raised like he was testing them.

John decided to call him on it. "Okay, but I get to be captain and drive the boat. At least for a year or so." He sat back and drank his wine.

"That's fine. But I want the stage planking, too."

Before John could answer, Remus cut in. "Hey, Jack, I wanna come, too." He was half-joking.

"You bet, Remus. 'Cause we're taking that piano upstairs."

They all had their glasses in hand and there was an odd moment of silence. Jack raised his and they followed suit.

"Good, that settles it. To the boat. But not a word to anyone *please*, not for a while."

They all drank. John shrugged looking at his wine and Remus laughed. Never in their wildest dreams. . .

CHAPTER FOUR

Italy

Licio Gella, now going by the name of Jack Stanley, grew up in Boston's North End. Like many of the neighborhood families, he and his parents had emigrated by boat from Italy. Jack's father, Giancarlo, grew up outside the town of Carrara. His family owned and operated three of the largest marble quarries in the area, the largest marble trucking business, and a vast shipping and distribution network. These quarries have produced fine statuary marble for some of the greatest masterpieces of all time. The family had also operated a studio where they sold their own works in marble.

Jack's mother's family owned more than thirty stables that had supplied horses and mules to the quarries for generations. When trucking became the future of marble transportation, the family switched over to thoroughbred breeding. These stables now produce some of the finest horses in Europe.

Giancarlo grew up with marble dust on his trousers, a chisel in his hand, and an eye for beauty. His masterpiece at age twenty-six was a seven-foot hazelnut cluster on the branch. It was commissioned by a confectionery that was headquartered in Turin. The piece was rendered approximately twelve times life-size, carved, and polished out of a single block of pink-veined marble.

One August morning, Giancarlo was riding his horse along one of the great marble ridges east of the city of Carrara. He had the unique skill of being able to spot the finest blocks in the quarry. Just off the path, he spotted an unusual piece. About the size of a football, it had a hazel tinge, a fine texture and veins of ochre that seemed to glow from within. "This is the most beautiful color I've ever seen," he said to himself. "I will save it for a very special piece."

Jack's mother, Giardinia, grew up in the rugged hillside town of Vignale. After a drunk driver killed her mother, seventeen-year-old Giardinia became head of the household, taking care of the laundry, cleaning, and most importantly, the cooking, for a healthy and hungry family of five. There were tiny wild strawberries and blueberries to be gathered and fall showers produced more porcini mushrooms than the village could grill, stew, and marinate.

Her father was a good man, and he continued to make a fine living raising horses. He loved his children, and he loved his wine. Giardinia's teen years were spent in and around the stables. Her days and dreams were filled with the aromas of saddle soap, horses, and the rich mountain foliage.

Giancarlo was on his horse when he came upon the stable built into the hillside. He saw the back of a lovely woman scrubbing saddles. She had long wavy brown hair, and a fine figure was revealed as she worked the heavy leather. Turning to greet him she stepped into a shaft of light. Her eyes, lit by afternoon sun, were a shade of hazel he'd seen only once before.

A month later, he presented her with a sculpture of a winged horse poised on one foot. The size of a football, it was made of finely polished green marble flecked with gold that mirrored the aura of her eyes.

Boston twenty-two years ago.

Thirteen-year-old Jack was sitting in the courtyard sculpture garden of his family's modest three-story building. His mother, Giardinia, watched him from an upstairs window.

Since they'd arrived, Boston had been good to them and Giancarlo was as busy as he wanted to be. He now had five helpers and more than enough sculpture commissions from Rome. The sculpture garden was outside and when it rained a cleverly designed roof was hoisted to shield the work area. In winter, the men worked around a fire built in a large iron tub. The rhythmic chipping of marble echoed through the courtyard and into the dreams of young Jack. As a child he was immersed in an aesthetic wonderland. He spent hours watching and listening to his father and the other men as they created beautiful forms out of rough and often large pieces of stone. This stone was marble. It was their daily bread, and it was in their blood.

The family had come to Boston based on Giancarlo's ability to create beauty and they'd all flourished. Giardinia cooked every day, feeding her family, the workers, and their families. And now when the men from Rome visited, young Jack began cooking for them. He never knew why these men were so important, but like many things, he took his mother's word. Sometimes arriving in full regalia, the men would sit and discuss things in large books with Jack's father. Then his father would make drawings for them.

As a child, his ears were filled with the "tat-tat-tat" of chisel on stone, the soft voices of Italian men in earnest, and the sweet sound of his mother's knife on the cutting block. Jack could always tell by listening, which tool was being used and at what stage the sculpture stood. From the sounds of the heavy flat chisel used to outline a project, to the endless rubbing with cloth and paste to make the stone glow.

In this childhood environment sounds were visual. Jack could also tell which vegetables were being cut by his mother's knife, he had such excellent hearing. The sounds echoed into the courtyard as he grew up. He regarded marble as divine and venerated the men in the sculpture garden as his heroes. His father explained to him that they never considered themselves masters; the medium was their master, and mastery was not for mortal souls.

He went on to say they were simply servants. Servants to those who came to them with ideas and servants to the marble. Their duty was to look into the rough stone, see the beauty within, and free it for all to behold.

• • •

It was late October and the cool, damp winds blew in off Boston harbor. Looking down from the bathroom window, Giardinia wondered what was going through her son's mind. Lico or "Licie" as he was called, fiddled with a chisel. He inspected the blade and idly wondered what it had most recently done and when it had last been sharpened. He kicked at the marble chips around his feet. His father wanted him to become a sculptor, but he and his wife both knew their son was meant to do something greater. She could not stand seeing her son dawdle any longer.

That evening, Giardinia was most outspoken. "Carlo, we need to *do* something with him."

His father shrugged in resignation. "If he doesn't want to be a sculptor, fine. He's talented. We can pray for him, and he'll find his course."

But his mother pressed on. "We need to do more than *pray* that someone or something will make him. He's a brilliant boy. He notices things." She was adamant that something should be done. "I won't stand by and watch that boy make his life on the street. I see him with the other boys on the corner. I know he doesn't like them, but in time he'll be working with Dano and his trash."

Giancarlo knew she was right, but he didn't know what to do about it. "Ginia, the boy is young. Give him time. What was I doing when *I* was a boy?"

"You were riding your horse through the Apuan Alps looking for strange pieces of marble." She glared at him with an eyebrow raised and he knew exactly what she meant. She was so beautiful. As she continued, her blood boiled, "That was *not* Boston, and I will not sit and wait with our boy! If you don't have a solution, I will take him from here myself. Back to Italy." She got up and went to the sink, cleaning up the area.

Giancarlo knew there would be arguing. While his work was his life, she was his love and without her his life would crumble. "I'll speak to his eminence tonight. I have an idea." The men from Rome came for dinner and later that evening Giancarlo spoke to them in earnest about his family's issue.

• • •

Back in Italy a few days later, three of the men and a visitor sat outside the villa at Castel Gandolfo. The table was simple but the view from the veranda was grand, overlooking the lake and stretching out across the lazy hills of western Lazio. It was late afternoon, and the hazy Roman light was calming. It set the tone once again, for the weighty conversations that had taken place there for centuries.

They traveled together often, and when men such as these were received, it usually meant much decorum and rich dining. It was always a relief to return home to their private conversations and simple fare. They ate communally from a large wooden trencher set on the table.

There was a small pile of Latvian sprats, the fine Baltic smoked herring prepared by a monastery on the Gulf of Riga. There was also a crock of Sicilian olives and a hunk of tangy cheese from Modica in southern Sicily. The men used their contacts and influence wisely and it showed on their table. The still mineral water was from Gandolfo's own spring. The oil came from the fruit of their olive groves.

The men rarely made small talk, but tonight they were avoiding the topic at hand. Donato Bramante finally broached the subject. "It's a mistake bringing this boy here. His father may be talented but what can the boy *do*? Cook? His meals have no sense of composition, and he spends too much concentration on individual dishes. He's simple-minded and besides there are no others his age here." He muttered the Latin equivalent of *humbug*. "What will he do?"

Julius Della Rovere was first to counter. "True, but what was Cesare Baronio when he started? Just a boy." He awaited Donato's retort.

"That *boy* is no Baronius!" Donato replied brusquely as he cut into a piece of cheese.

The other men at the table smiled. They knew well the comparison Julius was making to the famous Roman priest-chef of the Community of the Orations. Founded in 1575 by Saint Phillip Neri, the congregation was held together by Baronio's fine cuisine for years. In 1596, Baronio, at the time forty-eight years old and a poor man, was elevated to cardinal in reward for his dedication to his brothers. He lived to be eighty-nine years old.

Lorenzo Orsini skillfully nibbled an olive, tossing the pit over the veranda's rail. "The boy's talented. That's reason enough for me. You've seen him draw. He may have no sense of foreshortening, Donato, but consider his parents. His father's work is unrivaled. What was the first piece he did for us, the little satyr? He portrayed the rotten teeth so delicately I could almost smell the wretched breath," he paused.

"I know we've paid a pittance for the work his father's done for us. Giancarlo's work is the finest sculpture we've added to our museums for over a century. And I admit, the aging and reselling of the sculptures is a bit shady, but it was for a cause." Lorenzo held out his arms. "Anyway, I think in return the least we can do is bestow upon the boy some things he otherwise might not have had. Nothing material of course, but things along the lines of education, introductions, and experience. Perhaps then we can consider it reimbursement or compensation for using his father for our benefit."

Lorenzo picked up another olive. He knew he was right, and so did the others. The topic was a recurring one. Each of the men, in their own way, felt guilty for how Jack's father had been taken advantage of.

Julius broke the silence, instigating as he always did. "And his mother. Need I mention that there is scarcely another like her in all of Italy."

Jacapo Galli spoke next. "Eminence, with all due respect." Jacapo's expression carried embarrassment and friendship. Julius regularly offended his three friends with his talk of and exploits with women. "I'm certain we agree the boy's mother is the purest embodiment of feminine beauty, but this is not the point. However, I do agree there is something compelling in the boy's nature."

Lorenzo raised his arms. "He's simply *entertaining*. A genius and a creative prodigy. Consider the meals he's prepared and described for us in that little house in Boston. He conveys such alacrity and gusto through his food that he makes the performance of merely *cooking* seem divine." Lorenzo could, at his most persuasive, be both poetic and magnificent. His skill in debate was not simply to advocate his own wishes or ideas but to find a common ground. His friends respected his eloquence and were often united by his words.

Julius turned to Donato, who seemed the sole antagonist. The chief gourmand of the four, Donato was also a devout and pious man. He'd openly objected to the abuse of Jack's father, but at the same time praised the meals at the small town-house as exquisite and august. Julius played on both these angles. "Donato, I think Lorenzo has a point. If we do something for him, I think we can consider it penance for our behavior towards his father. We can achieve absolution and at the same time bolster the cuisine here at Gandolfo." He paused.

"Remember the braised veal shank with chestnuts in pastry? It would taste even better if we were freed from the guilt tugging at our cassocks."

Donato gazed at the food, picking up the knife and then resting it back down on the cheese board. He sat back in resignation. Lorenzo smiled faintly, bowing slightly. "Besides, he may come in handy someday."

And so, as was the way with such men, they justified their personal greed by bestowing grace upon others. Lorenzo got up from the table and went to the door. "Angelo, please, join us for a moment," he called down the hallway and then returned to his seat.

Angelo Vilotti was chief secretary of the estate. He handled transportation arrangements and security for these men and their guests. He was also responsible for all the estate's finances and directly responsible for management of the entire staff. Having been at this post for more than twenty years, very little escaped his watchful eyes. Translucent skin stretched across his bones with the bluish hue of low-fat milk. He smoked between three and four packs of cigarettes a day. He entered the room and addressed Lorenzo. "Eminence." He nodded to the others.

"Angelo, we have a boy coming to stay with us. His name is Licio. The length of his stay is uncertain, but we'd like to extend him every courtesy." This was indeed strange, and Angelo waited, his mind racing through accommodation schemes.

"He's the son of Giancarlo, the sculptor." Vilotti nodded, knowing well the situation with Jack's father. He himself had been personally appalled; the fact that they were reselling most of the works for nearly fifty times their purchase price was sickening.

Lorenzo continued. "He speaks no Italian, Angelo, and we would like to see that he is only spoken to in English." Angelo nodded, understanding. "Introduce him to Geraldo. Have him spend most of his time in the gardens. He should enjoy that. And take him to Casaroli. Have him teach the boy to ride horses. Sister Vicaenza will teach him some Latin. Now, Angelo, let him roam but keep him busy. And keep an eye on him. Geraldo and Casaroli, *English* only. Are we clear?"

Angelo blinked slowly and nodded once more. "Most certainly, Eminence." It was absolutely clear. Licio was not to find out about the true value of his father's sculpture. Or anything else going on at Gandolfo.

Lorenzo went on, "Good. First of all, we'd like you to take him to Gamaretti and have him outfitted with a wardrobe for evenings and banquets. Have Tesla fix some lights and a bed up above the carriage house. He can bathe in the spa area." He glanced out of the corner of his eye at Donato, who rolled his eyes, exhaling and shaking his head. "That's all, Angelo, thank you. He should be arriving in a week's time."

• • •

Giardinia spoke to her son in the garden. "Licie, you're going on a trip. I'll go with you until you're settled, and your father and I will come to visit you. This city is nowhere for a boy like you to become a man."

Looking at his mother, he knew this would not be an easy situation for him or for anyone. He began to cry. "Why, Mama? Why do I have to go? I love you and Papa. I love the sculpture garden, and I love your kitchen. I don't want to go on a trip."

Giardinia put her arms around him and held him to her breast. She too began to cry but could not let him know she was crying. "Oh, Licie, we love you, too. That's why it needs to be. You're very special and you'll do great things. But not here. Not in this city. You will come back as a man."

In his mother's arms, Jack smelled her body and felt her warmth. He wanted to stay there forever, and they embraced for some time.

The following evening, young Jack took his first ride to Boston's Logan Airport and got on a plane for the first time. In the end it was decided that his mother would not accompany him. They'd spent the day saying their goodbyes. "You're going to work in one of the greatest kitchens on God's earth. When you come back, you can show me all the wonderful things these men have taught you."

"But, Mama, I love your cooking. I know it so well. What could ever be better than that?" There were tears in his eyes.

She paused and looked at her handsome son wondering how he would change as he matured. "You will see the most beautiful things on Earth and taste wonderful things. Please believe me."

Jack always believed his mother. But this time, for the first time, he found it difficult. He didn't know what he would do without his mother, or how he'd cook without her. But she assured him just as she did when she began letting him decide what to cook for the men from Rome. "You can do anything you set your mind to." And so, whenever the men came over, he would decide what to make, he would serve them, and he would explain to them in English, never Italian, how the meal was prepared. This is why they trusted him. And when his father asked them if he could go to Italy and cook for them, they agreed.

He traveled with a single bag. His mother had packed a chef's knife, along with his favorite chisel from the courtyard. These were wrapped in a small piece of heavy Italian flannel Jack had grown up with. His "nightie night" had always been placed in his windowsill to freshen it with the outdoor breeze. As a child, he held it in his hand as he sucked his thumb. And so, as he slipped into twilight sleep and childhood dreams, the fresh smell of his mother's clothesline permeated his thoughts. All these things gave him comfort and while he knew he would miss his parents immensely, he also knew he would not be lonely.

The greatest gift his mother gave him was a final bit of advice. Shortly before he left, she pulled him into the kitchen to say goodbye one last time. With her hands on his shoulders, she looked into his eyes and said, "Licie, whatever you do, do not let anyone know you speak or understand Italian."

As he settled into the large leather seat on the elegantly furnished jet, he looked around. He wondered about the black and red motif, and he wondered why the men he now knew to be cardinals were taking him to a small town outside of Rome called Castel Gandolfo.

• • •

One of the first things young Jack noticed after moving to Gandolfo was the opulent luxury. His personal quarters were simple yet expansive. The carriage house was stone and had been built in the fifteenth century on one of the highest points on the property. The cathedral ceiling was wooden, rough-hewn beams that had been replaced less than ten years ago and did not leak during storms. But with the large, shuttered windows and heavy wooden doors, the space was drafty and cold. Windy nights were downright spooky, but the views through the great windows were spectacular. Looking west, he saw the rooftops of the old medieval village. Far to the east, he could make out Rome, and on the clearest winter days, the Mediterranean beyond.

Jack was introduced to Vilotti, who spent the first day with him touring the grounds and they were served lunch in the formal dining room. Lorenzo had set the menu and also arranged to have all the raw ingredients displayed on platters during each of the five courses.

The chef came out to describe the preparations with Vilotti translating in English. From the beginning Jack heard more than talk of food. The following day he was fitted for clothing at the tailor shop in downtown Rome. Enzo Gamaretti headed the third generation that operated the shop. He did Jack's fitting himself, explaining all the fabrics with Vilotti translating. This fascinated Jack to no end. To him, the uncut fabrics were luxurious and beautiful works of art unto themselves. Being measured by Gamaretti and listening to the two men speak Italian was mesmerizing. By the end of the second day Jack knew exactly where he stood.

In the beginning, he didn't cook and there was really nothing required of him. Still, he was up early each morning with the first stirrings of the day. Like any large estate, Gandolfo had a large staff. For the exterior, there were groundskeepers, gardeners, and maintenance men. The interior staff consisted mainly of nuns who cleaned the rooms and served meals. During the summer months, the staff more than doubled. Guests would often arrive with a staff of two or three and sometimes stay for weeks. It was a universe of chiseled Italian faces and incredibly beautiful countryside.

There were dialects of Italian he'd never heard before. Always true to his mother's words, he never gave the slightest inkling that he understood everything.

The kitchens were extensive and most of the raw ingredients came from within the grounds of Gandolfo. The estate owned plots of nearby farmland, which produced different types of wheat used for the bread, pastry, and of course the pasta. The estate also owned a mill in town that processed all the wheat products. There were barnyard animals — cows, sheep, goats, lamb, and water buffalo — that produced meats and different milks for the cheeses.

Then there were the gardens. Onions, tomatoes, garlic, potatoes, zucchini, eggplant, many types of beans, and an even larger variety of sweet and hot peppers. The largest crop by far was the olives, with numerous cultivars for table and oil production. Most of the forty thousand olive trees were more than two hundred years old. In one small section, the ancient grove, the trees were said to be more than five hundred years old. Besides the wheat and the olives, there were the artichokes. This was the third largest crop, and it seemed for some reason, that a lot of energy and attention centered on the artichokes. The estate was for the most part self-sufficient and any surplus was given to the town's monastery. The largest imports were coffee, salt, and office supplies.

Jack was in wonderland. His mother never had a vegetable garden in Boston, and he knew next to nothing about cultivation and agriculture. The chief gardener, Geraldo, spoke good English and it was here that Jack was most comfortable at Gandolfo. For him it was going one step further into the process of cooking. He'd never realized the work it took to produce the beautiful foods his mother so carefully selected at the North End markets. Geraldo grew some of the finest vegetables he'd ever seen.

The oblong and slightly curved plum tomatoes were larger and heavier than any tomato Jack had known. Seeing them cut, he was surprised by the deep red color and hardly a drop of moisture inside. Geraldo made a reduction of these tomatoes. After removing the seeds, he dried the halved fruit on large terra cotta plates in the sun. The plates were laid on top of the toolshed and Geraldo was careful to let them be lightly rained on but never drenched. The skin came off easily. The tomato pulp was pressed, scraped, and spread across the plates each day. Nine in all, each plate contained about two pounds of the seeded tomatoes. As they reduced, the plates would be combined and then mixed with fresher tomatoes.

Geraldo's family came from Southern Spain and so he called it "La Pommodoro Solera." It was flavored with the sea salt brought to Gandolfo from Cyprus in barrels. The salt was used extensively at the estate for the brining of the olives, pickling, and seasoning. The tomato reduction was then made into various *salsina*. Olive and anchovy were Jack's two favorites. It seemed to be a private project he kept secret from the cooks and other members of the staff. The salsina was put into jars and Geraldo sold them back to the estate through Vilotti.

Geraldo lived in a secluded spot next to the tomatoes and herbs. He was thirty-seven and had been working at the estate for nearly twenty years. His father, Bartonius, had been head chef at the estate, a career that spanned two Popes. When he died, his son was given a plot of land with a small barn and a job for life. Geraldo was an accomplished woodworker and over the years had constantly upgraded the dwelling. Now with a gorgeous wife and two small children it seemed a living fairy tale. Sunny afternoons on their patio with a breeze blowing through the fragrant plants were transcendental.

From the beginning, Jack wrote long letters in English to his mother. She saved all of them and after she died Jack read them all. He talked mostly of the vegetables and of Geraldo, his new friend. He described in detail the care and cultivation that went into the gardening and also Geraldo's preparation of the Solera-style tomatoes. What he did not mention was the disdainful chatter of the workers. Jack was thought of as a fool, but this didn't bother him. He quickly made his assessment of most of the staff, those he trusted and those he did not. His parents visited often over the years, and they vacationed on Elba at least twice a year.

Shortly after his arrival, Jack began lessons in Latin with Sister Vicaenza. Three days a week this gave him reason to visit the main building. The afternoon sessions were surreal. Sister Vicaenza's voice softly filled the exquisite parlor as they read classics in philosophy, humanities, and drama. One day, as he passed the *Camera Musica* (music room), he was drawn to an instrument with gleaming polish and intricate inlay. After being told it was a rare lute made by a man named Stradivarius, he picked it up gently and plucked one of the strings. "Sister, may I take this back to my rooms?"

She said she needed to ask Lorenzo, who thought it was a fine idea. "Have Garcia visit him in the evenings to show him how to play," he told her. Jerome Garcia was caretaker of the instruments. He taught Jack all types of music and brought him to his shop where he showed Jack the tools and techniques of the luthier.

The warm breezy days of summer rolled in and Jack began to help in the huge kitchens. Most of the staff decided he didn't have the ability or the desire to speak Italian. There were great banquets, intimate dinners, and all sorts of dignified guests coming and going. Jack was often asked to join them at table, and to entertain them with the renaissance dances he'd learned to play on the lute. It wasn't long before Jack heard all he needed to know about the true value of his father's sculptures. Then a very curious tale came to his ears one day, and a plot began to form in his mind. He wanted retribution.

• • •

Years later, with the help of Vilotti, Jack had done a fair bit of research before he found The Theatre. Truth is, he knew he was going to buy it before he met Phil. And so, he quit Rome and disappeared.

One of the constitutional mechanisms of Freemasonry is regularity. Because of this, one Masonic lodge can recognize another and its members with absolute transparency. Angelo Vilotti, now Vatican Secretary of State had been the estate manager where Jack worked when he first returned to Italy as a young man. It was he who arranged the introduction to Vic Sindano, the governor's brother and Worshipful Master in St. Louis. Vilotti had used the Cardinal in Chicago to facilitate the introduction but gave no information about Jack's real background or who he'd worked for.

His *cover* was simply that he was the son of a wealthy industrialist in Italy who'd recently inherited a fortune and wanted to move to the United States and open a restaurant. This in fact was true. Within the past year, both of Jack's parents had passed away. His father left him one of the largest marble concerns in Italy. The operation had been profitable for decades and with its assets was valued at more than $700 million. His mother had left him an extensive collection of stables and one of the most successful thoroughbred breeding operations in Europe. This too was extremely valuable and had been left solely to Jack.

He met Vic in St. Louis for a long dinner, and they talked about Italy, food, restaurants, and Jack's desire to find an out-of-the-way place to build a small trattoria. It was here he came to learn about some of the other members of the Samson

Masonic lodge, including Remus, John Tenyon, Heidle and Phil. Vic also told him about The Theatre and how he might be able to get it for next to nothing.

Jack's plan started out vague but progressed quickly. Now he had a place to hide out and keep his mind busy while he decided exactly how he would take revenge on his former employers.

After St. Louis, Jack made short stops in Chicago and New York, then went back to Boston to complete his final arrangements. This included getting a fresh passport and driver's license in the name of Jack Stanley and buying a car.

His father's passing away six months ago had started the whole plan in motion. After visiting New York, Jack spent three months with his mother at the townhouse where he grew up. Giancarlo's death was a horrific shock. She'd found him one sunny afternoon in May out in the sculpture garden. He'd been working alone, the massive aneurysm creating a pool of blood that flowed onto the hammer and chisel clenched in his hands.

Shortly after his death, she closed the studio. There was no one to cook for and she'd lost any will to go on. During one of their last conversations, Jack expressed his conviction that it was stress over the sculpture commissions from the men in Rome that had killed him. She saw his rage and knew he had a burning desire for revenge. Again, she gave him advice that would serve as a signpost to new space.

"Licie, you can do anything you set your mind to. Do something positive with your fire. Make them help others as much as they helped you and hurt your father." He'd already told her about how they'd been aging his works and reselling them and mentioned the recordings of their dealings. At that moment, Jack knew how he'd channel his desire for revenge. He would find a group of people of humble means for the men in Rome to make their reparations to. When he left Boston, he had the unmistakable feeling he'd never speak to his mother again. Three days later her neighbor Ricola found her in the bathtub dead, looking peaceful as if she'd fallen asleep reading the magazine. Ricola was his mother's best friend and had known Jack since childhood. They had lunch together after the funeral and she told Jack that his mother was somehow changed after his last visit. "She died when Giancarlo died. It was like that beautiful light inside her went out. But after your last visit a peace came over her. All she would tell me is you knew what you would do, and you would be all right."

Whether or not Jack knew what to do, he was relieved to know his mother was no longer living in pain and that she died peacefully.

From there, Jack drove out to Western Missouri to meet Phil. He'd bought the Cobra but having never driven in Italy he'd never really learned how to drive. After meeting Phil, he visited the top three tailors in St. Louis and ordered different parts of his new wardrobe from each. Tailors service a unique strain of clientele, men who are vain, rich, and some super-rich. This was Jack's target market. He befriended the tailors, and they were happy to drop names. His style was classically elegant and strong on local flavor.

• • •

Jack moved into one of the downstairs dressing rooms at The Theatre and lived there until just before the restaurant opened. A few weeks after moving in, he opened up to Remus about his past and revealed his future plans, beyond the restaurant. It was the day he'd gone to John's shed to see the bar. Jack cooked braised oxtail that night on a burner in Remus' suite. Remus had once mentioned it was a favorite dish when he told Jack about a Jamaican woman he'd been involved with.

It was late and they'd opened a second bottle of wine. Their conversations drifted far and wide, something of a ritual as the nights wound down. Jack quoted part of what's known as the definition of Freemasonry.

"Remus, I'd like to see this restaurant become a beautiful system of morality, veiled in allegory, and illustrated by symbols." He spun the stem of his glass without moving the wine.

"That would be an elegant restaurant, Jack." Remus raised his glass. "What lodge you comin' from?"

"I've been cooking for the core members of P2 for the past fifteen years," Jack did not say it proudly. *Propaganda Due*, also known as P2, is a secret Masonic lodge based in Rome. The neo-fascist organization is strongly anti-communist and thought by some to be a shadow government in Italy.

"Good lord, Jack. That's not even a Masonic lodge anymore. It's illegal. Don't tell me you're a member."

"No, I'm not a member. But I know what they're about and I have a lot of interesting information." Jack went on to explain how he discovered that the men from P2 in Rome were monopolizing sales of his father's marble sculpture studio to fund their endeavors. Not only were they keeping him so busy that he couldn't work for anyone else, but they were reselling his works for as much as fifty times what they'd paid him. Sculptures of all sizes were rubbed with cheese to impart mold growth in the pores of the stone, burned and buried. The patina was virtually indistinguishable from that of actual ancient pieces.

"One of their masons became so good at aging the stone that it was nearly impossible to tell the difference between the patina of my father's work, and pieces in the Vatican Museum from the 2nd century B.C. This went on for almost twenty years until the day he died. I began to hear dribs and drabs of it early on and finally Vilotti explained the whole thing to me. I spoke to very few people around the estate to begin with and only in English. But I understood Italian perfectly, everything they were saying. No one knew I understood. Imagine . . .

"You know it was one of the last things my mother said to me before I left Boston for Italy as a child, 'Don't let anyone know you understand Italian.'" Jack was quiet for a moment. "I think she knew what they were doing then. Even in the beginning she didn't let me speak Italian to them when they came to commission the works in Boston. She was protecting me." Jack shrugged as if he were simply lucky.

"Jack, that is some mean-ass business." Remus gave him an even look.

"I want to break their back. But the thing is, Remus, I believe in everything they work for, their fight against communism. Only problem is they're crooks. And of course they ripped off my family." Jack tensed and sat back, letting the rage pass, and then he continued.

"So Vilotti's been there forever and he knows everything. The night he told me; he was afraid I *would* kill someone. So, he gave me an idea. He said that if I used what I knew about some of their 'plans and activities' as he put it, it could cause them. . . *difficulty* was the word he used. At that point, I'd been cooking for them and doing my own menus for a year or so."

Remus relaxed in his chair. "Jack, you know something. I knew you didn't just come from nowhere. You came from *somewhere*. And you came here for a reason. And now you're going somewhere, right? You got a plan, but you're building this restaurant like you lettin' everybody else build it. I think it's a smokescreen so you can be a real puppet master with something else." Remus smiled at Jack. "I'm right, ain't I?"

Jack liked Remus more every day. He knew from the minute they met he had a sharp intellect and paid attention to details. He was also a very modest, very talented artist. These simple qualities showed themselves over time like an orchid in full bloom.

"Okay, okay, you're close, but let me finish. And it's not me who's the puppet master. I just want to cut some strings."

"You better be able to cut and run, 'cause from what I understand those boys got big ears and long arms. I've been following what's going on over there." Remus was excited. "Banco Ambrosso, right? The Vatican Bank doing some shady deals with the Mafia. And now the newspapers are talking about proof that they've been manipulating the Italian currency market for years. These dudes are into some heavy shit! It's just coming out now. Jack what do you got to tell me? I can't imagine what's next, 'cause I know you're not dumb enough to take on a gang like this."

"I'm not taking them *on* Remus. Thing is I cooked for them, and I recorded nearly every meeting for fifteen years. I have a very complete picture of their story. Really, ratting them out would be stupid because I'd never be able to run fast enough or far enough, right?" Jack nodded with his arms out. "Listen to this, how I copped on to them. I was playing the lute in my spare time. It was an incredible instrument, a Stradivarius. They had five or six… priceless. There was one man who took care of the instruments, Garcia. He did all the repairs and tuned the lute, the harp, the piano — I think there were more than forty instruments. If things work out, I'll show you some day. He played them all and he taught me how to play the lute. I played in the strangest ensembles. 'Dances of the Renaissance' the tunes were called."

Remus cut him off, "Jack, did that piano come from Italy?" He said as he stood up.

"Yes." He wondered if Remus was offended or surprised. "But let me finish."

"Damn, I knew it! I said it to Phil." He laughed out loud and swallowed almost a full glass of wine. "Hold on I got to use the john." Remus left the room and Jack was alone.

Jack decided he would tell certain things to Remus and no one else. Remus sensed this as he came back and closed the door so Jack could continue. No one else was in The Theatre but it was still a quiet conversation.

"Remus, you can't tell Phil or anyone any of this yet, please. I'm telling you 'cause I trust you. If any of this got out it would not be good for anyone."

"Okay, Jack. I understand. Nobody." Remus also felt that just knowing, let alone being involved, was risky. "I'm with you and I don't like them anyway. But go on, tell me how you stumbled onto their fool game!"

Jack laughed aloud, thinking he'd never taken this angle. He filled the wineglasses again. "It was an accident. I'd gotten access to a portable tape recorder so I could record and listen to what I was playing. I'd play the lute for them at dinner. And believe me it had to be good. I actually practiced a lot. One night I set up the tape recorder for a dinner when I was going to play. It was a special occasion, big-time menu and guests. I brought in the machine in the afternoon and set it up under one of the side tables where the silverware and glasses were stored. I wanted to record my performance, but I didn't want it to be distracting so I hid it." Remus was laughing, and Jack did not know what to make of it.

"I started recording just before they all came in. We served some hors d'oeuvres, they had some drinks, and just before dinner I played. When I finished, I put down the lute and went over by the table where the recorder was. The captain was opening wine and there was no way I could get to the recorder under the table to turn it off, so I just left it under there running."

Remus nodded. "I see where this is going."

"Okay, right. So, I take it back to my room. I didn't even know what I was into until I listened to what they were saying. I told Vilotti and he got me a bunch of miniature recording devices to put around the place."

"Jesus, Jack. When did you start and how long were you recording their dinner conversations?"

"Thirteen years. I stopped about a year ago."

"And this stuff coming out in the news was just being cooked up then. You must have the whole. . . You got the whole story."

"I do. I got the whole story, everything. Things no one would believe. Dates, names, I put it all together chronologically with a directory. The conversations read like a screenplay noir." Jack looked at Remus without blinking and they were silent. "Vilotti got me all the high-tech gear, same stuff the Swiss Guard were using. And no one knew."

"Shit." Remus said. "That must be something. What about the piano? You sent it here six months before you came by with Phil to see the place." Remus finished his wine.

"Yeah, that's right. I did. I learned about The Theatre, all of you, and the owner, and I just knew this was the place." Jack drank some of his wine. "Let's talk about the piano another time."

"Sure Jack. Whatever you say."

• • •

Jack's Café began serving dinner nine months later and it received a resounding acceptance. Plus, the food was excellent. The restaurant was comfortable, casually elegant, and seemed like it had been there forever. The bar, installed at stage right, was managed by Pamela. The Theatre's vintage costumes were restored, scaled back, and tailored to fit Pamela's figure perfectly.

Phil had convinced Jack to invest in an audio system similar to the one he'd designed at Evangeline's. This allowed him to separate the strings of the huge piano into groups using a set of unique electric pickups. After some testing, the speaker enclosures were placed around the auditorium. Reviews had declared the sound of Remus' piano and voice in The Theatre "otherworldly" and "metaphysical." Phil called it *sexaphonic.*

As *maître d'*, Phil answered the phone and managed the dining room. At five-foot ten-inches tall he was in good shape, but his clothes in the beginning consisted mainly of plaid shirts and blue jeans. Jack offered to split the cost of some new "work threads" and took him to Borsalino, his favorite tailor in St. Louis. He told Phil to invite his new girlfriend and the three went into town, had lunch, and drank some wine before Jack dropped them off at the tailor. Phil had never been to a tailor. In fact, the most he ever spent on a piece of clothing was $45 for a Cardinals baseball jersey. His girlfriend thought the tailor was a great idea. She sat with a cappuccino as Phil tried on different types of shirts, pants, and blazers. Jack knew and liked Phil's girl and had told Borsalino to listen to her. Phil reluctantly agreed to cough up $100 and never saw the bill. It had come to $3,700 and Jack never said a word.

The bar — and Pamela — made a significant impact on the dining area. Two of the original overhead stage lights had been turned to crisscross just above the bar. Late at night, the two beams enhanced by cigar smoke created a dramatic effect. Pamela could remain veiled in shadow or step directly into the light. At least once a night she would join Remus at the piano to sing and occasionally tap dance near the edge of the stage off the rug. On particularly special evenings she would get up on the bar and dance under one of the lights. These nights were especially memorable. The draperies, seats, and barstools were covered in a heavy deep red damask fabric. The paneling in the auditorium was a dark oil-finished walnut.

Vilotti had given Jack two large Turkish silk rugs that now covered most of the stage and defined the seating area. The rugs were identical in size with similar colorings and pattern. More than two hundred years old and in excellent condition, the pair was known to be extremely valuable. They'd never been separated and had a rich history. If the rugs had ears…

These days, three cooks work the kitchen's "line." Originally named for the gas line running behind the stoves and ovens and grill, it defined the cooks' work area during service. On the left was the grill. Jimmy Mack had been cooking meats and fish on the grill since the Café opened. His disposition, one on one, was quiet and articulate. Once behind the line his Ozarks roots produced a cocky, snarling mountain lion.

The center station prepared sauces, vegetables, and plated most entrées with Jack directly across the counter at the servers' pick-up area. Sarah Monet had held this spot for three years. By far the most strenuous job in the restaurant, Sarah had worked the lead position longer than anyone, man or woman, in the Café's seven-year history. To the right was the *garde manger* station. Paulo the dishwasher would jump back and forth to help Sarah with the cold items. Jack, usually in a simple gray pinstripe suit and white shirt, spent most of the evening in the kitchen or delivering food. Open six nights a week, the Café was closed for the month of August with the entire staff on half salary.

Late afternoons produced tangible energy in the kitchen. As all prep was completed, the stations were cleared, wiped down, and set up for service. By five o'clock, the kitchen was set and the staff sat down for dinner. Jack, Phil, and Remus usually sat at the bar with Pamela at her spot by the cappuccino machine. Pamela never sat down. Rumor had it that her legs were just too long, the skirts were too short, and she didn't want to show off her panties. Everyone loved her. She was incredibly beautiful, sharp as a pin, and epitomized the lovely character of the dancer. And she never stopped working.

During crew dinner, bottles of the house wine were scattered about the table. It was a young Bardolino that Jack imported by the pallet. It was produced on his uncle's farm (winery) in the rolling hills of Piedmont, south of Torino. There was no label, but guests and staff alike agreed its quality could not be found anywhere close to the bottle price. The café had "just enough for the restaurant" and unfortunately could not sell any of it retail.

Once every two months or so a delivery came in a large truck driven by a man who spoke only Italian. Approximately seven thousand bottles of wine, two hundred gallons of olive oil in twelve-liter flasks, and boxes of canned and dry goods were received and paid for in cash by Jack. This was all strapped onto five and sometimes six palettes. The containers were emptied while the driver ate lunch, and a large box of food and wine was prepared for his drive back to Boston.

CHAPTER FIVE

The Interviews

Three weeks ago.

Mike Ambrose arrived at Jack's restaurant the following day around 12:30 p.m. He carried a small leather satchel containing a notebook, pen, and miniature digital audio recorder. He saw a delivery truck on his way in and then heard the boxes coming into the kitchen as he crossed the stage and sat down at the bar to wait.

A few minutes later, Paulo came out carrying a box and put it on the bar.

"Hey, man. How you doin'?"

"Hey, Paulo. How are you?"

"Good, good, man. What's your name again?"

"Mike."

"That's right, Mike. Listen, I hear you writing a book about the kitchen."

"I'd like to, but it depends on what Jack says."

"Jack says we all gonna be movie stars."

Mike laughed. "A movie would be nice. You'll be the first to know, Paulo, I promise."

"Okay, man. Hold on. I'll get Jack."

"Thanks, Paulo."

Jack appeared in a beige T-shirt, blue jeans, and flip-flops. He looked like he'd just gotten off a sailboat. After seeing him command the restaurant last night wearing a suit, this was a mild shock.

"Hey, Mike. How are you?" Jack held out his hand.

"Good, Jack, good. Thanks. How about you?" Mike stood to shake Jack's hand.

"I'm fine. I'm a little busy right now, but I do want to talk to you."

"No problem. I'm not in a rush. I saw the truck out back. Checking in deliveries?"

"Dry goods."

"I see." Mike turned and gazed out at the auditorium. "I love the light in here during the day." The daytime scene in The Theatre presented a contrast equal to Jack's daytime appearance.

"So do I. It's one of the first things I noticed." Jack put his hand on the back of one of the barstools. He was in excellent shape and Mike put his age close to forty. His smile came easily as lines formed around his eyes. Dark brown eyes that looked straight at you, as if he was thinking hard about you whether he smiled or not.

"The morning sun comes in that side, and the sunset comes through there." Jack pointed up to the sides of the auditorium. Mike was surprised he hadn't noticed the windows last night. On each side of the auditorium were two large-paned windows with deep red drapery pulled back on both sides.

"Make yourself at home. Help yourself to the bar and have a look around. I heard you and Phil stayed here pretty late last night." Jack looked at Mike closely.

"That's right. Remus joined us. What an interesting man. I really like him. He brought us something to taste?" Mike scratched his chin and looked toward the bar. "A sherry, I think."

"Probably a '47 Madeira."

"Yes, that was it!"

"I gave him a case for his birthday recently. He loves the sweet wines and this one's special. Hard to find, too." Jack peeked over his reading glasses. "I'll see you on a bit."

Jack went back to the kitchen and Mike was alone in The Theatre. He pulled out his pad and started to make some notes. Twenty-five minutes later, Jack came out with a carafe of wine, a bottle of cold water, and two glasses. He asked Mike if he was hungry. Mike nodded eagerly with a smile. They sat at the large round table near the bar where the governor's party sat the night before. Jack poured the water as Paulo brought out a platter of food and two plates.

"Thanks, Paulo. Mike, I meant to ask if you were allergic to anything."

After a pause, Mike said "Starvation and sobriety." And opened his napkin.

"Hah! I like that. Bacchus couldn't have said it better. Cheers!"

Paulo left without a word. The two men made small talk throughout the meal. Jack finished first and pushed back his plate. "All right, tell me about the book you want to write."

"I've put together a brief outline for you." Mike said, reaching for his satchel.

"No, just tell me. I don't feel like reading. But I'd like to know a little more about how the project came about. Is this something you proposed to your agent?" Jack brushed the crumbs off his shirt and tossed his napkin on the table. He wasn't wearing his glasses. Mike hated giving a pitch face-to-face. He wanted to be the artist and not the salesman. Jack sat back and lit a small half-smoked cigar. It seemed to be slightly tapered and very dark and Mike wanted to ask him about it.

"Honestly the job came out of the blue. I try not to get too involved with the process, but my agent got a call from a publisher in Italy who wants to produce a book about American food, and they gave me your place to start with. Must've been because of my work on the wine book in Italy. Anyway, I got a large advance, and I try not to complain when somebody wants to give me money." Mike shrugged and Jack seemed satisfied.

The interviews were to take place with the kitchen workers — Jimmy, Sarah, Phil, Pamela, and Remus — at their convenience. Phil, Pamela, and Remus technically weren't cooks, but Mike said, "I like them and I'm sure nobody knows the story quite like they do. They're the ones who really see everything." Jack went along with this. Each person was to receive a list of questions and topics in advance of the interviews. The interviews would be recorded and run for an hour or so. The digital voice transcription software on Mike's computer would produce a rough text of all the interviews. This particularly interested Jack. *That could have saved me a lot of time once,* he thought. Mike offered to print the texts and give them to the restaurant crew with a separate copy for Jack. "I think it would be good if everyone knew what was being said."

"Sounds like you've given this some thought. But I think we should wait until the end to let anyone read it. Don't worry about any questions in advance either. Just keep it casual." Jack got up and asked Mike if he'd like coffee.

He returned carrying the cups, sugar, cream, and a plate of cookies. *This guy could be a waiter in a fine restaurant,* Mike thought to himself.

Jack was talking to Sarah, who'd followed him out to the stage. She was wearing gym shorts, a chef's jacket, and an apron. As she took off the toque, her light brown hair fell onto her shoulders, and her eyes were on Mike as she laid it down. He inhaled her perfume, while catching a full glimpse of her legs. She turned around and sat down next to him. Mike almost muttered something aloud.

Jack noticed Sarah's effect on Mike. "Mike, tell Sarah about the book." Mike's delivery the second time was not so smooth, and Sarah asked a lot more questions.

Jack and Sarah shared a similar, honest quality of allowing you to follow their thoughts. A seamless, involuntary verbalization of inquiry.

"Will you have the same questions for everyone?"

"No. Some questions would overlap but most would be crew-member specific."

"Will you be asking about peoples' personal lives?"

"No. The questions would be strictly related to food, the restaurant, and The Theatre."

"Will anyone else be reading the work in progress?"

"No. When we're finished, Jack will see the results of the interviews. Anything published would first need to be approved by Jack and the crew." The questions went on.

Sarah stood up and the sun grazed her hair, shimmering highlights of red and gold. She swung it around and put the toque back on. There was an aesthetic grace to her movement and Mike once again drifted in the aura of her spirit.

Sarah dominated the surrounding space as she put a foot up on the seat of the chair next to Mike and re-tied the laces of her shoe. She spoke directly to him, and he wanted to reach out and touch her.

"I like it, Mike. I think it'll be fun for everyone. I also like your whiskey story. The sex was a little strong, but it was well written. When do you want to start with me?"

Mike fought to keep eye contact. "I'll put a sign-up sheet, and you can tell me when it's good for you." Sarah was having a severe impact on him, and he wondered how he was going to be able to concentrate on the project. The facets of the restaurant grew like a forming crystal. Jack found all this very amusing.

"Okay." Sarah stood up and adjusted her apron. She sparkled in front of the curtain as the sun bathed her from head to toe. "Jack, what about the tomatoes?" She put her hands on her hips. Her eyebrows were light brown and fine. They pointed in a frown and Mike wanted a closer look at her brown eyes.

"I know, I know. Leo's coming back in a week. You know he won't give me any of his sources when he goes away. Let's just eliminate the fresh tomatoes for a few days. Change some things around."

"Right." Sarah looked up toward the windows and went back to the kitchen.

Mike's eyes involuntarily followed her walk and then returned to the table, shaking his head. Jack laughed and shrugged when Mike looked his way. "Can't get any good tomatoes."

Jack paused before continuing, "All right, Mike, you're on. You got everyone's approval. Work with Jimmy when he needs you. You can come and go as you like and eat with the crew. The bar is yours, but don't overdo it. Mind the personal quarters downstairs as well. Remus, Paulo, and I live here. My office is down there, too."

"I didn't know that. How interesting."

"We're a family and this is our home. We don't often invite people in like this. Keep that in mind."

"Thanks, Jack. I appreciate that."

"Good." Jack leaned back in his chair and puffed. Paulo came to the end of the bar to check on them and had heard the last few words. Jack turned to Paulo and motioned toward the wine. Paulo poured for Mike first.

Jack leaned back and scratched his jaw as he looked up to the rafters. "So, what kinds of things do you want to ask *me* about?" His tone was indignant and curious. Paulo made eye contact with Jack before they both looked at Mike for his response.

Mike picked up the recorder. "Do you mind?"

"Not at all." Jack watched Mike as he switched on the recorder. Paulo lingered.

"Jack, there's something going on here and you have a lot to do with it. What do you think makes this place so special?"

"We have a lot going on here. There's a lot of people involved. Paulo, would you like to join us?"

"Thanks, Jack. But Sarah's got me busy."

"She's upset about the tomatoes, right?"

"Yeah, man." Paulo's smile was big.

"Okay. Thanks, Paulo. Tell her Mike's coming in to help with the menu adjustments." Jack's gaze returned to Mike as Paulo headed for the kitchen.

"Mike, what do *you* think is so special here?"

"I'm not sure. That's what I'd like to find out. How long did it take you to build the restaurant?"

At that moment, Jimmy came out from the kitchen to get ice from the bar. "Jimmy, when did we start building the kitchen?" Jack called over his shoulder.

"I think it was the summer of . . ." Jimmy pretended to count on his fingers. "It's been almost nine years. We're still not finished! Phil's building a big stand for the olive oil. We're going to start bringing in barrels. Not sure if I told you." Jack leaned back. Mike exhaled and tossed his notepad onto the chair with his satchel. So much for the list of questions.

Jimmy took a seat at the bar facing them and lit a cigarette. Mike looked at them both. They were sneering gargoyles. Jack took another puff on his cigar and said, "What else would you like to know?"

Mike leaned back in his chair, "I knew this wasn't going to be easy."

Jack leaned forward with his elbows on the edge of the table looking straight at Mike. "Mike, nothing's easy here. If things seem relaxed, it's because the crew is seasoned. We've been at this for some time. But it's a very busy restaurant, run by a few talented people who work very hard. There's no tales here for a glossy coffee table book."

"Jack, I don't read those books. Besides, I feel there's a deeper layer here, beyond the actual food and cooking. That's what I want to get at."

Jimmy was making a face, rolling his eyes and moving his lips. He seemed to be mimicking Mike. Jack grinned, looking over Mike's shoulder. Jimmy stopped just as Mike turned around to look at him.

"Jimmy, what's kept *you* here all these years?" Mike asked.

Jimmy took a drag off his cigarette and gave a thoughtful pose. Then he pointed at Jack with the cigarette in his hand. "Hatred, pure intense hatred. I'm just waiting for this guy to let his guard down and screw up. Then I'm really going to let him have it."

Mike held up his palms in a gesture of resignation. "You guys are impossible."

"Relax, Mike. Jimmy, hand me the Sambuca, would you? Bring a few glasses. You have time? We're one-sixty-four tonight. Sarah won. Again."

"Damnit! Mike, you're workin' tonight, right?"

"I don't suppose I have a choice, do I?"

Jack poured the velvety thick clear liquid into three small glasses. "No, you don't. But let's just say that today is special. It's not every day we sit around drinking Sambuca after lunch, is it, Jimmy?" Jack glanced at Jimmy out of the corner of his eye.

Jimmy was looking at his glass and shook his head. He raised his glass, looked up and turned to Mike. "No, it's not. We're all glad you're here."

Mike looked Jimmy in the eye as they touched glasses. "Thanks, Jimmy." Mike drank and asked, "What's this about 'Sarah won'?"

"We have a pool that bets on the number of reservations." Jack said

"So, you're gamblers?"

Jimmy nodded through a swallow of Sambuca.

Mike rolled his eyes and turned to Jack. "Jack, when you thought of building a restaurant, what did you have in mind and how does that compare with what you have today?"

Jack held up his hands, "Mike, can't you come up with something more original?"

"Come on, Jack." Mike looked at Jimmy, who laughed aloud through his smoke.

"Okay. Honestly, what we have here today has gone beyond my wildest dreams. You know Phil brought me to The Theatre in the very beginning. He owned a real estate agency at the time." Jack glanced at Jimmy and shook his head.

"Dick Welch. Hah! That's a story in itself." Jimmy leaned back on the bar.

Jack cut in with a sharp glance at Jimmy. "That's a story for another time Jimmy. Anyway, Remus was the caretaker here." Jack paused. "Phil and Remus had been good friends for years. They grew up here in Sampson. So, I learned about the history of The Theatre and John Tenyon's connection. You'll meet him and also Heidle, who owns the German café around the corner. It was a discovery. Mike, I'll let you in on a little secret. You see the food part is easy, really, if you know what to do. But The Theatre itself is a living entity. A lot of people have connections and ties to it. I couldn't have found a better setting. Remus and I have talked about it over the years. He knew something was going to happen here. It was a driving force for him. He didn't know what, but he knew something would bring The Theatre back to life. So, in a way he willed it to happen. Truth is, Mike, I'm a good cook but this would not be what it is without Phil, Remus, Pamela, and Jimmy, and of course, Sarah. I was just lucky."

Jimmy chipped in. "Sarah's really the boss."

Jack sipped his drink and looked at Mike before continuing. "Mike, you'll come across a lot of confidential information, and I'll let you in on quite a bit, but I'll tell you right now, there's certain information that never leaves the building, on paper or whatever. Got me?" Jack was serious and Jimmy looked closely at Mike.

"Sure, Jack, no problem, I don't really…"

Jack interrupted. "I know. I just want you to understand you're in, and I don't mind letting you in. Understand?"

"Kind of a confidentiality agreement?"

"Something like that." Jack finished his drink and got up and walked to the kitchen.

Mike turned to Jimmy. "That was weird."

"Don't worry, Mike. Jack's a weird dude. Especially when it comes to business. All black and white. But I'll tell you he's one of the smartest guys I've come across. And he thinks you're okay."

"What was that about sensitive areas?"

"He was probably referring to the corporation and maybe some other things. You see the restaurant is set up like separate businesses and we're all shareholders. Jack and Pamela run the liquor and the rest of us run the food, with both of them as directors. It's very creative and I don't think it's been done before. As far as I know it's legal, but Jack isn't really part of it. The restaurant doesn't accept credit cards, and we all make a lot of money." Jimmy shrugged. He got up and headed off to the kitchen.

Mike poured himself another Sambuca and laughed out loud at the table. Sarah came out to the bar and began making herself a cappuccino.

"Mike, you're all alone," she said without looking at him.

"Hi, Sarah."

Mike looked at Sarah's back, her hair was still a bit wet, hanging in long dark curls over her shoulders. Mike downed the Sambuca and got up to sit at the bar.

"Would you like a cappuccino?" She whacked the old grinds into the knock box.

"I'd love one. Sarah, you look and smell like you just got out of the shower. Do you always come to work straight from the gym?"

Mike thought he saw a tinge of a blush as she put her hand on her hip and turned to him smiling.

"Mike, your observations are startling. You look and smell like you've been drinking Sambuca."

Mike grinned sheepishly as he looked at the table with the bottle and glasses. "Touché."

Sarah turned back to the cappuccino machine. "It's okay. Besides, I busted Jack and Jimmy on my way out here."

"There's something about cooks being very sensory aware or sensually aware, one of the two." Mike was looking at her shoulders as she turned to face him. Time stopped as they locked eyes.

Sarah blinked first. "Mike, what makes you think I was at the gym?"

"Well, first of all, couch potatoes don't dress like that. You also have great posture and you're very agile."

Silence filled the moment and neither Mike nor Sarah was uncomfortable. She placed his spoon on the bar and then set down the cup and saucer.

"You're not a fan of Sherlock Holmes, are you? This sounds a bit like deductive reasoning." She looked at him coyly.

"Funny you should say that. I just finished a recent biography on Conan Doyle. You know the process of deductive reasoning was actually a method of diagnosis he studied in medical school in Scotland before starting his literary career."

"You're too much." She whacked the espresso grinds again. "I just finished *The White Company*. I'm looking for copies of his writing in the *Strand Magazine*."

"Really? I was in Scotland recently and I found three volumes bound in blue leather. I have a collection of nearly two years of his work as it was published in the *Strand*."

"Oh, Mike, I'd love to see them." Sarah put down her spoon.

"They're beautiful. Printed in two columns, typeset on fine paper. They're at my house in St. Paul."

"Mmm," Sarah took a sip. "Anything else you'd like to try and deduce?" Sarah was directly across the bar, and their faces were about two feet apart.

Mike looked appraisingly at her eyes, lips, shoulders, and hair. "Well..." He let the moment hang as Sarah watched him admire her. "You're either a dancer or a yogi." He sat back.

Sarah immediately smiled and tossed her head back. "I've got to get back to work," she chuckled.

As she walked to the curtain she called out "Yogi" and then turned to face him.

"How'd you know?" She was blushing with a hand on her hip. She sparkled once more, bathed in sunlight in front of the dark curtain.

"It's all in the tailbone," called Mike.

With a girlish flip of her hair and a laugh, she disappeared behind the curtain.

The evening passed and Mike was once again amazed at the operation of Jack's kitchen. He arranged to spend some time with Remus the following morning.

• • •

After talking with Mike before lunch, Jack left the table and went downstairs to speak to Remus. He knocked once. "Yeah, Jack. Come on in." Remus was sitting at his table reading. Jack sat down and pulled out a cigar. "Remus, I have a problem."

"How's that?" Remus said, putting down his book.

"It's Mike. I suppose it was bound to happen sooner or later. You know, the only guy who knows where I am, or who I am is Vilotti." Jack tapped his cigar in the ashtray. "Actually, he just became Vatican Secretary of State."

"Really." Remus got up to make coffee and raised a cup to see if Jack wanted any.

Jack shook his head. "Nah." He looked over at the bottle of Madeira and picked it up off the side table. "Maybe some of this?"

"It's all you, man." Remus put a glass on the table.

"Vilotti told me now's the best time to make my move. I know things are heating up over there with the investigations into Banco Ambrosiano and the Vatican's involvement. I guess the time's come. He said he'd send a message and the calls about the piano confirm it. Maybe he started the ball rolling by making this thing with Mike happen. He's a crafty old bird. Probably wants to see it all happen before his time's up. He's gotta be pushing eighty," Jack marveled, as he sipped his Madeira.

"I bet," said Remus, putting down his coffee. "He probably put the whole thing in motion without anybody knowing." Remus picked up a fresh cigar from behind the piano and sat down at the table.

"Yep. I'm sure you're right. I have a feeling he started by putting Mike on the whiskey story. I'll have to ask him." Jack poured another small Madeira.

"Sounds like these guys got a lot to lose. But you could put the nail in the coffin." Remus said and relit his cigar, letting Jack continue.

"Lorenzo is into big international shit. Plus, I'm pretty sure he and his partners are covered. Likely toss a few low-levels to the wolves and be fine. He's always removed and always has a cut out. But honestly, you know, his ideals focus on the fight against Communism and I don't disagree with him on that."

"But you still got your agenda, don't you?"

"I do. I think what I'll do is let Mike in on some of what's in the recordings. I'm sure he's going to have to report to Rome at some point. But I need to somehow let them know that I know what they're into."

Jack sat back and relit his cigar. "I trained the guy they have cooking for them now, Gianario from Veneto. And he's a clown. I've contacted Vilotti a few times since I left and he tells me Lorenzo's always asking Gianario if he's heard from me. Of course, I've never contacted either of them, but maybe I'll send Gianario a message. 'Hey, how's it going, remember the old days. . .' He'll tell Lorenzo and it might plant a seed."

"No. Be more specific," Remus said. "Mention some big night and some of the guests. You know, some of the fat cats involved in the bank crash."

"Remus, you're right. That's it! I have all that information here. I'll send him a list of some of the dinners and guests and dates. I have all of it. He's sure to pass it on to Lorenzo."

"Don't send it from here," Remus chuckled.

"No, I'll make sure it goes out from Florida or something. Hah!" Jack stood up with his cigar. "I think you just solved my problem." He went to the door and turned around. "This poor guy Mike doesn't know what he's into." He opened the door. "Or at least I hope he doesn't. Thanks, Remus."

"No prob, boss," Remus took a sip of coffee and Jack shut the door. He looked closely at the empty Madeira glass as he relit his cigar.

• • •

At ten fifteen the following morning Remus met Mike in the kitchen and led him down to his suite. Mike was immediately comforted by the atmosphere in the room. If ever there were a direct reflection of a man and his surroundings, it was here. The smell of coffee lingered with a hint of cigar. The space reflected Remus' perpetual demeanor — casual, gentlemanly warmth laced with Southern elegance.

A beautiful baby grand piano dominated the space. Off in the corner was a long wrap-around settee covered in cordovan leather. The low table in front of the settee was topped by an incredible piece of wood. Roughly oval shaped, it must have been three inches thick and nearly seven feet long. Mike had never seen anything with such luster. Looking deep into the grain it was unclear if there was a coating at all. Mike touched the surface and his hand moved over it as if on a Ouija board.

He sat back on the settee and looked around Remus' suite. It spanned three quarters of the length of the back of The Theatre. The front room, where he sat, was separated from the rest of the space by a dark green velvet curtain that ran floor

79

to ceiling. It left a four-foot gap in the side behind the piano. The black and white tile floor imparted a regal feeling, and it looked like it was hundreds of years old. The tiles were not identical in pattern but carried a cohesive grade of sparkling silver-gray flecks throughout both the black and white tiles. Mike leaned over and clicked his ring on one of the tiles and realized it was marble.

Remus came out with their coffee service and laid it on the round table, suggesting that was where they should talk. Mike stood up and came around to Remus.

"Remus, thank you so much for meeting me here," Mike said as they sat down. The table was covered by a heavy ivory-colored linen and off to one side was a large ashtray, a book, and a pair of reading glasses. There were three chairs and Remus sat with his back to the wall. Mike put his satchel on the chair next to him and once again decided to ignore his list of questions. He felt like a time traveler in another era as he considered the impression of the moment. There were a million things he wanted to talk to Remus about and none of it had to do with the restaurant.

"Okay, Mike." Remus smiled. He had liked Mike from the start and was glad he was comfortable. "I'm glad to have you here. We're all intrigued by what you want to do — I'd say nearly flattered — but I won't speak for anyone else. You know, after Jack got your whiskey story, he tried to locate you. It's interesting that you showed up like this." Remus put cream in his coffee and didn't stir it. He raised the cup to his lips and with a slight nod said, "Here's to you, Mike."

Mike took his black, and it was some of the best coffee he'd ever tasted. He considered the grace of this man facing him, who'd spent his life in an old theater in southern Missouri. He sat back in his chair and moved so that he could look at the rest of the room.

"Remus, The Theatre reveals itself layer by layer. I'm surprised at every turn, but it all fits together like a classically crafted tale." Mike paused to take a sip and Remus let him continue. "And this room is beautiful. I feel like I've stepped into the past, but really, I'm just having coffee with you in your sitting room."

Remus was pleased with Mike's honesty. "Well, you're right, Mike. This room hasn't changed much at all, except for the floor."

"Really? So, the floor's not original?"

"Nope. It's the only thing that *has* changed. It was a gift from Jack. The floors were wood in here before. I think it's nice like this." He picked up his cup.

"It really makes the room, Remus. Black and white tile is one of my favorites, but these are so unique. Are they marble?"

"Yes, they are. You see, Jack knows quite a bit about this. His family's been involved with marble in Italy for generations. This is a particularly fine set of selected pieces. The black and the white were each cut from a single block. They call it a vein, and that's nickel that runs through it. What makes these really special is the way the flecks of nickel are so consistent and evenly distributed. It's a very rare collection. The marble was mined about five hundred years ago and was never used for its intended purpose. Jack received it as a gift."

Mike watched Remus as he ran his fingers across the edge of the tablecloth. He wore a fine white cotton shirt that was ironed and had the sleeves rolled up. The top two buttons were undone, revealing a small gold medallion on a fine chain. The patina of his skin was a cross between polished ebony and worn black leather. His fingernails were neatly trimmed with a satin ivory-vanilla tone. Mike let the moment drift as they both slipped into personal thoughts.

Remus looked up and said, "It was a surprise. In the very beginning you know, there was a lot of work to be done. Everything from downstairs was moved up to the stage and Jack had all the floors down here done. Mostly I'd left every-thing down here untouched before Jack bought the place. When the work began, I couldn't really stay here with all the cleaning and sanding and varnishing, so Jack asked if I'd like to go to Chicago for a few weeks. He knew my family was up there 'cause I'd visit them once in a while on weekends. He set up a place for me to stay that was close to downtown. See, I have a lot of musician friends up there and I usually sit in at some of the clubs when I visit. You know, real St. Louis blues piano is hard to find. My buddies had been busting me for years to move up there, and I was considering it. But I couldn't let go of this place. The landlord wasn't the nicest guy, but he was paying me to stay here. Not much of course, but this place has been my life." Remus arched his eyebrows and turned his palms upward. "Anyway, I got back, and the floors were done with the tile. Jack told me it was a gift for keeping The Theatre in such good condition all these years." He drank some more coffee.

Mike smiled and shook his head. While he never would have imagined this, it seemed perfectly natural. "How in the world did Jack come into possession of five-hundred-year-old marble?"

Remus sat back, crossed his arms, and regarded Mike for a moment before he spoke. "It was a gift from the Vatican."

The word hung in the air and Mike knew there would be no more talk of this. He continued without missing a beat. "Wow, okay. . ." he turned and motioned toward the table. "Remus, that coffee table looks like something from outer space. I've never seen anything like it! What kind of wood is it and what makes it shine like that?"

Remus broke into an easy smile. He stood and picked up the cups. "Yes, that's a very special piece of wood. It's been here since The Theatre was built. You like another coffee?"

Mike nodded to his host. "I sure would, Remus. Thanks." Remus went behind the curtain to make the coffee and continued speaking to Mike, who'd gone to have another look at the table. "John Tenyon's grandfather was something of an eccentric. In the process of designing and building The Theatre he spent a lot of time and money selecting the wood. Most of it came from Central America up through Mexico, and the rest came from California and the great northwest. Nearly all of it came by rail car, raw and simply dressed. These were giant trunks with most of the bark still intact. There are photos of the shop. John's grandfather was a master woodworker, and his three brothers had worked in the North American hardwood trade for most of their lives. John's grandfather was the oldest. I think he was twenty-seven when they moved here in the 1890s."

Remus returned with the coffee and took a seat on the settee at the opposite corner. He picked up his coffee and saucer and sat back, crossing his legs. "You know, wood was relatively cheap back then. And the resources and connections they had gave them a lot of leeway. That big shed out back next to the railroad tracks was the mill. All the machinery, the saws and such, is up at John's place on the river. So, they just dumped these giant logs right there. Cut every plank themselves. Have you seen the photo albums?"

Mike shook his head, remaining silent.

"I think John has them now. You really need to have a look. One of the brothers made a hobby of photography. He had a big German camera." Remus sipped his coffee, noticing Mike's fascination. He was pleased that Mike was interested, and if he wanted to know everything, there would be time. For now, he would stick to Mike's original question. "The tabletop is Hawaiian Koa. It's cut from a six-foot section of a trunk that was probably five feet in diameter. It's cut on the bias." Remus held up his forearm and traced a line from the outside of his wrist to the inside of his elbow. "It's a pretty extravagant cut. In fact, I don't even think there's many Koa trees of this size growing anymore. It only grows on a certain island in Hawaii at higher altitudes."

Mike touched the surface of the table once more. "This finish is unearthly. Did you do this?"

"Yes, I did. It's a Danish oil finish I learned from my mother. Only I add shellac so it's kind of a French Polish. Try not to spill your coffee on it. It's pretty, but sensitive to hot liquids. It repairs easily though, and I enjoy treating it every now and again."

The morning sun streamed in across the surface of the table. It seemed to glow, and Mike marveled at the grain's depth. "It's almost as if it's translucent. I feel like I'm looking into a golden velvet curtain," Mike said.

Remus chuckled and drank more coffee. "I know, isn't that something?"

"It's like magic. Isn't shellac made from beetle shells or wings?"

"No, it's a secretion from a beetle-like bug. They live in the jungles of India, Thailand, and other places like that. You see the bug eats into the wood of these tropical trees. The wood is very oily, like most tropical hardwoods, and the bugs eat the sap. The secretion is the result of a chemical change that happens when the sap is digested by the bug. I buy it raw, in flakes, and mix my own shellac. The flakes I get are high grade and highly refined. This gives it the pure, crystal clear, deep golden color. Before the sprayer came along, French polish was the way most stringed musical instruments and fine furniture were finished. I finished the raised paneling in the auditorium this way." He scratched the center of his forehead, wondering if Mike understood the gravity of this last statement.

Mike shook his head and smiled. He wasn't sure how the conversation came to this point. "You know I did some research recently on the Stradivarius and Guarneri instruments of the eighteenth century. It seems a lot had to do with the finish they used." He watched Remus' response as he sipped his coffee.

Remus sat back and stretched his arm along the back of the settee, regarding Mike in a new light. "True, a lot had to do with the varnish. I've been told they steeped shrimp shells and pearls into it. Also, that they added blood and wine to some of the varnishes. But the leading theory is that a soaking method was used to prevent worm damage and fungus growth in the woods, and this is what created the acoustic properties. The unsung hero was a chemist who'd helped both families with treatments to preserve their wood. They never knew how crucial this was and a generation or so later, the methods and formula disappeared." Remus gave a rare smirk, implying that he thought these facts odd, and that they might interest Mike. "I think it's been proven that they soaked the wood with a mixture of spring water, wood ash, and sea salt."

Mike laughed out loud. "Remus, that's great!" He was supremely pleased with his encounter here and at the same time perplexed that he'd originally come to talk about food. Somehow the conversation echoed with talk of wood being preserved in spring water and sea salt and finished with a concoction of alcohol, shrimp shells, and beetle excrement. Once again, the completely unexpected made perfect sense. The layers of The Theatre peeled away into the corners of Mike's imagination.

"Remus, what was it like when Jack came here?" Mike was speaking without thinking. Neither of them had anywhere to go, and Remus considered the question.

"What do you mean? What was it like the day he came here, or how did it go once he moved in?"

Mike's smile escaped from the corner of his mouth. "Yeah, both I guess." He knew that at best, he would barely scratch the surface of what he wanted to know. In any case, he wanted to hear anything Remus had to say.

Remus examined his fingertips, one by one, rubbing his thumb across each nail. He displayed a ring with a motif of a compass and a ruler. Seeing that Mike took no notice, he looked up at Mike with raised eyebrows and slightly drooped lids. As was his way, when it was his turn, he spoke slowly, and for some time.

"You know, Mike, when Jack came here it was like divine intervention. He pulled a lot of people together in this town where nothing was really happening. That may sound strange, but the way he did it was like he didn't really have any-thing to do with it. He had this idea. I don't want to say he used people, because everyone has benefited, but he just conducted the whole thing from the sideline. It was all very loose. He never gave much instruction or said exactly how he wanted anything. He was also very lucky because everyone involved is talented in their own ways. Still, I think he sized these things up, because he's observant like that. He just let people go and do things the way they wanted. I didn't see a lot of the actual interactions, mind you, I just watched from the sidelines. I know he was able to impart his vision somehow, because he built the place, and it's all Jack." He paused, and Mike waited.

"It's like the way the food is prepared here. Jack says: 'Mother Nature does most of the work and we just nudge it onto the plate.' That's exactly how he did things when he first came here. I suppose I'm lucky, too, since I didn't really do much of anything. I just watched it grow over time. And I've been here a long time with nothing happening with the place. I think everybody was so involved with his or her own projects that it may have been tough for them to notice how the big picture was evolving. Jack and I would stay up late and talk about things while the restaurant was being built, but we didn't talk much about The Theatre, or the projects going on. You know, Jack is really a philosopher, and this place is just a way to express himself. Believe me, food is the main focus here, but I think it's just the vehicle. The Theatre really stands for something much deeper. This may sound like I've got it all figured out, but I don't. It's still a mystery to me how these things work. And you know, Jack isn't the same guy these days either." Remus stopped. "Mike, there's some personal things here and I'd rather you not get public with some of it."

Mike had crossed the threshold to the alpha moment. He shook his head with a frown. "What do you mean, Remus? Is Jack okay? Is he healthy?" Mike asked gravely.

Remus chuckled. "Yes, Mike, that guy is strong as an ox. With the amount of garlic and prune juice he consumes I'd be surprised if anything could grow inside him." Remus paused, looked at Mike as if considering if he should go on, and then shrugged. "Building a restaurant like this is a long process, and there's different stages. Now, it's kind of chugging along.

"You know the story of the transcontinental railroad? It was a lot of work even before they swung the first pickaxe. And then imagine building it over the mountains and through the tunnels and into the desert with all the different nationalities working together. Nothing like it had ever been done before. So where do you go from there, after completing something like that? Don't get me wrong, and I'm sure you can see this operation is a pinnacle. One of the greatest restaurants ever. That's what he set out to do, and he did it. Just like now they operate the railroad. It's still a huge undertaking but it's not the same as the exhilarating turmoil and miracle of building it. Probably an anti-climax if you ask me." Remus sat back as if he'd explained it all, and there was no more to be said. "Has he said anything to you about the boat?"

"What do you mean by 'the boat'?" Mike furrowed his brow. He had been following Remus' words like he was on a blind run through the woods. Now this.

At that moment the recorder clicked, tape finished. Remus laughed. Mike looked at his watch. He was five minutes late for his appointment with Jimmy. He made a mental note to schedule the interviews further apart. "Shit, Remus, I gotta go! I'm late for Jimmy. Thanks again for your time here. It's been great." He stood up. "I hope we can continue soon."

Remus stood with him and nodded with an understanding smile. "Okay, Mike, any time. Tell you what, next time I'd like you to explain to Jack and I how they make that sweet sherry wine. I think it's called *Solera.* Anyway, we've never managed to look up the process, and Jack said you were the man to explain it."

Mike nodded. "Sure, the Solera method. No problem. I'll bring a big piece of paper and draw it for you."

"All right, deal. And, Mike, not a word about the boat, okay? No one knows, but we can talk about it later."

"You have my word, Remus." They locked eyes and shook hands. Mike picked up the recorder and switched it off, tucking it into his satchel on his way out. At the door he turned for a final glance at Remus' sitting room. He gave a thumbs-up and Remus replied with a wave. They each laughed aloud to themselves after Mike closed the door.

After talking with Remus, the mention of the Vatican stood out in Mike's mind as he walked upstairs and into the kitchen. He was infinitely curious and at the same time sure he would never get to the bottom of it.

• • •

When he reached the stage, he found Jimmy sitting at the bar. He was reading the paper and smoking a cigarette. There was a glass of dark brown liquid next to the ashtray. Mike had no idea what he was drinking. Jimmy stood up and greeted Mike with mocking hostility, hands in the air. "Mike, what the hell? I told you I don't have all day!" He lowered his right hand to shake with Mike.

They shook and Mike gave an exaggerated hiccup, then with a slur in his voice said, "I was *invertorying the richo room*. Jack's got quite a *correction*." Another hic-cup followed.

Jimmy looked at Mike with dismay and then slapped him on the back with his left hand before breaking the handshake. "Hah! Good man. I knew you'd fit right in. So, how's the book coming? And how did you manage to end up at Jack's Café?" Jimmy took a drag and put out his cigarette, his eyes on Mike's as they sat.

Mike was confident he had disarmed Jimmy, but he wasn't ready for an inquisition. "You know, if I could just get some information on the restaurant, I might get somewhere. So far, it's been nothing but struggle, and to tell you the truth, I'm not making any headway." The minute the words left his mouth he knew this was the wrong angle to take with Jimmy.

"Aww, pitty-poo. Nothing but struggle, not making any headway. What d'you think this restaurant is about? I'd say you're right on track. Don't let Jack hear that prissy shit or he'll have your ass." Jimmy turned to the bar and took a drink of the pulpy brown beverage.

"What are you drinking?" Mike asked.

He took another gulp and made a mild face. "Prune juice. Why, you want some?"

Mike made a face and squinted like he'd smelled rotten eggs. "No way, man. My grandfather drank it. Gross." He pulled out the recorder and changed the tape smoothly like a veteran soldier cleaning his weapon. Switching it on, he looked up at Jimmy. As Jimmy watched, his wicked demeanor evaporated, and he and Mike were united in frame of reference. They were not more than a year apart in age and though quite different, the two men seemed to share a common thread.

"Come on, let's talk about the Café. When did you meet Jack?" Mike began.

Jimmy scratched the side of his neck and looked around. "Well, it was before the place opened. In fact, the bar wasn't even here yet and the kitchen was just being built." Spinning the stool around, he rested an elbow on the edge of the bar. He looked out at the auditorium and pointed up to the center of the rows of seats. "We met right up there."

Mike followed Jimmy's gaze out into the auditorium. As a writer and human-ist, these were the moments of pure experience. While words were just a tool he used to craft his work, his ultimate master and true medium was people. Provoking folks into thought and memory, especially in such a sublime setting as The Theatre, was both fodder and bliss for a writer. Pondering what it was actually like here in the early days, he tried not to distract Jimmy. In anticipation of his response, he wondered if anyone would ever talk about the food. Jimmy began by talking a bit about the early days before the restaurant opened.

Seven years earlier.

Building the three tiers of seating rows was the first major project Jack wanted to complete. It was the most dramatic change that would transform The Theatre into a restaurant, but most importantly he just wanted to see what it would look like. After the supports were installed and the concrete poured, it was deemed solid and to everyone's agreement, a great idea. Shortly after, he moved his office space up to the center of the second row. Then the stage was cleared, and John's crew began refinishing the stage. The planking used was a rare collection of Iroko milled on twenty-five-foot lengths eighteen inches wide and three inches thick. This lumber had arrived at The Theatre as raw trunks. John's grandfather had personally selected the trees in Nicaragua. Most of the trunks had been cut down by hand and were more than thirty feet long. It's virtually impossible to find wood of this type and grade today.

The large walnut desk was originally a makeup table that dated back to the 1860s. The two turned posts that once held the mirror were all that remained of a spit curl vanity. A large flat panel computer monitor was now fixed to one of the posts. It was on this computer that Jack and John modeled a three-dimensional rendering of The Theatre's interior. With Jack's ideas and John's design skills, they planned the seating rows and kitchen layout.

With the stage refinished, work started on the cooking area. Jack knew what he wanted as far as equipment, workspace, and refrigeration. Then with the help of Vilotti, he lined up the metalworking crew, five men from Italy. With a simple plan in mind, he began looking for suitable cooks and their input, to finalize the task of building the kitchen.

It was raining the day Jimmy came to meet Jack. It seemed that it had been raining every time he met one of the key players. Inside it was always relatively warm from the movement of people and he and Remus both mused that The Theatre was happiest when it was damp. He remarked that the wood wanted to be moist and tight at the seams. Remus was sure the acoustics were superior on rainy nights. They talked about how to measure this and after a while it became sort of a joke, one of the many conversations that would remain in Remus' sitting room. Jack was most uncomfortable on the dry, windy days of winter. It was as if a demonic presence would steal in through the cracks and peck away at his soul. It reminded him of a time long ago, when a fifteen-year-old boy moved to Italy.

Jimmy hustled in the door that first day with a wet shiver and looked around. He was instantly at ease and Jack felt once again that the rain was an omen. He enjoyed having his desk in the center of the auditorium for two reasons. One was that he could see everything going on at a glance. But what was really interesting was that anything he said from this vantage point would amplify through the space. He waited for Jimmy to notice him and then called out, "Jimmy Mack?"

"Yeah. You Jack?"

Jack nodded and waved, motioning for Jimmy to join him. Jimmy walked across the stage, taking a close look at the work going on there. As he made his way down the steps at stage right, he looked up at the windows, stopping for a brief moment while taking in both sides of the auditorium. Jack saw that The Theatre was having its usual dramatic impact and was pleased.

"Jimmy, Jack Stanley." Jack stood up and they shook hands.

"Hi, Jack. Nice to meet you." Jimmy paused and pointed toward the stage. "I like it."

"Good. Have a seat." Jack nodded toward the chair next to his desk and they sat. Silence became the moment as they both looked at the scene on stage. The spotlights were on, and the work area was bright as day. The men did not look like metalworkers. If they had been wearing black felt fedoras with shotguns over their shoulders they could have easily been a hunting party in southern Tuscany. Or perhaps Michael Corleone's security detail during his Sicily exile. They were old country and didn't talk much while they worked. When they did, only a local would understand the dialect from the Roman province of western Lazio. Jack was the only one who spoke to them. He also recorded everything said in the work area and so had an intimate relationship with the metal-working crew.

At stage right, was a rack holding a neat pile of stainless-steel tubing. There was also a large crate of fittings and a small stock of stainless sheeting. The framework for the line of cook tops, grill, and preparation areas was being completely custom fabricated. There was a large bending machine near the pile of sheet stock and one of the men was cutting a piece of counter with an acetylene torch. The gleaming metal of the half-built kitchen was, to a cook, completely amazing. This sight, with the bright overhead lights focused on so much detail, was awe-inspiring.

Jimmy looked at Jack, who was clicking away on the keyboard and mouse. The big flat panel displayed a 3D drawing of the kitchen space on the stage. He made the drawing spin forward and back, up and down, and then looked at Jimmy.

"So, what do you think?" Jack laughed.

"No way. That is outrageous! Did you make it?" Jimmy looked at the monitor and was beside himself.

"I have a guy helping me."

Jimmy noticed a drawing on paper that looked like the finished project and pointed to it. "Can I take a look?"

"Please, be my guest."

Jimmy looked at the drawing and scratched his chin. He looked over at Jack's ashtray and pulled out a pack of cigarettes. "You mind?"

Jack gave a backhanded wave. "No, go ahead." He reached for the ashtray and pushed it toward Jimmy.

Jimmy lit a cigarette while looking at the drawing and exhaled as he looked at the stage. "So, where's the refrigeration going?"

Jack frowned and scratched the back of his head. "Well, I'm definitely going to put some under-counter below the service area. Probably build a small walk-in downstairs. There's also room behind the line for an upright or two." Jack had been pointing toward the stage and when he finished, he crossed his arms. "What do you think?"

Jimmy blew the smoke out slowly and tapped his cigarette butt into the ashtray. "Mind telling me what kind of food you'll be serving?"

Jack smiled. He knew about Jimmy's reputation, both as a cook and otherwise. For the past thirteen years, Jimmy had run the grill at Seven's Top, St. Louis' premier steakhouse. He was also a gambler; he owed his boss money, and he liked to drink. On and off the job. But he was the best grill man within miles. In this type of situation, Jack usually gave people a three-minute test and Jimmy had passed.

"I'm glad you asked. I'll be serving Italian food and lots of steaks. You ever cut steaks, Jimmy?"

Jimmy gave a sly laugh and said, "Yeah, I cut steaks." He had no idea Jack knew anything about him. He was simply sick of his job and the drive in and out of the city. This was just an interview for a job he'd heard about from one of his purveyors; a bug carefully placed in his ear.

"Okay, good. Here's a rough idea of what'll be on the menu." Jack started making a list on a small yellow notepad. "And about how many seats I'll have with an estimate of the volume I'd like to reach. Think about it for a week and give me a call if you're interested in the job. I want to do most of the butchering here. Tell me what equipment you'd need and what you think that volume can support as far as the larger primal cuts." Jack stood up and tore the sheet off the pad. Jimmy took the yellow sheet from Jack and followed him.

Jimmy was a bit mystified, being offered a job after about three minutes of very little interviewing. Not to mention he'd spent an hour and a half typing a resume this guy didn't even want to see. "Come on, I'll show you the rest of the space," Jack said, and started down to the stage.

"Right, okay, I'll just leave a copy of my work history here on your desk." Jimmy put down his neatly folded resume.

"That's all right. I know all about you, Jimmy. But please, leave it anyway."

Jimmy looked down at the resume and wanted to stuff it into his pocket. Turning to look at Jack's back he thought, "*Who is this guy?*"

• • •

Jimmy turned back to face Mike. "Yeah, Jack had his desk up there like he was perched on his little throne. He could see everything going on and he had this big computer screen hooked up. The funny thing was that with all the stage lights on for the guys building the kitchen, you couldn't really see anything from the stage, and you never knew if he was there. And then anything he said would boom through the place. He would say things in a certain tone, sort of change the pitch of his voice, not louder, just a little deeper. It's the 'resonating frequency' of the auditorium. You know, like when you sing in the shower or hum, and just as you hit the right note it goes all through your body? That's when you've hit the resonating frequency. Remus told him about it. It's not so strong anymore with all the tables and things, but here, check it out."

Jimmy got up and walked up to the center of the second seating tier. "Okay, listen." Jimmy made a loud *aaahhh* sound and then in three steps he went up in pitch, until suddenly the room seemed to reverberate. Jimmy stopped making the sound and when he did, he cupped his ear and pointed to the piano. Faintly but clearly, it was resonating the same note. "Remus has the piano tuned to the auditorium."

Jimmy came back down to join Mike at the bar. "I'll tell you, I did not know what to make of that guy. See, I came here after hearing about a new place that might be needing a grill cook. But it turns out Jack had gone to The Top, where I was working, and asked who was cooking the steaks." Mike held up a finger with a frown and Jimmy stopped.

"The Seven's Top? That's where you were working?" Mike asked.

"Shit, thirteen years. And my time was up at that joint." Jimmy lit another cigarette.

"That's one of the greatest steakhouses in the Midwest. And what a view! My grandfather took me there when I was a kid and we sat at one of the window tables. I'll never forget it. He told me that when you get a steak you cut down the middle, so your first bite is from the center. That way you get the best part when your appetite's keenest." Mike looked at Jimmy for a response, and he nodded.

"That's right. How a gentleman eats his steak. Some people just plain live their life that way. What did you say your name was? Ambrose? Your grandfather wasn't Al J. Ambrose, was he?"

Mike nodded. "Yes, he was. A great man. Very well-known."

"Hell yes, he was well-known! That guy was a legend at The Top. President of the bank, right?"

"He put himself through night school in the thirties. Yeah, he talked about that restaurant. And the steaks." Mike looked at Jimmy with respect.

Jimmy nodded again. "I cooked for him for years. Now there's a true gentleman — real class and grace. I met him when he came into the kitchen many times. Always with the cigar and that ivory white hair."

"That's him. He passed away about seven years ago." They were silent for a moment and then Jimmy spoke.

"I'm sorry Mike. You know, when he came to eat, it was a bigger deal than when the mayor came in," Jimmy added.

"Wild stuff, Jimmy. Listen I don't want to be rude, and I really enjoy being here, but I told Jack I was going to write about the restaurant and food. Every time I sit down to do one of these interviews, the subject goes into space. I just feel like I got to get something together to show Jack. You know he lets me eat and drink here."

Jimmy shrugged. "Hey Mike, nobody here really wants to sit and talk about food. Or their work. This may sound weird, 'cause I know you can probably see it's our heart and soul. But if you do something so deep and dear to you, all you can do with your discipline is exercise it and express yourself. Talking about it doesn't really cut it. To tell you the truth, I think you'll learn more about our work by talking about other things. Then just watch us cook and taste the food. Don't worry about what Jack thinks. You're doing a good thing, man." Jimmy pointed with the prune juice in his hand.

Mike smiled back at Jimmy with such genuine sincerity that his eyes nearly watered.

Sizing Jimmy up in an instant brought to mind a scraggly cat. He wore a goatee, an old ball cap, and his hair hung straight, just over his shoulders. It wouldn't take much to imagine he'd slept in the clothes he was wearing. But the clarity came through his eyes, his aura was pure light, and there was order to his words and message. The appearance and identity clashed paradoxically, but Jimmy was truly an artist, able to affect your emotions with both his work and his words.

Almost without thinking, Mike asked, "Can I come watch you cook?"

Jimmy laughed as he put out his cigarette. "Sure, Mike, you can watch me cook."

• • •

The moment they entered the kitchen, Jimmy became a different person, back to his old cocky self. "I got veal racks. Six pieces, six bones each. I'm going to braise three of the racks and cut the others into chops as the orders come in. I might pound one or two and bread 'em depending on who comes in. You ready to work?" It was not voiced as a question and this wasn't what Mike had in mind, but he agreed all the same.

"Sure, Jimmy. What do you need?"

"Okay, listen up. I want you to take that big pot of veal stock and strain it. Use the big colander over there. Strain it into this pot and stop pouring it through the strainer when you get to the last few inches. Got me? I want the bones and everything to stay in the first pot. Then take the strained stock and put it on the stove over a low flame. Bring it to a simmer for about ten minutes and skim the scum off the top. Put the pot a little off the center of the flame. That way the foam'll end up all together on one side. After that, we'll put the pot on the floor so it can cool. Okay, next, while that's simmering, you're gonna cover the bones with cold water and bring that to a boil. Then turn it off and let it cool. This'll be the remouillage we use for the braising liquid." Jimmy paused and looked at Mike to make sure everything was clear. "You with me?"

"Wait, so you strain the stock and then make stock again out of the same bones? Isn't that kind of lame?"

"No, man, it ain't lame. What the hell's the matter with you? Those bones are still loaded with flavor and covered with gooey vegetables. I'm not making demi-glace out of it." Jimmy stopped and rubbed his chin and started again, this time a bit mellower. "Think of it like the first time you strain stock as the extra virgin, okay? Then we make a second stock by pouring water over the bones once more. This is the *remouillage*; it means 're-wetting.' It's an old French technique. So, when I make the next stock out of freshly roasted bones, I use this remouillage as the cooking liquid to pour over the roasted bones. Beats water right? It's also good for cooking rice and blanching vegetables. So today, if we ever get around to it, I'm using it as the braising liquid for the veal racks. If that's okay with you."

Mike was frowning as he thought about this new technique he never would have considered. Then he smiled and nodded his head eagerly. "Cool, Jimmy. No prob." Mike headed off to the stove, but Jimmy stopped him by grabbing the back of his shirt.

"Hold on there, Escoffier. Put an apron on and next time leave the Dandy Don shoes at home."

Mike looked down at his cordovan loafers and then up at Jimmy sheepishly. "Okay, Jimmy."

• • •

An hour later, the stock was strained and the remouillage had been brought to a boil and turned off. Mike marveled at the velvety rich body and clarity of Jimmy's veal stock and made sure he tasted everything he could. The remouillage was cooling on the floor in the corner of the kitchen. He went downstairs to find Jimmy, who was in the walk-in putting away the meat order.

"What's next, boss?" Mike was pumped from this high-caliber style of cooking.

Jimmy was wiping a sheet pan, which he then covered with a full-size piece of parchment. He laid the last of the four full strips from the box onto the pan and hefted the pan onto a shelf. "Okay, dude, how'd you make out with the stocks?"

"Good. I strained the stock into the sink and put the bones back in…"

"You what!?" Jimmy's eyes were on fire.

"Just kidding, Jimmy. Everything's cool."

"That's not funny. We actually had a butthead who did that his first day. He was supposed to work Sarah's spot. Imagine. Jack almost punched him out. Yeah, Jack worked the line that night. We've had a few clowns over the years, but fortunately nobody new lately. Jack does a kind of background check when somebody comes to work. He sure did on me, and that was in the very beginning. You'd be surprised at the value of personal information."

"What do you mean by that?" Mike put his hand on the shelf.

"Don't worry about it, buddy. You'll find out in due time. Come on, let's get outta here. I'm freezin' my ass off." Mike followed Jimmy out and back up the stairs to the kitchen.

"Okay, grab that giant rondeau over there. I want you to dice up about five pounds of carrots. Peel them first, and I want them diced nice and even, about quarter inch, right?" Jimmy used his hands. "Put the diced carrots in the rondeau. It should be about two inches deep on the bottom. Start that on medium heat with a little salt and some flavored oil I'll give you. Then dice up some celery and onions, same size, equal parts celery and onion, the same volume as the carrots. You with me?"

"Yep, twenty-five percent each celery and onion, fifty percent carrots."

"All right, Galileo. You got it. See that crock over there by the grill? That's the fat from the bacon cooked with garlic. Use that, about a cup. Put a handful of black peppercorns and a bunch of bay leaves in with the vegetables. Use that wooden paddle. Stir it gently and cook it slow." Jimmy opened what looked like a military briefcase. Inside were knives and other cook's tools, neatly arranged in their own spaces. He pulled out a chef's knife and stroked it across a sharpening steel seemingly without thinking. He gave the handle to Mike. "Here's a knife, *coochie coo*. Don't cut yourself. The carrots and celery are in that fridge, and there's the onions." He pointed. "Remember, I want everything uniform and don't take all day. I'm going downstairs to clean the veal chops, and I'll be back in a few." Without another word, Jimmy turned and went downstairs. Mike looked around at the kitchen in a whole new light.

Twenty minutes later, Jack came in and noticed Mike after a second glance. "Mike, what's going on? What the. . .?" Jack instinctively looked down at the cutting board where Mike was working. He'd nearly finished the carrots, and they were a beautiful uniform dice. "Mike, where the hell did you learn how to cut vegetables like that?" Jack was surprised and pleased at the same time. Mike kept working as he looked up at Jack.

"An old man taught me."

"Taught you well, it seems. Where's Jimmy?"

"Downstairs. Cleaning the veal racks." Mike turned his attention back to the cutting board.

"That for the braised racks?" Jack nodded toward the carrots.

"Yes, sir."

"Good. Don't cook that base too slowly and brown it a little more than he tells you. And don't forget the damn coriander seed. Add as much of that as you do black pepper." Jack headed for the stairs.

"You got it, boss." Mike called after him. This was already getting fun. He was cooking this dish to Jimmy's specifications but was now taking a new direction due to an override by Jack. *Woohoo! Bite this, Jimmy.*

Fifteen minutes later, Jack and Jimmy came upstairs and went out to the bar. Mike had finished the vegetables and they were simmering, with the spices and oil, in the rondeau. This was a beautiful pan; a piece of functional art. It weighed more than thirty pounds and was nearly three feet in diameter and a foot deep. It was solid stainless-steel construction with a plate covering the exterior bottom of the pot. This plate, designed to evenly disperse heat across the cooking surface, was nearly a quarter-inch thick. Heavy bronze handles were bolted to the sides. The pot was obviously old and well used, but the bottom was perfectly flat. It was a pure joy to work with a piece of equipment like this.

Jack and Jimmy came back into the kitchen. "Jimmy, where'd you find this guy?" Jack asked him.

"He just kind of wandered in off the street. I don't know where he came from.

I think we need to check up on him just in case. He looks a little sketchy to me." They both were looking at Mike, who had turned around, standing proudly in front of his pot of vegetables. Jack laughed silently to himself.

Jimmy said, "Mike, where's your hat? Jack, you mind if he wears your stuff again tonight?"

"Whatever, Jimmy. Just make sure you brown those racks a little more this time, okay?" Jack headed to the stairs.

"Yeah, okay. Mike, come on. We gotta get the potatoes going. Here, fill that small pot with the little red and white potatoes. Cut 'em in half and then into half-inch slices. Nice and even, right? Perfectly parallel. Fill that other big pot with water, add a handful of bay leaves and bring it to a boil. Once it boils, put a bunch of salt in and blanch the potatoes for two minutes. Keep it rolling, but no more than two minutes, okay? As soon as you put those potatoes in the water, go and get a pot full of ice, stop up that sink, and fill it with cold water about a foot high and add the ice. You cool with that?" Mike nodded in somewhat of a daze, but still sure that he understood. "Good. By the time the water fills, the potatoes should be done. Strain them in the other sink with that colander. Hah, you washed it, good man. Okay, so strain the potatoes in the other sink and then dump them in the ice water. You with me?"

"Roger that, Cap'n."

"Good. When you finish that, get back to me. I'll be downstairs."

Mike was thoroughly invigorated. These directions were the mark of precision cooking. He was starting to care even less about the book. He was simply enjoying himself.

Half an hour later, Jimmy came up to the kitchen and Mike was nowhere in sight. The vegetables were nicely caramelized, a little dark but just barely simmering. The blanched potatoes were in even layers on two sheet pans, and all the pots were clean. Something told him Mike was out at the bar, and there he found him drinking a glass of red wine, talking to Sarah as she made a cappuccino.

"Mike, what the fuck! That mirepoix is burnt to shit! Those racks need to go in now if I'm gonna serve 'em tonight. Come on man, I thought we were cool, damn it! Get in there and clean that pot, now! Shit, I'm in the weeds thanks to you." Jimmy was being loud. Mike nearly spilled his wine getting up, as he grabbed it and went to the kitchen. Jimmy winked at Sarah, who laughed into her cappuccino.

Mike ran into the kitchen and over to the big pot of vegetables. He gave them a stir, bewildered until he realized Jimmy was messing with him. The bottom of the pan was perfectly clean as he scraped it with the large wooden spatula. The vegetables were a rich golden brown and had reduced to about a quarter of their original volume. They smelled really good. He heard Sarah and Jimmy come in and turned around as they stood opposite him, at the pick-up area. They were both looking at the pot and Sarah made her way around to the cooking area.

"Nice cut, Mike. And it looks a little darker than usual." Sarah gently took the spatula from Mike's hand and stirred the pot. "I think we have a conspiracy here." She looked at Jimmy over her shoulder. "Finally, someone's giving this dish some depth and character."

"This is my dish, and I'll make it however I damn well please. Mike, what the hell? Why'd you cook this base so dark? I said sweat the vegetables with just a tinge of color. Does this look like a tinge of color? And what's with all the coriander seed?" Mike looked at Sarah, who was smiling at him and then to Jimmy, who had his hands on his hips and was glaring in an exaggerated way.

He shrugged. "I had a little man on my shoulder guiding me, I guess." He grinned as he took a sip of his wine.

At that moment, Jack came upstairs and over to the pot to see what was going on. He took the spatula from Mike and stirred. "Ahh, there we go, nice and dark. Good man, Mike." Jack clapped him on the shoulder. Sarah looked up, rolling her eyes and headed out to the bar. Jack followed, asking about the produce order.

"You little shit." Jimmy took the wine from him and tossed it into the pot. "Season those three racks over there and when the grill gets hot, sear 'em in three directions. *Golden brown!*"

As Mike walked away, Jimmy stirred the pot and tasted a bit of the vegetable mixture. He got a burst of flavor from a soft, whole coriander seed and was pleasantly surprised. He laughed but would never admit how good it tasted.

The grill was getting hot and Mike scraped and oiled it, preparing to sear the racks. He rubbed the racks with the flavored oil and spices.

Jimmy was cutting onions in half, leaving all the skin on, preparing to roast them for another dish. He brushed the cut side of the onion with the flavored oil and then seasoned them with a ground spice. As he was putting the onions in the oven, Mike crossed over to the pot and said with an uninterested tone, "So what next with this?" As Jimmy turned and pointed in the other direction, Mike grabbed the small crock of ground fennel seed and smelled it.

Jimmy continued. "Okay, pour a bottle of white wine in and reduce it by about half. But add the wine a cup or so at a time. You can turn the heat up a bit and stir it a little. And add a bunch of thyme tied with string. When that's done, add two or three gallons of the veal remouillage — up to about the handle — bring it to a boil, skim the foam, and then bring it back down to a low simmer. I just want to bring it all together; I don't want to reduce it. So low heat, one bubble at a time. Now, be careful with those potatoes. The only reason I blanched them was to get most of the starch out. If I didn't blanch them the juice would be cloudy, right? I don't want them to cook away and melt into the juice either and I definitely don't want them broken up. So be real careful when you stir them. Add the potatoes just after you put the racks in. Bone side down.

"Okay man, your grill's smoking. Wipe it down once more with a clean oily rag and toss those babies on. Remember, three directions on the grill, forty-five, forty-five, and one-eighty degrees. Nice and even, and not too dark. Don't forget to scrape and oil the grill each time you flip them. And pay attention to the backside and the edges. I want two nice crusty end cuts from each rack. Here, add some fennel and more salt and pepper." Jimmy handed him a small crock.

Mike nodded again, silently thinking about what Jimmy had just told him. It was perfectly clear, and it seemed simple as waking up and brushing your teeth. But he knew there was nothing simple about it. It was the product of years of experience and hours of attention to detail. He stepped up to the racks and with both hands massaged the oil and spices into the meat. He thought about how this same scene could have played itself out centuries ago. A similar relationship between a kitchen apprentice and his master, and a similar cut of meat. With a similar insistence that protocol be followed, leaving just the slightest leeway for evolution. Mike once again marveled at one of the most vital, powerful, spiritual, and oldest disciplines known to mankind… cooking.

A half hour later, the three racks, seared to Jimmy's order, were in the huge pot with the potatoes. They had just come down to a gentle simmer with a single bubble here and there, perking through the caramelized vegetables and translucent, nut-brown broth. The bones rose an inch above the surface of the liquid, just as Jimmy had intended and the aroma was wonderful. Jimmy came by and poked one of the racks with his finger. "Good. Shut it off. They're rare and I want them to stay that way for now. Turn them over and come on downstairs." Mike was gliding a foot off the ground after preparing the incredible pot of braised veal chops and wondered what was next.

Outside the walk-in, Jimmy handed Mike a thin, quilted work coat. He opened the door and said, "Okay, I want you to take everything out and mop the floor with the pine bleach. And wipe down the walls and shelves with it, too." Mike's euphoria quickly dissipated as he looked around at the trays of meat, bins, and crocks on the shelves. The refrigerator smelled and looked very fresh and clean. He already knew by watching that Jimmy was quite fastidious and neat despite his appearance. But he had to wonder if he was being neurotic or just giving him a hard time. What he would never know was that it was Jack's idea to have him clean the walk-in, *after* Jimmy had put the meat order away.

Mike came upstairs after cleaning the walk-in. He was tired and chilled to the bone. He'd cut his hand on the bottom of one of the shelves, which made him uncharacteristically irritable. Making his way to the bar, he just wanted to grab his things and slip out unnoticed. It was just as he stepped around the curtain that he bumped into Sarah. She was carrying an empty coffee cup and saucer in her left hand. Instinctively she raised it as they collided. Mike was neither concentrating nor looking up when his hands landed on her waist. His thumbs rested on her belly just below her navel. Her right hand was on his forearm, and as he looked at her face and into her eyes she didn't flinch. For a moment they were still. Her hand slid up to his bicep and gave the slightest squeeze. He wanted to pull her close, but simply pressed his thumbs gently into her belly. He tasted her breath as she slowly blinked and exhaled with her lips just slightly parted. They heard someone on the stairs and at that very moment gave each other a firm hold while remaining six inches apart. Their hands relaxed and reluctantly let go. The five-second interlude ended and they parted; Mike to the bar and Sarah to the kitchen. Jimmy came out to the bar and found Mike standing behind one of the stools.

"Mike, the fridge looks great. You must've been in there for forty-five minutes. You gotta be freezing."

"No, Jimmy. Actually, I'm not cold at all," he said, slightly out of breath.

"Well, your cheeks sure are flushed. You okay?"

"Yeah, sure, Jimmy. I'm fine." He just wanted to look at Sarah again. To look into her dark brown eyes, with her hair spilling across a pillow…

"Okay, thanks man. I'll be back in an hour." Jimmy went out the side door.

Mike returned to the kitchen and saw Sarah from behind, standing at the sink. Wearing a beige T-shirt, her brown shorts came to mid-thigh. Her proportions and posture were perfect. Her feet were spread slightly apart and her shoulders, though not broad, were held back and square. The raw purity of her sexuality hammered into Mike's core. He approached her without a touch and commented on the shrimp she was cleaning at the sink.

"I think that's the most beautiful bowl of shrimp I've ever seen. They don't look like they've been frozen." He picked up one of the whole shrimp and gave it a smell. Like the others, it was in perfect condition. He made a point of looking closely at the shrimp's head and eyes as she turned to him.

"Jack gets them fresh from Florida. They're called *Key West Pinks*," Sarah said without looking up.

Mike nodded. "Mmm. Look at the eyes. They're like polished ebony." He turned and looked at Sarah.

Sarah had brown eyes, so dark they were nearly black. Combined with her brown hair and a light tan, Spain came to Mike's mind. Sarah was absolutely stunning to him. In the instant that he looked into her eyes, he saw honesty. The muscles of her face and eyebrows relaxed. She was demure. And he knew that now, in this kitchen, was neither the time nor the place for it. He broke off the shrimp's head and cracked open the shell, gently removing the vein as he did so, basically cleaning the shrimp in one smooth move.

"Yeah, they're fresh all right." He gave Sarah a sideways smirk with an eyebrow raised. He tossed it into the other bowl that held the cleaned shrimp.

Sarah smiled. "That was well done. Can you do it again?"

He picked up another shrimp and repeated.

"Very nice." She nodded her head as she spoke.

"Look at the flesh. It's so fresh it's almost transparent. Soft and moist like jelly. You don't rinse them, do you?"

"Mike, please. No, I don't rinse them. But I usually de-vein them with a small knife. I try to score them just off center to avoid cutting into the vein. Then it comes out in one piece, but I like the way you pulled it out with the head. They'll cook so nicely without the butterfly cut down the back."

"That they do. But you can only clean really fresh shrimp that way. The first time I had them that way was at Commander's Palace in New Orleans. I was down there doing a story on Marcia Ball."

Sarah interrupted. "I love Marcia Ball! I saw her in St. Louis at Johnny D's. I'll never forget. She must be over six feet tall."

Mike smiled, adoring her enthusiasm, and her smile, her teeth, her eyelashes. . . He chuckled. "Right, she plays piano sidesaddle. She was at the Maple Leaf." Mike paused, wondering if she had the tape.

"You've got to be kidding. I have this tape of her from the Maple Leaf in New Orleans." Sarah tried to remember the details.

"Nineteen eighty-three? Dr. John, The Neville Brothers? Is that the one?"

"You were there?" She was incredulous, beautiful.

"I was working and I'm telling you it was insane. I made my spot by the sound-man. He was on a platform at the back of the room, so it was a great spot to listen. Just after the second break, who walks in but Dr. John! He nods to the bartender and then to the sound guy, who points with his thumb in the air like a gun. And it was like nobody noticed him, just ole Dr. John strolling in to have a drink. He sits down and watches the whole set without moving. Next thing I know, Aaron Neville walks in and gives him the high-five. I could not believe my eyes. They closed the doors at two. Whoever was in, was in. I didn't leave till noon the next day. By the time it was all over, I'd met this amazing group of people, including Taj Mahal, Maceo Parker, and Mickey Hart from the Grateful Dead. And they all jammed! Early on the sound guy said to me, 'I'm running tape. They can throw me in the jailhouse if they want.' Turned out everybody was glad he did, and they all wanted a copy. I got a first generation right off the original DAT direct from the soundboard. You really need to hear it. It's crystal clear. There were no contracts, and they all agreed to let the tape go around for free. That's probably how you got a dub."

"A couple years later. I'd love to hear your copy."

"Sure, it's on my laptop. I'll bring it by tomorrow."

It was almost comical. Like children they'd gotten so excited. But as adults they both knew there was so much more to it. And there was nothing either of them could do about it.

"Mike, I have to get to work. Maybe later you can tell me more about the shrimp at Commander's Palace. And the evening at the Maple Leaf." She did not want him to leave. But two hours before service was no time to be social. And she had two specials going that evening.

"Okay. But don't forget about Arthur Conan Doyle." He opened his eyes wide and pointed.

Sarah twinkled. "And Arthur Conan Doyle." They both waved but did not make contact.

"Okay, see you, Sarah."

"Bye, Mike."

Mike went out to the bar and sat down. His hand wasn't hurting as much as it had earlier, and he badly wanted to go back into the kitchen. He considered how busy Sarah must be, but as he looked around at the interior of The Theatre a voice said to him: "You only live once." He went back into the kitchen.

"Sarah, you mind if I cook some of your shrimp?"

Sarah assumed an agreeable air. She continued stirring the large pot she was working in. "Sure, you know where everything is."

"Great, thanks. How have you been cooking them?" He gave her a hard stare, pretending he didn't know she was busy.

Sarah laid the wooden spatula across the rim of the pot and turned with a hand on her hip and a straight face. "Ground coriander seed, chili, grated garlic, and olive oil. Just like everything else. Deglaze with a squeezed orange." Turning back to the pot of lentils, she was clearly busy now, fully perturbed, and Mike had achieved his objective.

"So, you're not salting them until they're on the plate." Mike almost laughed aloud and couldn't wait for her response.

She gave the pot a final stir and then whacked the spatula on the rim. There was a slight pause before she turned to him. "Cook them any way you like. And then get the hell out of here." Sarah managed to keep a straight face while Mike couldn't erase the grin. He quickly realized he'd gotten more than he bargained for.

"Okay, I'll just work over here. The recipe sounds so good I can't wait to see if it measures up to my imagination." He went to the cold station to get the peeled garlic. Lucky for him she wasn't there.

Sarah grabbed a sauté pan and when Mike turned around she jammed it into his gut. "I'm sure you can't imagine what it would be like. Make sure you get the pan hot before you put the shrimp in."

Mike cooked the shrimp, ate at the bar by himself, and didn't return for dinner service. He'd made plans to talk with Jack at The Theatre the following day.

• • •

"Jack, it's clear you run the kitchen. What's your background as a chef?"

"First of all, Mike, Sarah runs the kitchen. I'm just louder and taller. As far as being a chef goes, I don't really like the term. I think it's used much too loosely these days. Chef." Jack nearly spat. "I picture some pansy ass on TV with really white teeth and an expensive watch."

Mike scratched his head and was frustrated. He wanted to shake Jack by the shoulders but decided to try another tactic and looked at Jack.

"So how did you learn to cook?"

"My mother was a cook."

"So, it started early?"

"I grew up in the kitchen."

"And you watched your mother cook?"

"I watched, I smelled, I tasted, and I listened. I started cooking when I was young. She made me try everything. She taught me how things act depending on how you treat them, and the stages of flavor. One of the first basic steps in cooking is to understand and respect the character of your ingredients. Then you can start telling stories with it." Jack shrugged as if this were a simple, uninteresting fact. "We ate very simply."

For some reason Jack did not look like a cook. Mike watched as Jack picked up a cigar from the ashtray. His cigars looked like dark, half-smoked twigs that were wider on the ash end. He meant to ask him what the hell kind of cigar it was. Before Mike could speak, Jack continued.

"My father was a sculptor. Generations of his family worked the marble quarries around Carerra, in Italy. They cut blocks for the finest statuary on Earth from those mountains. You see, Mike, sculpture is unique because you take away to get to the end-product, where most other art forms are created by adding to get to the finished product. Michelangelo said a sculptor has to see the theme within the block. You need to know what it looks like before you go there. It's not like painting or drawing, where you can keep adding to it. And you can't cover up something you don't like." Jack stopped, thinking how to make his point. "In a way it's like bringing out the truth, with no safety net. That's sort of how I learned to cook. Use good ingredients, like a fine block of marble, and bring its beauty to light. Without adding on." A drag on the cigar revealed it was dead, so he put it down and drank some water.

"Sounds easy, right? Bring people into the equation and it becomes infinitely more complicated. The people you work with and cook for have all sorts of require-ments. A meal is like an opera. You have a setting, intro, the acts, a climax, and the finale. And add to that an audience and orchestra. That's the big picture. When I did private work, I needed to look at a whole week that way. Say you have a group staying at a villa. They eat your food every day, so the menu becomes even longer. It's now a meal lasting a week. So, it needs to be a graceful wave day to day. I'd carry them through the forest and then down to the sea, with some days light and breezy and others dark and stormy." He motioned with his hands. "Easing from light to heavy as the days go by."

As Jack lit the cigar, Mike said, "So you worked as a private chef. Where?"

"In Europe." Jack exhaled, thinking Mike wasn't listening to what he'd said.

"Really? Where in Europe?"

"Europe. It doesn't matter where in Europe. I'll tell you about that some other time. Go on." Jack put the cigar down.

That was weird, Mike thought as he looked down at his notes. "Tell me some-thing else about your mother."

"My mother? What I got from her were deeper, more universal things. She taught me to have respect. That was the beginning. She refinished woodwork — antiques and such." He took a slow puff. "One of the laws of refinishing she taught me was that 'your final coat is only as good as all the coats beneath it.' That's one of the great things about watching a master of anything. There's an understanding that's so basic and fundamental, it can be applied to any discipline. And it can usu-ally be explained in a single sentence. That's what I believe. I suppose it depends on your philosophy." He drank some more while Mike was silent.

Jack sat back with the cigar in his mouth, holding out his hands. "But nobody wants to hear about somebody caring too much." He took a puff and put down the cigar. "It's like money: 'Take care of the pennies and the dollars will take care of themselves.' It's the same with a lot of other things. With cooking, I think if you pay attention to the ingredients and the details of your technique, you'll have more leeway further into the dish toward final composition and assembly, where all the real chaos happens. If you stand strong from the beginning, you're more likely to get your point across when the shit hits the fan. Assuming you have an open mind."

Jack stopped talking and Mike took a moment to respond. "I think improvisational music can be described that way. If you have the arrangement and score set up, then the musicians are free to take off and explore as long as they stick to the beat and keep count of the measures."

Jack laughed. "Yeah, that's it. Improvisational cooking! The live culinary experience."

"Jack, what is it about prunes? I hear you insist that everyone cook prunes at the restaurant?"

"Insist is a strong word. Sounds to me like you've stumbled onto a conspiracy." He looked toward the curtain. "Yeah, it's true, I put prunes on the menu. And everyone has to cook them. Mind you, they're also allowed to do as they please. One of the privileges of owning a restaurant."

The cigar was out and so he put it down. He stood up to grab the water and poured for them.

"Truth be told, I do exhibit a certain amount of control here at my restaurant." Jack was mocking dignity as he sat.

"Why prunes?" Neither of them moved. Mike suppressed a grin.

Jack sat back. *That was fast*, he thought. "I like prunes," he said.

"What do you like about prunes?"

"It has an appealing character to me, dark and deep. Keep in mind, most of our clientele are, let's say — middle-aged or beyond and can always use a bit of water-soluble fiber. I'd like to think of this place as a dietary spa."

Jack was suddenly bored with Mike. He began to play with the glasses as he went on. "I also put a lot of garlic on the menu. I'd also like to think of the restaurant as a healthful retreat. It is a service business, right? I'll tell you one thing: I've seen a lot of new ways to prepare things since I've been here. That's part of the fun. When you become chef, you step up a bit higher on the food chain." He stood up. "I suppose you could say I'm an evangelist of sorts. Preaching a doctrine of garlic and prunes for older folks."

Phil had come out to the bar to make a coffee. He'd heard the last bit and added, "Don't forget lots of onions and chilis."

Jack had his hands full of dishes as Sarah was on her way out of the kitchen. They nearly collided, but nothing dropped.

She was saying, "And tomatoes if we're lucky!" And went back into the kitchen.

"Whatever!" shouted Jack.

Remus came in the side door and crossed the stage. He was carrying a newspaper and a clear plastic bag that held a half-dozen or so cigars. "Mike, you causin' trouble again?" Remus smiled and stood behind the chair next to Mike's.

"He's stirrin' the pot all right." Phil said, with his back turned.

"Well, I think that's just what we need around here. To get some of these issues out on the table and talk about things," Remus said as he sat at the end of the bar and put down his newspaper and cigars.

Sunlight blasted through the windows on the left side of the room. Mike bathed in the warmth of this friendly place and wondered how something like this was made or came about. Still, he knew it wasn't easy working here.

Phil turned around. "An intervention. That's what we need. Straighten out this dysfunctional restaurant."

Jimmy came out and stood at the edge of the curtain. "Hey, I kind of like the idea of a dysfunctional restaurant. I would've quit by now if this place was normal."

"I had a normal job once," Phil said as he finished wiping the coffee area and went downstairs.

"Aw, come on. Can't we have a normal restaurant? Please, Jack?" Remus stood up.

"Okay, okay." Jack came to the bar. "Everyone's hereby on notice to be normal. For the sake of our esteemed lexicographer of humanism, Mr. Mike Ambrose." Jack was now orating.

"Finally!" said Remus as he reached the stairs.

• • •

Jack followed Remus downstairs to the VIP suite and closed the door. "Remus, I put together the package I'm sending to Rome. It's actually a lot more than what I envisioned, but what can I do? Gotta go for it."

"What've you got?" Remus was intrigued. Jack was excited.

"It wasn't too hard. I have it all on my laptop. I took all the menus Gianario and I did together over the last three years I worked there and included the guests for each meal. Honestly, it wasn't until this period that I started taking notes on who was there. But I was also recording the men's room. There was a phone there. You know, I'm just now remembering what it was like. It was really exciting! Not just the thought of getting caught, which was a big concern, but what they had going on was beyond anything I could've imagined." Jack was brimming as he continued. "And you know, I was so concerned with this stuff that I was having Gianario do most of the work. That was when I really started thinking like a chef. Until then, I was just cooking, but when you have other people cooking your food you really get to look at things from outside the box. So much came back to me, looking at these menus."

"Sounds like being a bandleader," Remus said with a laugh. "Then you gotta start dealing with personalities."

"Yeah, I was just saying that to Mike. But I think it adds to the product. It would be difficult if you're hung up, but I had my own agenda and just wanted to get it done. You know, I let him do things I'd never have done. He also gave me a lot of ideas."

"It sounds like a restaurant I know."

"Hah! Yeah, here's to the big picture."

"Yeah, the big picture." Remus paused. "What about Mike?"

"I talked to Vilotti this morning. It's a convoluted route, and we use this weird code, but I was right. He put Mike into the picture. He also put him onto the whiskey story. Told me it was a gift. He always knew I loved Scotch and we could never find a book about it. It was also a test for Mike, before he sent him here. Can you imagine?"

"That's a beautiful thing Jack. And being able to think in long timelines."

"Sure is. Hopefully you'll meet Lorenzo when we're in the Med next year. I'll give you some of the transcripts. These guys thought in really big pictures."

"I still think he was tired of waiting to see how the whole thing would pan out. Anyway, Mike doesn't know anything and Vilotti said he's going to be called to Rome soon. He thinks sending the menus and all the details is perfect. Thanks again, that was a great idea."

Remus shrugged. "So now what?"

"I think I'm going to contact Gene Nogara and have him check up on Mike. He's tight with the cardinal up in Chicago, who knows most of what Rome has going on here in the Midwest. I'll see if he can find out anything. Hopefully nothing. Far as I know, nobody here in the states knows anything about me. At least who I really worked for. Vilotti is good at this sort of thing.

"You know he's really a genius. He put this whole thing together for me. And all the introductions that basically gave me a new identity here. He really felt they abused my family and it's because of him that I have a chance to get some justice. I think it's kind of an absolution for him. He's spent his life working for them and facilitating a lot of things he knew were wrong. So maybe this last gesture is his way of doing some good in exchange."

Jack picked up his cigar again and held it still for barely a second before looking at Remus. "You know, Remus, during one of the last conversations I had with my mother we talked about revenge and retribution. Her take on it was that I should turn it around and do something good with all the negative energy it created. Her suggestion was that I should force them to do something positive, and to let that be the equalizer. It's funny. Two of the people who've been closest to me over the years have come up with similar solutions. I think I'll let Mike in on a bit about the recordings, so if he does get called to Rome, they'll get wind of it."

"Careful, Jack. I don't trust those guys."

"Yeah. What the hell. Only live once."

Remus wasn't quite comfortable with this, but he trusted Jack. "So, what happens when we go to Italy?"

"Well, first off, I think it's gonna happen sooner than later. Maybe you, Pamela, and I will go to Rome while the boat ships. That's when it will all go down. I'm planning to get Vilotti to arrange a meeting with Lorenzo."

"Jack, I don't know if I want anything to do with it. This is *your* big gamble, isn't it?" The fact was, Remus wanted more than anything to be there and see how it all went down.

"Remus, I want you there. It'll help with what I have to propose."

Remus crossed his arms. "Which is?"

Jack paused and sat forward. "That they employ us as a company to cook for them and pay all our expenses while we travel in Europe. We'll be free and I'll make sure everybody's well paid." He sat back, having made his case.

Remus considered this and he still had reservations. But he thought about staying back in Samson, Missouri for the rest of his life and there was really no question in his mind. "Jack, you know when something big comes up, I can usually place a good song that helps me make the decision. But I ain't heard a song like this ever and I think the bandleader's got a part for me. So, what about everybody else? Pamela? Jimmy? Sarah? Phil? What's their take on all this? They all in?"

"Phil's in on some of it, but not all. You know everything, Remus. The rest of 'em don't know a thing except it'll be working like we've been, but just on a boat. They're baffled, I think, but yes, they're all in." Jack trailed off.

"Okay, man." Remus let it go at that.

• • •

Upstairs, Mike was alone in The Theatre, wondering how this joking came about.

A few minutes later, Sarah came behind the bar to get some ice. "You are trouble, aren't you?" She was facing him, confident, strong, and very sexy.

Mike tried to think of something interesting to say, unaware that she was already quite interested in him. He paused only a moment. "Sometimes I don't know what I am."

"You're ambrosia, Mike. I looked you up on the internet." She leaned forward and looked toward the curtain. Then in a hushed tone added, "You're marked." She straightened up, turned, and continued filling the bucket with ice. "You know what ambrosia is. It's food of the gods. Something very pleasing to the palate. Have you heard of the ambrosia beetle?" She didn't turn around.

Mike was severely intrigued and a bit unsettled by the crafty delivery. "No, tell me about the ambrosia beetle." He went to the bar and quietly sat across from where she was working.

"The ambrosia beetle bores into a branch or limb of a tree and begins to feed on the wood. Then they create a symbiotic fungus that they feed on." She turned around and was ever so slightly startled by his sitting at the bar.

"A symbiotic fungus. Would you care to elaborate on that?" He was watching her.

110

She stood tall and took a beautiful drink of water. The light came in and grazed her from behind as she looked at him with shaded eyes. "I think you have your work cut out for you. You've got a group of strong personalities here. Everybody's so hung up on their own work that I don't think anyone truly realizes how interesting it all is. So now you're trying to get to the bottom of it and you're getting nothing but jokes. They're all puffed up." She stopped, wondering how he'd respond.

"Sarah, you're so right. It's a battle. I just want to be a fly on the wall. Or a beetle maybe." He stretched both his hands out on the bar. She smiled as he looked at her. "I can't just sit here. I need to try and prime the pump somehow. Right?"

She picked up his hand and turned it over. She pulled her thumbnail down through the center of his palm and up his middle finger. Then she took the finger and shook it lightly, pulling his forearm. "That's your job, Mr. Writer." She held onto his finger.

Mike smiled and took her hand in his. "Well then, Ms. Chef, why is everything such a performance here?" He let go.

She held up her glass and looked around dramatically. "Duh, Mike, this is a Theatre." She lowered her voice a bit. "But it's funny you say that. I was sitting here with Jack once when I first started, asking him about his past. He was telling me about when he was a kid in Italy and he would be invited to these high-profile din-ners. What he said was, 'The room was so beautiful, the table was so beautiful, but it was the people that were the most beautiful. They would sing to the opera.' He went on telling me there was nothing as elegant as people. That he would sit and watch these people eat and drink. I remember him describing ladies drinking from long-stemmed water glasses as if it was a ballet. That sitting in these dining rooms was like being a performer and spectator all at the same time. So, what's *this* place? It's a museum, and people are the art."

Mike looked at her squarely. "The guests or the cooks?"

Sarah turned around to pick up the bucket of ice. "That's a good question."

Mike was staring out into The Theatre. "Far out."

"Yeah." Sarah went back to work.

• • •

Twenty minutes later, Mike was twirling the stem of his glass and Jack came out to the bar to light his cigar.

"Mike, what the hell? What are you doing?" He was lighting the cigar.

111

"I'm sitting here. What?"

"I thought you were writing a book, that's what." He tapped the cigar into the ashtray on the table. Still standing.

"I'm in the design phase. Putting the pieces together before I attack the project."

"Design phase." Jack sat at the bar.

"I need more background. Tell me about your father. What did he teach you that applies to cooking?"

"He taught me about art. His whole family worked in marble. My grandfather said to me once, 'An artist is a servant to his discipline, and the medium is the master. Don't you forget that. You have to look for the grain.'" Jack's eyes seemed to glaze a bit and Mike let him continue. Jack tapped the ash and looked up before putting the cigar down and sitting back.

"You see, Mike, all of us, the crew, we're just the vehicle. Our job is to bring the food to our guests by featuring the ingredients. A lot of work's gone into lining up the purveyors and making sure the ingredients are top notch to begin with, right? I mean the stuff is dynamite before we even touch it. What's the main attraction at this restaurant? The food. Certainly not us."

Mike wondered about this last statement. The cooks here were in fact rock stars, and the restaurant was famous for miles around. The irony was that while this was a theater, Jack insisted that the star of the show was something besides people. Only truth can prove philosophy through contradiction.

Jack continued. "This menu is actually very flexible, even though it uses relatively few ingredients. Everything is raw and we just sort of nudge things into the dining room." Jack paused to relight his cigar. Mike felt his hair begin to bristle. *Now* he was getting somewhere.

"Jack, it seems like there's a bit more than nudging going on back there at night. I mean, at times it's downright loud. I don't want to say there's tension, but the energy is very high."

Jack laughed. "Sarah's tough. And she gives Jimmy a hard time. He needs it. He's a little cocky, but there's no other grill man in the Midwest as good as him. I'm sure of it."

Jack puffed and glanced toward the curtain, as if making sure no one was listening. Mike made a mental note to watch Jimmy more closely.

"I'm really very lucky, Mike. Those two work quite well together. They're both very skilled, talented, and intelligent. But they're opposites, and that's the key, I think. This is high volume, and we have very little waste. Everyone's conscious of what everyone else puts out. And there's a vested interest. So, we're all watching each other. That may be what you perceive as tension.

"It seems like you and Sarah are at odds."

Jack smiled. "We argue incessantly. She's good. We keep each other on our toes." Jack stood and picked up the coffee cups. "But the fun part for me is that we have to play by my rules."

"Why, Jack?"

"Because it's my ball. I gotta go, Mike. I'll talk to you later." Jack headed for the curtain.

"Thanks, Jack."

"Okay, Mike, okay."

Mike smiled and shook his head as he switched off the recorder. He spent the evening with Jimmy behind the grill. He carefully studied Jimmy's methods and was impressed. He studied Sarah even more closely.

• • •

Mike had been looking forward to sitting with and interviewing Pamela. He'd only spoken to her once or twice at this point and he still wasn't sure what she was about. She was a dynamite-looking woman with a personality to match. He asked if she'd mind meeting at Heidle's on Saturday afternoon, and she said that was fine.

"Pamela, thanks for meeting me."

"No problem, Mike." She lit a cigarette.

She's as sultry as anything I've ever seen, he thought to himself. Mike was immediately attracted to her, and she'd found her mark. He switched on the recorder and sat back and looked at her. Unlike Sarah, Pamela was flirty-sexy. She wore red lipstick and that was about it for makeup. Her skin was virtually flawless, and he couldn't guess her age. He noticed her nails and decided to comment on them. The response might be as interesting as the interview.

"Nice manicure, Pamela. It matches your lipstick perfectly." Mike kept his eyes on respectable areas of her body.

113

She gave him a dazzling smile, and her eyebrows curved in an interesting way. Her expression was an art form in itself, more than simply sexy. There was a certain feminine intellect that he'd never seen before. It was beginning to seem that everyone connected to The Theatre was quite unique.

"Thanks." She took a drag on the cigarette.

He noticed her toenails were done to match the fingernails. They were in a nice pair of open-toed heels, not too high, which were also red, in polished leather. She'd done herself up for the interview and probably enjoyed doing it. She was very entertaining.

"Pamela, how did you get involved with Jack and his restaurant?"

"First of all, Mike, I'm not involved with Jack." *No mistaking that statement*, thought Mike, *people told you just what they thought around here.* She took a drag and tapped the butt into the ashtray.

"Sorry, Pamela, that's not what I meant." But it was. Check that off the list.

The cigarette was in the ashtray between them, smoking away. She left it there and sat back. "I know. Okay, let's see. When did I first meet him…" She reached for the cigarette but didn't pick it up. "Jack came to Evangeline's one night, the place I'd been working. Remus played piano there, and Phil was always around because he did the sound. So, we had chitchat about things going on. It's a small town, right? And we'd all known each other forever." She picked up the cigarette. "So, they'd been talking about this guy who came to look at The Theatre and how he was going to build a restaurant in it." She played with her cigarette, looking down. "I didn't believe it. I mean, I believed them, I just didn't think anyone would actually do it. Certainly not like that." She took a drag. Smiling out of the side of her mouth, she kept her eyes on him as she exhaled. "But he did."

Up close, Mike now saw that Pamela was in fact fantastically beautiful. The play of her eyes, teeth, and lipstick was captivating. He was overwhelmed at first and then realized that it wasn't just simple beauty. "A gorgeous gumshoe dame," came to mind. She was such a shining star. He needed to ask Phil if there were any black and white glossies of her working the bar at The Theatre. And if not, could he take some.

"So, you were there through the whole process of building the place. What was it like?"

"Mike, what do you mean, what was it like? You're talking about years. How much time you got?" She put the cigarette out.

"Okay, okay. Let's start at the beginning. Before it opened. What was your part in it all? When it was being built."

She looked over his shoulder at Heidle's daughter and smiled as she came to the table.

"Mike, this is Heidi, Heidle's daughter."

"Hello, Pamela." There was no accent, but her stance, fine skin, and strong features spoke clearly of her German roots. Wearing a plaid apron with a hand on her hip, she faced him directly with her brown eyes.

"Heidi, this is Mike. You know, he's writing the book about Jack's Café." Pamela reached out with a beautifully manicured hand and touched his arm. Socially elegant.

"Yes, I know. When do we get to see it?" Heidi's inquisitive gaze reminded him of the vicar, who at that moment came in and sat at an adjacent table. Heidi turned toward the people at two tables that had just sat down and were looking their way.

Mike answered. "Heidi, when it's finished, I promise there'll be a copy for anybody who wants one." He put both hands out onto the table as he looked up at her.

Heidi shrugged with eyebrows raised as she looked at Pamela. "Okay. We'll wait and see."

Heidle called out from the deli something in German. He was holding a bottle of Riesling.

"Would you like something to drink?" she asked, looking from one to the other.

"I'll have…" Pamela's eyes drifted over Mike's shoulder toward Heidle at the counter. "Some Riesling."

Mike smiled. "That'll be fine for me also."

"And you're eating, too?" Heidi nodded slightly, answering the question herself.

Mike looked at Pamela and she answered, "Lentil soup. And a bottle of water please. Mike, would you like sparkling?"

"Sure."

Heidle called out again in German and Heidi said to Mike, "My father says you should try the Kassler Ripchen."

"Is it a chop?" Mike asked.

"Yes, it's on the bone. The whole pork rack is smoked and then sliced. He just finished them yesterday."

"That sounds great."

"Would you like one or two?"

"Two."

"One cut?"

"Yes, please. With some cabbage . . ."

Heidi cut him off. "And spätzle. Well done."

Mike smiled and nodded as Heidle came to the table. It's always nice when people know how you like things. On a tray he had placed the bottles of Riesling and mineral water, four glasses, and a stein of beer. He put the tray down and then went to give the vicar his beer, taking his order and chatting in German. Heidi poured for Pamela and Mike.

"I'll be there Sunday," said Heidi with a grin, as she poured water and wine.

"Good," Pamela said with genuine sincerity. Heidi turned to speak to the vicar and then followed Heidle back toward the deli.

"What's up on Sunday?" Mike picked up his glass and held it up.

"It's a special party at The Theatre. Yes, cheers, Mike." She picked up her glass delicately by the bottom of the stem and touched his. Graceful indeed. "You didn't know?" She made direct eye contact.

"I'm surprised at how little I know. Here's to Jack."

"Yeah, Jack." She kept her eyes on Mike.

"So, Pamela. The Theatre. What about before Jack bought it and before the restaurant opened?"

"Well, before Jack, it was empty, and Remus had been living there forever — I mean forever — mainly keeping up the woodwork and playing piano. Nothing ever went on there. Phil was probably in there more than anybody. They've been friends for a long time and share a lot of common interests, like woodworking and music. They both read a lot too." She drank some of her water. Mike drank, watched, and listened as she continued.

"I know Phil always loved The Theatre. And Remus, well it's his heart and soul. It's the only home he's ever had. You know, I think he always knew something would come of it." She looked at him closely and then continued. "Phil's real estate business had the listing, and it had been on the market for as long as I can remember." Pamela noticed someone across the room and waved. Another flash of gorgeous teeth. "So, if someone wanted to see it, Phil had to show it. It was kind of ironic. He'd go over there and get Remus to give the tour, and nothing would ever happen." Pamela reached for her wine, smiling with her shoulders high.

"They never really wanted it to sell, did they?"

"Nobody did. In fact, I've heard Phil say he never gave the real asking price. I don't know if it's true, but it's a joke they had. He says he'd always give an inflated price if they didn't like the person."

Mike nodded. "So, they liked Jack?"

"I don't really know what happened. The previous owner was shady. Small time mobster or something up in Chicago. I never met him. I think they said Jack made the deal directly and paid Phil his commission in cash. Nothing else was ever said and I never asked. But yes, they were intrigued by the restaurant idea."

"And John?" Mike moved on, pondering her last statement.

"For John it's a family heirloom. But he didn't own it. Imagine that." She drank some wine.

"So, in walks Jack and he buys it. Then what? What does everybody think?"

Heidle brought out the plates and put them down. He motioned with the pepper mill to Pamela, who declined. Without asking, he gave two cranks to Mike's plate, refilled all their glasses, and left without a word.

Mike continued. "What did people think of Jack at first?" Mike inspected the pork chop, gently probing it with his fork. It was nearly two inches thick, with a single bone. A beautiful cut. The fat had been trimmed off, and Mike knew the chops on either side of his ended up thinner. A few tablespoons of thin gravy had been spooned over the top. It smelled smoky. He looked up to see Heidle watching from the deli and gave him a smiling nod of thanks.

Pamela took a spoonful of lentil soup, raised it to her lips, and blew on it. It was too hot, and she put the spoon back in the bowl. Probably didn't want to melt the juicy lipstick. She picked up her wineglass and watched Mike as he cut into the chop.

"You know that's a loaded question. I don't know what anyone else thought. What I can tell you is that he made some waves here when he came to this little town, but he did it in a classy way. He knew what he was doing and what it meant.

Some people here just plain didn't want a high-end fancy restaurant that people would come to from miles around. But he was switched on to that. That's one reason for the kind of success the place has."

She tried the soup again and took a spoonful. Not a trace left on her lips. "Jack is a very intuitive person and sensitive, too. That's what it takes, to come into a small town and build a restaurant like this. The food is important, but it's really a small part. Don't get me wrong. The food needs to be great for a restaurant to succeed, and our food is. People can't describe it." Another spoonful of lentils and still the lipstick was flawless. Mike dug deeper into the chop. "Jack also has no problem kicking people out of the restaurant for misbehaving, whether or not they've eaten or paid."

"So, you're saying he asked people what was and wasn't okay as he went about starting it up?" Mike wiped his mouth with the napkin and drank his wine.

"No, he didn't ask anybody anything, Mike. The thing is, he did very little. The bare minimum, really. I think he used the least amount of effort with just a little guidance. He just let people do what they wanted. That's what he did with me."

"How so?" Mike wondered what else Jack did with her as Heidi came to the table to check on them.

"Good? Everything good?"

"Mmm, wonderful, Heidi. You know, I'd like some greens." Pamela looked up, awaiting a response.

"Arugula today, with mustard dressing. Would you like some cheese?"

"That would be perfect. Anything but Limburger."

"Of course."

Pamela returned her attention to the soup and took another spoonful.

"I'll have a little more sauerkraut, Heidi. Please." Mike held up the bone and sliced off some dark bits with his knife. "So, what did he do with you, Pamela?"

"He let me choose the coverings for the chairs and barstools. And the draperies. And then I went about setting up the bar. Jack said to me, 'Whatever you want to do. Just tell Phil what you need, and he'll take care of it.' And that's how it went."

"So, he really trusted you," Mike said.

"Trust? I don't know if it's trust with something like this. I think trust is reserved for other things. He liked enough of my ideas, and I think he just believed in me. One thing that makes the restaurant great is that he lets everybody do what they want. My mother said to me that there's always something you can like about a person, anyone. I think in each of us he found a positive quality and set the stage for it to be showcased. That way we were each able to make our mark, like it's our own show. So, in a way, everybody owns a piece of it. But it's a difficult way to run an operation. And it can make things pretty chaotic at times. But I think that's where Jack likes to operate, on the edge of chaos."

The greens arrived and she picked up a slice of cucumber. She bit into it without it touching her lips and looked at the remaining crescent. She was beautiful to watch. She looked at Mike and went on. "It's easy to go in and say, 'This is how it is, this is how it's going to be, and there's not going to be any exceptions.' But it takes a lot more genius to manage something with minimal intervention than it does to use an iron fist."

Heidi had been behind Pamela and waited for her to finish speaking before refilling the wine and water.

"For me, a project like that is more interesting because you have a variety of input. And it's more creative. Then you have a whole that's greater than the sum of its parts. Like a gem with more facets." She raised her left eyebrow and shoulder and took a drink of wine.

"Here's to you, Pamela. That's a beautiful thing."

"It is."

They talked for another hour or so. After the meal, Pamela had a cup of Earl Grey tea and Mike finished the wine. He paid the bill, and they said goodbye outside Heidle's before going in separate directions. Mike left the following day, saying he had to drive to his house in Sioux Falls. The job was going to take longer than he'd planned, and he wanted to bring some things back to the motel where he was staying. He'd mentioned it to Jack, who didn't seem to care, saying, "Okay, see you in a week, then."

Remus was curious about where he was going, Sarah couldn't wait for him to get back, and Jimmy missed the prep help.

• • •

The day Mike returned from his home in South Dakota, he walked down to Heidle's and took a table at the rear of the seating area. It was late afternoon and only one other table was occupied. Heidle's daughter took his order of spätzle and sausages with a glass of Riesling. He knew he could drink a bottle but decided to be poised and drink by the glass. He settled into the transcripts and began to read through the interviews.

Heidle saw Jack regularly. Whenever sausage, bacon, or any other type of pork was called for in the restaurant, he got it from Heidle. Jack often came in to sit and read, or to just get away from the restaurant. He'd known men like Mike before, though none quite so peculiar, who needed a variety of public places to drink alone.

This affliction affects many men, and it's dealt with in many ways. Mike, though, was never one to sit for idle chat, nor was he one to pour his heart out to strangers. He was constantly working, writing, and researching. Prolific and productive was his mantra, and this he was.

Jack's life experience taught him to keep his eyes open. Wisdom told him to lace suspicion with magnanimity. And his lessons had served him well. So, while he gave his full backing on the book project, he kept a close eye on Mike.

Heidle called Jack while his daughter was taking Mike's order. "Your man's back. Yeah. He's at a table, looks like he's camping out."

"Right, thanks. See you in a minute," Jack answered and hung up. This meant that Mike was in for another of his long afternoon sessions of reading, writing, and Riesling.

Jack had nothing pressing at the restaurant and was at The Tavern twelve minutes later. He walked in, and pretending not to see Mike, went to the deli counter to talk to Heidle. Mike saw him come in and while he was looking forward to talking with Jack at some point, he subconsciously reasoned he needed another place in town where he could go and hang out unobserved.

As Heidle turned from the counter to go to the back room, Jack turned to Mike, who was looking directly at him. "Mike, what are you doing here? I thought you were back tomorrow," he called from across the room.

Mike put down the wineglass. "Hey, Jack. Yeah, I'm back. Guess I had my dates screwed up." Heidle came out carrying an ice bucket with a bottle of Riesling and another glass.

Jack came to the table with his eyes on the transcripts. He took the ice bucket and glass from Heidle and put them on the table. "You mind if I join you?"

Mike summed up the situation in an instant. "Please, Jack, I insist." He smiled as Jack thanked Heidle.

Jack sat down. "This Riesling is one of my favorites." Jack refilled Mike's glass before filling his own. "You know it comes from Heidle's family's hometown." They both reached for and raised their glasses.

"I can't imagine it coming from anywhere else, Jack." They locked eyes as the glasses touched.

"So how was the trip? Sioux Falls, right? Nice town. The river goes straight through it, if I remember."

"Yeah, I like it. But the river's mostly falls in town." Mike gave Jack a blank look and decided not to add, "hence the name." He unceremoniously reached for the recorder and after turning it on, placed it in the center of the table standing up. "How's things at the restaurant? Busy?"

Jack smiled. Touché. He picked up his glass and sat back. "Yeah, it's busy. We're always busy now. You know, day to day at this point." He took a sip. "How's the house?"

Mike did not want to talk. "It's fine, Jack. My wife died two years ago, and I still think she's going to walk into the room." He picked up his glass and before drinking said, "You ever get lonely, Jack?" At that moment he wanted to be alone and had no problem making that clear.

Jack softened. He knew what it was like to be lonely, but his solace didn't come in a bottle. "I'm sorry, Mike. And yes, I do. It can be a daily battle keeping the demons away." Jack was looking at the small crock of mustard in the center of the table and straightened its lid. He picked up his wineglass and looked up. "Gotta stay busy. You look good, Mike. I'm glad you're back, as I'm sure others are. Cheers." Jack raised his glass once more.

"Thanks, Jack. I'm happy to be here." Mike was indeed glad to be back, and although he didn't want to talk to Jack at the moment, he was in particularly good spirits. This and Jack's last statement resonated with thoughts of Sarah. "You keep looking at the transcripts of the interviews. Would you like to read them now?"

"I don't know. I'm definitely curious about what everyone's saying. But in the interests of serendipity, I think it might be best to wait."

Heidle came to the table with a cold bottle of sparkling mineral water and two glasses. He put them down and left. Jack poured and Mike spoke.

"Honestly, Jack, my experience in this sort of thing says the same thing. I think it would be best if no one reads them until the end. The content of the interviews will be more pure and innocent, if those are the right words. Best there's no unnecessary influence. I know I said everyone could read the work in progress, but that was mostly a courtesy. Presenting a project like this is never easy, 'Can I come interview all your staff and hear what they have to say about you and your restaurant?'" Mike shrugged and took a drink.

"Okay, Mike, I'm with you. I agree. That's just what I was thinking." And it was exactly what Jack was thinking. Of all the restaurants, in all the towns, in all the world… He knew Mike had no idea what he was into.

"Good. So, we're on the same page," said Mike.

Jack nodded in agreement as Heidle came back to the table. He was carrying a large platter of grilled sausages and spätzle, two plates, and under his elbow, a large pepper mill. He put the platter and plates down smoothly, and with a single crank of the mill, dusted the entire surface with ground pepper. The spätzle were browned and the burnt butter smelled delicious. Coarsely chopped flat parsley had been added after the food was on the platter and Mike was certain the mill contained white pepper.

Heidle held out both arms as if in benediction and said, "Enjoy." No one, certainly not these two men at the table, could deny the beauty of the aroma and presentation.

They smiled as they looked up and Jack said, "Thanks, Heidle." Heidle filled the wineglasses and left with just a nod.

The food became the moment and neither spoke as they started into their first portion. It was Jack who broke the silence. "Jimmy tell you about the lamb shanks?"

Mike frowned. He loved lamb shanks but had not seen any at the restaurant. "No. Why?"

"I just got some yesterday. I don't think we've had any since you've been around. They're from Malta. You know, the island near Sicily?"

"Yeah, Jack, I know where Malta is." He didn't dignify the question with eye contact. He continued eating before wiping his mouth and finishing his response. "And Sicily? You've been there?"

Jack perked up. "I don't get the Ragusano cheese from Wisconsin! I have friends in Ragusa. What about you? Been there?" Jack took a sip of his wine, watching Mike.

"Sure. I love that cheese. In fact, I love the whole region. How about Taormina? Do you know *The San Domenico*?"

Jack smiled. "Where else does one stay in the south of Sicily?" He returned his attention to the food. "That's one of my favorites." He looked up with a perplexed grin, knowing why Mike had mentioned *The San Domenico*.

Before he could say more, Mike cut in, "So what about the lamb shanks? You were saying?"

Jack looked up and scratched his chin. He opened his palm and looked at the five outstretched fingers. "They're from Malta. As in the Knights of Malta." He closed his hand to a fist and turned it over. Waiting for Mike's response.

Mike wiped his mouth again, smiling this time. "Hah! If only Machiavelli and Borgia had an army like that."

Jack had not heard these words in years. He repeated them softly. "If only Machiavelli and Borgia had an army like that." He looked at Mike, resolute but speechless. The words were a "mark." He'd anticipated this moment. There was nothing to dwell on and he abruptly changed the subject.

"I know someone in Malta with a farm. He's breeding lamb with goat. I suppose if you've been further east to Cyprus and Rhodes, you know lamb is hard to find." Jack raised his shoulders, as if it were common knowledge. "And if you've ever ordered lamb over there, I'm sure you've eaten goat once or twice." As Jack told the story, he began to raise his voice. Another sip of wine. Three tables were now occupied in the rear seating area, and a threesome was at the counter with Heidle. They'd all heard Jack and looked over as he talked. "And if you're from Denver, you're used to the big fat American domestic lamb, right? With no flavor?" He said louder.

Heidle laughed and Jack looked around at all the faces sharing the mirth. "I wouldn't recommend the lamb if you're going to Cyprus," Heidle called out.

"They feed the lamb olives there," Jack made a sour face and laughed.

"Canned olives, from Spain!" quipped Heidle. Everyone laughed aloud. "And it's usually goat anyway!" They all laughed a bit more and the moment subsided.

"Anyway, they've been breeding this lamb-goat animal for years." Jack spoke more quietly, more directly to Mike. "It's cheap as goat, to raise and feed, but milder and more — say, acceptable — than goat. It's a cottage industry. There's farms that are exporting totally organic grass-fed meat. Top quality. Occasionally he ships me ten or twenty pounds. It's scented and strong, but not like pure goat. Jimmy's doing it his way, and we usually sell all of it in a few days."

Mike liked the topic. "So how is it that everyone at your place just cooks what they want? It seems like anarchy. And they're constantly telling each other how something should be done. It's awesome. I mean, what happened to the good old menu? You know, the same items day in, day out?" Mike was pretending to be quizzical and cut into a piece of bratwurst.

Jack held up his hands as if making a miniature marionette dance on the table. He talked with his head bobbing back and forth. "Yeah, yeah. Then I can have my little masterpiece, that I've perfected, and I'm going to do for you over and over," he paused. "Chef!" he spat out loudly, as if the word itself tasted bad.

Jack's voice carried the room. Chairs moved, silverware clanged on plates, and glasses rang. The room was alive again and Heidle called back, "Don't ask Cheffy to butcher a pig!" A few of the patrons nodded in agreement.

"Yike, yike, yike!" Jack animated even louder.

The communal banter reminded Mike of French barrooms he'd been in. How therapeutic it must be to have a place to go where one can freely speak and even shout across the room — an age-old camaraderie. The high ceiling lifted the voices, and the wood of the interior softened the acoustics. Mike was content and had nothing to add. He finished the glass of wine and smiled at the tape recorder. The wheels turned slowly inside.

At a table across the seating area was the vicar, who sat with two older men. He picked up his half-full stein and tilted it toward Mike. "You're not a chef, are you?"

Mike looked up from the recorder. The room was looking at him. The demons were back, snarling and ready to pounce. They wanted to know who he was and what he was doing there. "No sir, I'm no chef. I'm just an observer." The room quieted down. *This is one small town*, thought Mike.

"An observer," replied the vicar in a caustic tone. "And what have you come here to observe?" The room became still.

Suddenly, Mike realized that probably just after he arrived the whole town knew about him and wondered what he was up to. It was indeed a very small town and Jack's Café was the largest operation within miles.

"Sir, if I were able to tell you what I was here to observe, I'd have already come and gone." He wasn't sure what to say next, but this seemed to satisfy. The vicar grunted and turned around. The noise of the room perked up, and everyone returned their attention to their own tables.

Mike looked at Jack, who was eating his spätzle. Mike filled his wineglass and said to Jack in a subdued tone, "So who's the old man?"

"Vicar Aceto," Jack said, in the same tone without looking up.

"Dour old root."

"Can be."

They ate in silence for a moment, and Mike once again noticed the woodwork inside The Tavern. The style of the raised panels was identical to the interior of The Theatre, and the finish was absolutely stunning. Mike asked Jack about it and got a brief history of The Tavern and its connection to The Theatre.

• • •

Shortly before the completion of The Theatre in 1926, John Tenyon's grandfather was asked to design and build a small bar for the artists to gather after the performances. His wife had already set up a kitchen and small brewery in the bottom floor of the building, where they were living, four blocks away. It was a fairly large kitchen that fed the four men, two wives, three children, and another six to ten men working with them on The Theatre. They all lived on the two floors above the kitchen area. The original ground-level floor space was more than two thousand square feet and completely open. There were six eighteen-inch square vertical beams supporting the upper structure. Along the back left and side walls were two large heavy trestle tables. On the right was the cooking, preparation, and staging area for the meals. The midday meal often lasted hours. The women of the house produced fresh sausage, a variety of mustards, and brewed the malty, Marzen-style amber lager beer their families had been drinking for generations. This space soon became known simply as The Tavern, a semi-private, very local gathering spot.

The men building The Theatre usually worked late and evenings at The Tavern ran into the wee hours. There was always beer and platters of cold meats as the women cleaned the kitchen and prepared for the following day's midday meal. The original equipment is still there to this day, mounted to the same spots on the floor, fully operational and used by Heidle nearly every day. The meat grinder, sausage stuffer, and mixer are German. The slicer is Italian. All are in perfect working order, having remained state of the art since the turn of the century. The two large copper vats for making the beer are also still in operation. Birthdays and holidays were quite memorable, and the large format camera was often brought to The Tavern to record these events.

* * *

"Mike, you've really got to see the photo albums," Jack said. Mike made a mental note to visit John to see the albums and also to visit Heidle's back room where the equipment was. Jack put down his fork. "I'd like you to see the journals, too. I think there's an interesting project there."

Mike knew when he was in the right space, having the familiar overwhelming feeling that there were not enough hours in the day. He still didn't think Jack was ever going to say much to help with the book. But that was all going to change. Mike didn't know it, but his life would never be the same after Jack told him this next story.

"Mike, listen to me. You're into something I'm not sure you want to be into." Jack looked closely at Mike, wondering how he was going to take it all in. He liked Mike and he kind of felt sorry for him. He knew if he were in Mike's shoes he wouldn't be happy, he'd be mad. This split-second reasoning told Jack something about himself… He had anger inside and he needed to somehow get rid of it. *Get over it*, he told himself.

Looking at Mike, he saw no anger whatsoever and liked Mike even more. He envied people like this and wanted to get there. His mother was right. Transferring the desire for revenge into a gift for others was the ticket to a new future.

Mike wondered what Jack could mean as he reached for his glass of wine. Maybe it was Sarah. Was she his girlfriend? He broke Jack's gaze and looked at a corner of the room. The woodwork was really nice. *If it only had ears*, he thought.

"Mike, turn that thing off." Mike snapped out of his reverie, turned off the recorder and Jack continued. "Between you and me, I have some issues with the people I used to work for. The short story is they'd been screwing my father really bad, going back to when I was a kid. I went to work for them in Italy while it was going on. I was about fifteen when my father got them to send me over there to work for them."

Mike became a deer in the headlights and spoke without thinking. "Who did you work for?"

"Don't worry about it. I'll give you the whole story in time. Basically, it was a group of businessmen financier freaks and some other characters who worked for the Church in Rome."

The phrase "Vicar of Rome" came to Mike's mind. "The Church in Rome is St. Peter's. Did you work for the Vatican?" He said, remembering Remus' comment about the marble in his sitting room.

Jack held his palms a few inches off the table and said quietly, "Sort of. Just let me finish."

Mike sharpened his focus and looked at the recorder with no lights on. He gently gulped the last of his wine and refilled the glass a bit high. He sat back and gave Jack a gentle nod.

"Good." Jack spoke softly and gave Mike a brief outline of the Banco Ambrosiano scandal that was now beginning to crack open. He then told him about the recordings of nearly everything that was planned, aborted, and executed leading up to one of the greatest politico-financial fiascos in European history.

Mike wanted a pencil. He had to remember Banco Ambrosiano. "Far out, Jack. What…" He had a million questions. "What does this have to do with me?"

"They're the ones who hired you. Your agent has nothing to do with it really. They just wanted to find me. They want me to come back and cook for them."

"Cool. What's the big deal? Sounds like a good gig."

Jack suppressed a smiling laugh best he could. He filled his water glass while thinking once again how lucky he was to have found this group of people. And he knew they were worthy of all the retribution Rome could afford.

"I just might go back and work for them. Thing is, Mike, they're probably going to ask you to go to Rome so you can tell them everything you know about me." Jack drank some wine.

Rome. Mike got excited. But he had a strange feeling there was more to it. Still, it sounded like big fun. He wondered if he could bring Sarah with him. There was an uncomfortable itch in the back of his mind as he looked at Jack. "So, what do you want me to tell them?"

Jack smiled, Mike got it. He talked for another five minutes, outlining what he wanted Mike to say and not say and what they might ask. "That's it." Jack held up his hands with a slight shrug and wondered what Mike was thinking.

Mike knew there was more. And he had to look into Banco Ambrosiano. "Sure, Jack. Whatever you want." He had to get up. This was way too much. The crystals weren't just growing, they'd just expanded into a universe, and he was stuck in a crack on one of the small ones. He finished his wine and stood. "I gotta use the bathroom." Jack nodded.

• • •

They walked back to The Theatre. Arriving in the kitchen, Mike found Jimmy cooking lamb shanks. "Hey, Jimmy, these must be the lamb-goat shanks Jack was talking about."

Jimmy looked at Mike with a confused air and then noticed Jack behind Mike, waving and making circles with his index finger. "Yeah, that's right, lamb-goat shanks. Why?" Jimmy said, as he turned back to the pot. He was gently shifting the simmering pieces of meat in the broth. It smelled awesome.

"Jack just told me about them. What a concept." Jimmy turned from the pot looking for Jack, who had disappeared. Lamb-goat shanks were a complete fabrication. Nothing of the sort existed.

"Oh, it's a concept all right." Jimmy said. He knew well of Jack's storytelling abilities. The hoodwinking usually went on when someone new joined the crew and Jimmy was expected to keep up the game. "You know the village they come from is famous for making stock out of the family laundry." Jimmy gave an affirming nod with his eyebrows raised as if to say, "You've heard of this before?" His left hand was holding his rag and rested on his hip. He gestured as he always did, with the tongs in his right hand. Mike found it interesting that a pair of tongs was Jimmy's primary utensil. "There's no mistaking a family aura when you enter someone's home, right?" Mike stared as Jimmy continued. "Well, these people make a broth out of T-shirts to incorporate the family aroma into their food."

Mike frowned. He was a bit drunk and not in the mood to work that night. Sarah must've been out on break, which was fine. As much as he wanted to see her, he felt it would be better to go home, wash off the dust of travel, and be fresh when he saw her next. "Far out, Jimmy. I want to hear more about the lamb shanks, but I gotta go back to my place and organize some stuff. I had to get up early this morning to get my flight, and I'm beat."

"Yeah, okay, cool man. I'll see you tomorrow then. I'll be doing more shanks. I got some osso bucco cut and I'm making confit with the scraps. You can help me out." This was true.

"Deal, Jimmy. I'll be here." He was interested in the shanks but looking forward to a shower. "See you then."

"Right on, dude." Jimmy pointed with his tongs and went back to his work. Mike went out on stage and looked into the auditorium. He was tired but didn't really feel like going back to the motel and decided to grab a glass of wine and sit in the upper row on the left side.

Jack came out on stage and stood for a moment without seeing Mike.

Phil called upstairs and told Jack he had a call from Gene Nogara. Jack went downstairs and saw Phil in the hallway with a towel in his hand. "Thanks." Jack went into his office and picked up the phone.

Phil overheard Jack's side of the conversation.

"Gene, what d'you got?"

"You're kidding. Mike Ambrose, you got nothing?"

"Nah, just wanted to be sure. You checked the photo and the address in Sioux Falls?"

"Thanks, Gene, I really appreciate it."

"Okay. Listen, Gene, let's keep in touch. I still need to get you back from last Sunday."

"Yeah, Gene, you and Vic."

"It's going well. Yeah, good, good, the boat's good. We're planning to launch it in February now. Shake down a bit on the river and stop in New Orleans. Plan is to be in Key West by mid-March. The boat ships from Miami around the twentieth. Our first official date is in early May."

"Yep, South of France. I hope to be over there by the end of April."

"Yeah, John's gonna drive. Says he wouldn't have it any other way."

"No, he's never been to Europe."

"That's right. Gotta find out sometime."

"It's the Grand Prix in Monaco. But we'll be in Nice. I'm putting the races up on the HD screens. Bern Calvi's booked it."

"Yes, he does it every year. Paris then Monaco. He's anxious to see the boat."

"Yeah, and eat, too."

"No, the kids are leaving the day before the races. They'll see the boat though."

"His wife will be there for the first few days. Then the races and a few day trips to the beach and she leaves. He'll be using the boat for ten days."

"No, they're all staying at the Eden Rock. There's a driver and about eight or ten guys."

"A few meetings on the boat, a few nights out, a few dinners on the boat. You know."

"Yeah, Val, too. I'm really looking forward to it."

"You'd better stop over. Think about sometime in the summer."

"I'll see you in Italy then."

"Yeah, ciao, Gene. Ciao."

This was good. Rome had sent Mike, but no one stateside knew anything about it. Jack hung up the phone.

• • •

Phil thought about what he'd just heard. So, Jack was having one of his friends check into Mike to see if he was who he said he was. Interesting.

Phil was in the studio packing up the cameras, monitors, and the rest of the video equipment that was going out to the boat for a test fitting. He'd overheard a lot of things at The Theatre and knew how to keep things under his hat.

He turned around to see Jack standing in the doorway. "I thought you were going out to the boat."

Phil had a coil of cable in his hand and was fixing a wire tie to it. "Later, why?" Phil was wearing a poker face.

"Phil, look at me. I can hear you typing when I'm next door in the office. I know you just heard me. Here, put that down, I need to talk to you." Jack came into the room and shut the door. "Turn some music on." He reached into the small refrigerator and pulled out an open bottle of Riesling. Taking a glass from a shelf above it he held it up. "You want one?"

Finishing the last of his water, Phil nodded, "Yeah." He stepped over to the gear and started up some Cuban piano music.

Nothing in the far reaches of Phil's imagination could have prepared him for what he was about to hear.

"For now, this is strictly between you and me," Jack said as he poured.

"Sure, Jack." Phil took a large sip of wine as they sat down.

"Good. You know when I was a kid I lived in Italy. And I worked for some pretty powerful people there. Most of them were connected to the Vatican in one form or another," he paused.

"You told me about Italy, never much about the Vatican." Phil's hair began to bristle, and he took another sip of wine. He was sure there would be another bottle opened shortly. "I didn't think you went to church."

"I don't." Jack twisted his ring. "But everything that had anything to do with my childhood revolved around the Church. So, I learned a lot about it, from the inside. Not much religion though." Jack twisted his ring again and waited.

"Jack I never noticed that ring before. I thought it was a simple band." He looked closer. "You wear it backwards with the insignia inside. Why?"

Jack stopped twisting it and held out his hand. "Ever seen one of these before?"

Phil looked closer. "The compass and square. Sure. The Freemasons. What was it? The square represents being square in your dealings with people or 'true' like a stone block that's square. And I think the compass stands for keeping straight."

"Yeah, that's it. Or to 'curb your desires' is a little more specific. Kind of ironic."

"Okay. I know Remus and John are Masons, and Heidle, too. There's a few more, Vicar Aceto and Vic Sindano and probably some of his friends. Jack, we never talked about this. I didn't think you were a Mason."

"I'm not. And I'm not really supposed to have this ring. It belonged to my father. He was a Mason and was made a member of P2 for some reason I haven't yet figured out. Have you ever heard of P2?"

"No."

"It's not important. Phil, not a word, got me?"

"Okay, whatever you say. So… what's up?"

"It's a long story so I'll give you the short of it. You know my father was a sculptor. Well, most of his commissions came from the Church. These men would visit, give my father a theme, and he would draw for them. My mother and I cooked for them when they came to visit. That's how I eventually ended up cooking for them in Italy. Anyway, they'd decide what drawing they wanted made into a statue and then my father and his crew of two or three guys would chisel and polish it out of marble. I didn't know it at the time, but a couple of the men were cardinals. One was from Boston and the others were from Rome. Most of the time they were in street clothes. One of them is now the Vatican Secretary of State."

"Wow. Real live fat cats," Phil said, refilling his glass.

"Yeah, big and bad. My parents had plenty of money. Both their families were wealthy, and I ended up with a huge inheritance. When my mother died, I basically got everything from both families. It's worth something like seven hundred million in U.S. dollars. But growing up we were simple. My mother cooked and I grew up a happy boy just watching her and hanging out with my father and his buddies chiseling away in the sculpture garden. A life aesthetic. I was a lucky kid."

"Far out, Jack." Phil wondered where this was going. He put down his glass and sat back. He'd never had any idea Jack had that much money.

"Yeah, right. Well, they were paying shit for his work, and they kept him busy enough so he couldn't work for anybody else. My father didn't know any better. It was a respectable way to make a living, and he didn't really need the money. I came to find out after I'd moved to Italy that these scumbags were making hundreds of thousands of dollars a year selling his work for twenty, thirty times what they'd paid him."

Jack downed the last of his wine and got up to get another bottle. "They actually buried and burned the statues and rubbed them with cheese to age them. Then they sold them as ancient relics from the Vatican collection."

Phil didn't finish his glass. Instead, he watched Jack get up and go to the fridge, wondering once again what his life must have been like growing up in Italy.

"Sure, it's speculation, right? Wise investment? No, these fuckers were ripping off my father and the people who bought the stuff. And he knew it!"

"How long did this go on?" Phil spoke slowly.

"Damn near twenty years! And it had been going on long before I got to Italy."

Phil was speechless. He drank his wine and then said, "How old were you when you found this out?"

"About fifteen or sixteen, a few months after I moved to Italy. You know, I think my mother knew. One of the last things she said to me before I left was that under no circumstances should I let anyone know I understood Italian. I think she knew."

"She died shortly after your father. Just after you left Italy." Phil knew this and had expressed his sorrow for Jack's experience.

"Shit." Jack paused and pulled a cigar from his pocket.

"Wow, Jack, that's awful." Phil meant it but wondered if there was more.

"Yeah. Well, now it gets interesting. Let me go back in time. Are you familiar with any of the Catholic Church's history?"

"I'm sure you're about to tell me. Far as I know there's been some pretty nasty business, but please go on." Phil finished his glass. "You mind if I open up that bottle?" Jack shook his head and handed it to him.

"Nasty doesn't quite do it justice. Does the 'Lateran Treaty' ring a bell?"

"Vaguely. Mussolini, before World War II, something about making the Vatican a sovereign state. That's about all I remember."

"That's it. It was in 1929. When they created The Vatican City. Okay now, imagine what it was like. The Catholic Church is broke. They're winding down centuries of global power and at this point the Papal States have dwindled to a few small regions in Italy. Now picture Mussolini on a mission to build a fascist state. Okay? The Catholic Church doesn't exactly fit into a philosophy that's based on the needs of the state and totalitarianism. Right? They'd been used to doing just about anything they wanted, regardless of what anybody else thought or said. But they had a huge following and Mussolini needed that support." Jack spun the stem of his wineglass while looking at Phil. "You with me?"

"Yes, Professor Stanley."

"Okay, stay with me. Just a little more background."

"I got nowhere to go." Phil sat back.

"Okay. So, the deal was that Mussolini would lend the Church nearly a hundred million dollars in cash and also pay the salaries of all the clergy in Italy. In exchange, the Church would give up claims to what was known as the Papal States and basically become a sovereign country within Rome. As an added bonus, The Vatican would be exempt from taxation and accountability. Even today you can't put an exact figure on the net worth of the Vatican's holdings, right?" Jack stopped. "The catch was that the Vatican was beholden to, and allied with, Mussolini and fascism in general."

"Genius."

"Yeah. It gets better. So here they are in bed with the *fascisti* because they're all strongly anti-communist. Then who becomes the biggest fascist of all time?" Jack leaned forward.

Phil was nodding slowly. "Hitler."

"On his rise to fame and power. Hitler realizes the power of the Catholic Church as a body whose support he needs. But qualities like 'excessive formal freedoms' didn't fit into Hitler's own idea of a perfect world. Adolf got it right thinking money would outweigh morals, so he offered them a deal. This was the 'Kirchensteuer.'" Jack paused. "Does that ring a bell?"

"Yeah, vaguely. A lot of this I didn't know, but I have heard of the Kirchensteuer. Church tax, right?"

"Right. Nine percent of every Catholic's income in Germany. Payable directly to the Vatican Bank. And this guarantee required another big formal agreement, or 'concordat,' that included among other things that the Vatican insist that all members of the Catholic Church support Hitler's policies. The Catholic Church now recognized the National Socialist State in exchange for millions of dollars a year. Even more genius, right?"

"I suppose that added up to a lot of reichsmarks."

"It still does to this day. Millions." Jack took a small sip. "And it gave the Vatican its jumpstart on the road to riches it's riding on now."

"I never knew any of this."

"Look it up. It's history man. I have some books on it if you're interested. But let me finish. Shortly after the agreement, around 1936, things in Germany start getting ugly. Pope Pius got wind of Hitler's plans and realized he was bad news. But keep in mind the Vatican was bringing in hundreds of millions of dollars from the Kirchensteuer and even the pope had a tough time deciding between right and rich. But in the end, the very end for him, he knew it wasn't right. So, he had an 'encyclical' drawn up." Jack drank some of his wine. Phil seemed dazed. "Okay?"

"Yeah, Jack. I'm with you. It's fascinating and yes, I'm going to look it up."

"Good. I'll give you a few books on this and some other interesting things." He took another drink. "So, the encyclical is drawn up. This is a hundred-page legal contract the pope writes. There were copies in Latin and I think the top five worldly languages. Jesuit priests in Paris did the translations. Remember the pope is the law. But he's no dummy, and this is no simple process. Popes don't just go writing encyclicals every day and they need a lot of support. But this was a big deal. The letter was circulated as it was being finalized. Now, naturally this horrified a lot of high-ranking cardinals. Imagine, Pope Pius wants to say 'Screw Hitler, he's up to no good and I don't want to have anything to do with him.' This would have caused trouble for both sides. For Hitler, it would mean losing the support of the Church — no small contingent — and for the Vatican it would mean no more Kirchensteuer. Something like one hundred million dollars a year, tax free." He took some wine. Phil couldn't think of anything to say.

"So, this encyclical was to be 'promulgated,' or made law, on the twelfth of February, 1939. That's when he was going to announce it, in effect saying, 'This is how it is now, and how the chuch and Catholics believe.' "

"What do you mean *was to be*? It didn't go through?"

"No man! It did not go through. See, Pius was very sick these days, in bed most of the time. Psychosomatic I'm sure, and a lot of people were convinced he was being poisoned. He begged his doctor to let him live another forty-eight hours so he could, and I quote, 'Warn Catholics everywhere not to support Mussolini and Hitler.'" Jack stopped as he realized he'd been talking nonstop and decided to slow down.

"He died on the tenth of February, two days before he was to publicly sign and announce the encyclical and the Church's — or at least his — stance on racist persecution."

"Wow, Jack. This is fascinating and well, thanks for the history lesson but what does this have to do with you — or me, for that matter?" Phil sat back and drank.

"Okay, here it is." Jack took another small sip. "All the copies of the encyclical were to be destroyed so that it was as if the whole affair never happened. Case closed by his successor. But a Jesuit priest found an unsigned copy in the early forties. He was ordered to be silent, and the document was declared a forgery because it wasn't signed." Jack sat back and picked up his wine. "See, if anyone knew that the pope really tried to stop Hitler in his early years, and was not allowed to follow his course…" He shrugged and held out his arms as if it were a question.

Phil sat back with his eyebrows raised. "The Catholic Church would have prevented the Holocaust by not supporting Hitler in his early years. But in the end, they let him proceed so that they could go on collecting the Church tax."

"Exactly."

"Jack that's… wow! Is this for real?"

"Phil, I couldn't make this up."

"I believe you, I guess."

"You will. Here's the good part. Pope Pius was so paranoid that he signed a copy of the encyclical the day before he died and gave it to his doctor."

Phil finished his wine and stood up to fill both his and Jack's glasses.

"The doctor was so freaked out about what to do with it, he just hid it. He put it in the leg of a piano that was at the pope's summer residence. The only person he ever told was his son. It was said the doctor was never the same after the pope died. Some say the doctor knew he was being poisoned, and a short time afterward, the doctor himself was poisoned. The Italian solution, and I'm sure I know why. They knew he knew. Anyway, the doctor's son stayed on and eventually became manager of the estate."

"That's the estate where you worked when you were a kid? And the estate manager used to come to your house when you were a kid. Vilotti the current Vatican Secretary of State? Jack, you're scaring me. Don't tell me it's that piano out on the stage."

Jack laughed, bowing and nodding his head up and down. "I swear."

"So, the encyclical is in there and you're going to use it to take revenge on the men who ripped off your father. Jack, come on."

"Not exactly. I have another card to play."

"It was you who had the piano delivered here. Anonymously, a year before you came here. Before we met." Phil was talking to himself, looking straight through Jack as he finished the story.

Jack nodded and went on. "The estate manager, who was the doctor's son, knew what the men had been doing to my father. In fact, he's the one who told me about it. Marc Vilotti, now the Vatican Secretary of State. He's sort of my benefactor."

Jack got up and grabbed a bottle of water from the fridge and poured some into his glass. Phil took some more wine. There was a sinister feeling in the room, and again Phil wondered what it was like for Jack to have lived with this. But he had a feeling Jack had a plan, so he sat back and let him continue.

"So, they let Vilotti in on the sculpture scam, gave him a few pieces he could sell. Sort of a guarantee that he'd keep quiet about the whole thing. That's the way those P2 fucks operate. Propaganda is gathered and then they own you. Anyway, he'd always felt terrible about it and one day he told me everything. First about the art scam and then the story of the encyclical. The piano was technically his and when I told him I was leaving, he told me he was giving it to me and eventually had it shipped here. With the signed encyclical still in the leg."

Phil blinked. "I don't believe it."

"He always wanted to see The Theatre but that would never have been possible. He'll come to the boat at some point when we're in Italy. We'll show him your photos of The Theatre."

They heard someone coming down the stairs and Jack grabbed a deck of cards from a side table. He was dealing just as Sarah opened the door. "You guys seen Mike?" Her eyes went to the table with the cards, two bottles, and the glasses. "What the hell? You guys got nothing better to do than play cards and drink wine at four in the afternoon?"

"No." Phil said. Jack shrugged.

She shook her head and went out. Phil scratched his chin and Jack crossed his arms.

"I got some info on Mike you might want to hear." Jack said quietly. "Let's take a ride out to John's place. I want to see what's going on with the aft cabin."

They got up and Phil went to pack up some gear.

"So, what do you have on the broadcast channels?" Jack picked up the glasses, and he looked up expectantly.

"It's looking good. Vivien's got me local stations all over the coast that will take half-hour programs. Production quality worthy of advertising. Hah." Phil turned around. "I know the music being produced there and what people see. We'll be doing some pretty revolutionary stuff. Definitely raise some eyebrows."

"That's where we want to be. What about the live stuff? Can we broadcast from the boat in the evenings?" Jack was clicking keys on the computer.

"Shouldn't be a problem on the mainland. Worst case we'd run a big cable to a truck on the dock with a satellite dish." Phil stepped up to the map on the wall.

Jack came to the map and pointed to the Cote D'Azur. "So, say Nice, Cannes, no problem. At the dock we can do the video conferencing and also be able to broadcast live if we want to?"

"The video conferencing will be good any place I can get a decent connection. I can always work the compression. There might be some delay if we have a slow connection. But broadcast and good video conferencing will always need something high bandwidth, either satellite or a line into a trunk cable on land, which could be tricky." Phil seemed to wince a bit.

"But with a satellite truck we're all good. Anywhere we go we can conference, broadcast…" Jack trailed off.

Phil was nodding with a smile. "Yes. If we had our own satellite truck we could do anything we wanted, anywhere we went, as long as it's close enough to the boat and we could run a big fat cable to it. TV, Internet, video in and out. With a good rig we could call the space station." Phil put down the cable he was coiling. "Hey, we can ship it, too. I mean we could design something inside a small container that could be put on a cargo ship or a tractor trailer." He stopped and looked at Jack.

"Well, fuckin' A, then," Jack said obviously.

"Fuckin' A, then I'll find out. You want the space station?" Phil was excited.

"Everything but the space station."

"Okay, no space station. I'll get you a price."

These moments of inspiring people to take on a mission were Jack's finest memories from his time at The Theatre.

"I've heard coverage is terrible around Marseille," Phil went on. "Something about the mountains or the weather."

"Fine. I have no interest in Marseille. It's a big ugly commercial port."

"I've heard it's got character."

"Yeah, character. If Jimmy goes to Marseille, we may never see him again."

"Hah. You're probably right." Phil picked up the duffel bag full of cables.

"I know I'm right." Jack corked the bottle and put it in the fridge. "You sure you're gonna have time to do all the editing and the broadcast production, too?"

"I don't think it'll be that bad. I got a streamlined plan in mind how we're gonna run tape and there won't be lots of editing to do. You know what else? I was talking with Mike yesterday. It turns out he's familiar with editing and camera work. You mind if I use him if he's coming with us?"

"No, not at all." They made eye contact just before Phil hit the light switch.

In the hallway, Jack stopped. "Shit. I just remembered Jimmy wanted to video conference Jono about some weird cut he's doing with the veal racks. You're all set up, right? It should only take a few minutes or so."

"Yeah, no prob. Jono's ready?"

"Yeah, he said any time this afternoon."

"Okay, I'll give him a call and get him online."

"Good. Thanks. I'll get Jimmy."

Jack came back up to the kitchen and called from the end of the line, "Hey, Jono's online for the demo." He noticed Mike standing beside Jimmy. "Mike, I thought you left."

"I was up in the raised seating area. You didn't see me." Mike smiled.

Jack kept a straight face. "Oh, is that so."

Jimmy laughed. Jack didn't.

"Bring your sidekick, Jimmy. Let's go."

"Yeah." Jimmy wiped his tongs with the rag. "Come on, Mike. I'm doing a video feed to the cattleman in Kansas City." Jimmy followed Jack and Mike scratched his head.

Mike entered the room downstairs opposite Remus' quarters. He hadn't seen it before. Like in Remus' suite, the ceiling seemed high for a basement and the massive overhead beams below the stage were exposed. The raw unfinished wood of this room seemed to have been scrubbed clean. Like so many other things around The Theatre, it was old, worn in, and beautiful. Phil stood at a small chest-high desk against the wall that held a keyboard and trackball mouse. A large computer monitor was mounted to the wall. In the center of the room was a long table with a chopping block and a few chairs scattered about. There was a video camera mounted to one of the beams pointing down at the chopping block. Jimmy came in and tossed a package of meat onto the chopping block and opened it. At the other end of the table were two large TV screens mounted to the wall. Phil came over and adjusted the camera above the chopping block as he looked at one of the screens. On the other screen was a headshot of a man sitting at a table outside with a pasture and forest in the background.

"Okay, Jono. Thanks for waiting," Jack spoke to a camera mounted between the two screens. Phil stepped to his desk and worked the keyboard and mouse. The screen showing the chopping block switched to a full shot of Jack and Jimmy. Video conferencing, the man at the other end could now see Jimmy and Jack.

Jono Kinney looked out from the other screen. "Okay, Jack. I play cards on Saturday and today I cannot seem to lose." He looked away, smiling, and there were voices in the background. Mike stared at the picture, wondering where Jono was and exactly where his Midwest accent came from. His voice was surprisingly clear through the speakers.

"Good for you, Jono. Then you're feeling generous today?" Jack said.

"Yeah, Jono, things have been really slow lately. We're wondering if you could you help us out," Jimmy said as he arranged the meat on the block.

"Yeah, sure, Jimmy. I know exactly how slow you are. That's an interesting chop I see. Looks like the number three and four veal ribs together — the king's loin chop. And how, pray tell, did you bevel the bone like that?"

The chop Jimmy was holding was a three-inch thick veal T-bone. He turned it around in his hands like a heavy cube. What made it unique was the way the bone of the chop seemed to be cut into a twisted pyramid. Also on the chopping block was a whole bone-in veal loin with a set of odd notches cut into the bone. He pointed to the notches along the chine bone that connected the chops. Phil switched the computer to the overhead shot so Jono could again see the view of the meat.

Jimmy started. "The only difference is that the band saw cut down the chine bone in what is now two cuts. About fifteen degrees off plane, they meet just past the number three chop. Then you just notch it twice at about thirty degrees perpendicular. All the cuts are straight. It takes about a minute or two to do it." What Jimmy didn't mention was how many racks he'd gone through to find the perfect design. There'd been a lot of strange looking veal chops served lately. "I get two of these out of each rack."

On the other screen, Jono sat back and held up his hands. "Jimmy, I'm not a custom meat cutter. Why don't you just do it yourself?" Phil switched from the cutting board shot back to the Jack and Jimmy shot.

Jimmy replied, "I know, Jono, but I'm busy. Just have Pat cut the loins like that and I'll break it down from there." Jimmy knew that for anyone but a master meat cutter it would be a difficult cut. And it would only be a matter of time before he lost a finger.

"I'm busy, too, Jimmy. Jack, what are you doing for beef these days?"

"Gus Dolan," Jack was short.

"Damn it, Jack. I'm doing twice as much beef as Gus Dolan! You know I can beat his prices."

"Didn't I hear you were taking over Pierce Provisions?" Jack said.

"Jack, that was a few months ago. I told you about it before it happened."

Jack looked over at Jimmy, who turned to face the camera and spoke. "Jono, we're doing more than fifty bone-in veal loins a month with you. What can you give me for whole beef strips? Prime niners."

Jono rubbed his chin, looking out from the screen. He picked up his phone and pressed a few buttons. "I don't know your volume, Jimmy. How's seventeen sixty-five a pound?"

Jimmy looked at Jack, who was looking down at the huge chop, turning it over in his hands. Jack didn't look up. Jimmy turned back to the camera and said, "Jono, I'm using close to sixty whole beef strips a month. How about if you do the cuts on the veal racks for me, say twenty a month, and I'll give you my orders for the whole strips at seventeen fifty."

This was indeed large volume. Jono knew Jack's was closed for the month of August but also that Jack did a very high volume through the fall and into the holidays. He pressed a few more buttons on his phone. "Okay, but I need at least twenty-six fifty for the veal racks with the special cut." He looked out from the screen, waiting for Jimmy's response.

"Jono, come on. That's a lot of beef. Let's keep the veal at twenty-two even and I promise I'll stick with you through the holidays for the beef. How long have we known each other?"

"Jimmy, I've known you too long. I remember when we met, you were at the Seven's…"

Jimmy interrupted. "Okay, okay, that's enough. We have a guest here, Jono."

Jono picked up a pen and made a note. "Okay, fine. Twenty-two even for the veal and the prime niners for nineteen fifty."

Before Jono could finish, Jimmy and Jack both retorted, "Whoa! Hold on. Seventeen fifty for the beef!" They shouted in confusion.

Jono held up his hand, smiling. "Sorry. My mistake. Now Jimmy you need to set up a conference with Pat and show him that cut." Jono spoke to someone off camera.

"You got it. We'll set up by the band saw."

"Okay, boys. I'll be in touch."

Jack and Jimmy said goodbye. Jono reached his hand forward and the screen went black.

"Phil, are we offline?" Jack squinted into the light.

"Yep."

Jimmy let out a whoop.

"Nice job," said Jack. "If the chops slow down, give the beef order back to Gus."

"Don't worry, they'll move. Maybe I'll give the beef order back to Gus anyway."

Jack laughed. "That's it. Keep those cattle fuckers on their toes."

"Jack, didn't you say Billy the Kid stole horses from Jono's great-grandfather?" Jimmy asked as they came around to the other side of the table. Phil was shutting down the video lights and Jack noticed Mike looking around the room. Jimmy picked up the meat and was heading out.

"I think Billy the Kid *shot* Jono's great-grandfather," Jack said, making eye contact with Mike as he walked past him on the way out the door.

"Phil, are we meeting Dirk at the boat?" he asked from the corridor.

"Yeah, he just texted me. I'll be right up," called Phil.

"Hey, Mike, welcome back," Phil was putting his laptop in a waterproof briefcase.

"Phil! You didn't tell me all this stuff was down here. How cool. Man, this thing looks like the Saturn Five rocket." There were three video cameras, one a bit larger, and three small powerful lights. Everything was neatly wired and mounted to the overhead beams. Mike was pointing at one of the lenses.

Phil smiled. Everyone got a kick out of Mike's enthusiasm. "It's been here a while. Kind of evolving. I'm producing cooking videos for Jimmy. Jack set up the video conferencing. He uses it a lot and we also do meetings down here for some of Jack's friends." He picked up his backpack and the laptop case. "We have to go out to John's place on the river. You… hold on Mike." Phil went out in the corridor and shouted, "Jack, are we going in the Cobra?" He stood still waiting for Jack to answer.

"He's not sitting on *my* lap!" Jack called down from the kitchen. Phil looked at Mike, who looked like a beagle ready to run out the door. "All right, Mike, you got time to take a ride?" Phil seemed skeptical.

Mike nodded his head eagerly and shrugged.

"Jack's driving and we're sharing the passenger seat. You okay with that?"

"Sure." Mike wondered what the big deal was.

Phil lowered his voice. "Mike, Jack doesn't drive much because he doesn't know how to drive."

"Come on, let's go!" Jack called down.

Phil handed Mike the laptop case. "Here, take this." They went upstairs and followed Jack out to the Cobra. It was a Sunday and the restaurant was closed. Mike didn't know when or how he'd get back, and he didn't care. He marveled at the buoyancy of life. He didn't have to worry about where he was or where he was going. It all seemed to take care of itself. All he had to do was write and there was a lot to write about.

When they got to the car, Jack opened his door and settled into the driver's seat. It was strange seeing him from above sitting in this car. Phil looked at the passenger seat and said to Mike, "Okay, I'm bigger. You sit on my lap."

"Shit," Mike responded.

It's surprising, but for such a small car, there's actually lots of room in the Cobra once you're in one of the seats. The big, heavy, handcrafted piece of machinery is made of wood, leather, and metal, and makes you feel like you've stepped into another era. Everything is old, worn, and perfectly put together. Jack put on the goggles and started the engine. The springs barely gave as Mike sat down into the car.

The ride was a nightmare, if only twenty minutes. Phil was right. Jack did not know how to drive. The car flew down the country roads like hell on wheels. It hugged the corners as if there were magnets holding it down and it seemed like there was no suspension. It was also very loud. Fortunately, there were very few other cars on the road. Jack seemed to know the roads and he talked the whole way, shouting above the engine and the wind. When they arrived at John's boatyard on the river, Mike couldn't wait to get out of the car. His first impression of John's property was that he could spend a lot of time looking around.

The road came in along the river and they parked in front of the dock. An old pine forest covered the opposite bank and stretched as far as the eye could see in either direction. Mike turned around to look up the gentle slope behind the sheds. It was mostly high grass with the craggy, dry scrub oaks in sporadic outcroppings. The day was crystal clear and sunny with a light breeze. The expansive area carried a silence that was punctuated only by the echoing of the tools coming from the big shed.

Phil put down the bag and said, "Give me a second." He walked over and onto his boat and Mike stared, taking a few steps in that direction. Mike's face showed his amazement, and his mouth was slightly open as he turned around, looking at the rest of the property. Jack laughed aloud.

"What do you think, Mike?"

"Unbelievable."

They walked up a path through the grass and into the large shed that held the huge boat. To stand and look up at a hundred-foot wooden boat under construction is a multi-sensory experience. First of all, there's the smell of wood. A lot of wood that's been cut and planed and screwed together. And it's all unpainted. The sheer tonnage of this massive hulk above you has a dramatic physical sensation. Finally, the realization sets in that what you're looking at is under water when the boat sails. Like an iceberg or the roots of a tree, this bottom view reveals a boat's seldom seen character. Very wide or "beamy" for its length, this boat also carried a lot of freeboard, putting the deck high above the water. The swooping shear of the deck gracefully lifted both the bow and the canoe stern. It looked like a giant whaling boat.

"Wow!" Mike said as he walked to the single five-foot diameter propeller and tapped it with his ring. A man in overalls came around from the other side.

Jack introduced them. "John, this is Mike Ambrose. Mike, John Tenyon."

"Hey, John. Nice to meet you."

"Mike Ambrose. You're writing a book about Jack's Café."

"I'm trying to."

"Just in time." John looked at Jack.

"Mike doesn't know anything about the boat, John."

"Oh, okay. Dirk just got a call." John turned and led them back around to the other side of the boat. "He'll meet us inside." John started climbing up a large wooden ladder that was clamped to the top of the hull. "Careful, Mike," he called down.

Mike reached for the ladder, but Phil held up his hand. John was three quarters the way up. "Let him get a hand on the deck first."

"Okay," John called, and disappeared over the rail.

They all walked down a set of steps built into the cavernous hull. There was no deck closing it off, so the boat seemed like an open shell. They were in a single large area in the center part of the boat. It was very well lit from overhead, including the forward and aft areas that Mike could see through the doorways. There was other work being done on the boat and the scraping, banging, and footsteps echoed throughout the solid structure.

John stood at a small plank desk similar to Phil's and faced a large flat screen display. On it was a 3-D rendering of the boat. John worked the mouse and began manipulating the drawing. First the sides and interior bulkheads turned solid brown. Then the ship rolled so that the view was from above. The deck and cabin top disappeared, and John zoomed into the main salon area where they were standing. The image on the screen displayed sharply and clearly. Mike looked around and then straight up. He felt like he was inside a giant piece of furniture on camera. Looking up he was barely able to see beyond the bright lights to the shed's ceiling, where shards of sunlight cut through. The scene was strangely surreal. Almost like a movie set, only the actors didn't seem to think it strange at all.

Mike laughed, pointing to the screen while blurting out, "I feel like we're on a CIA satellite feed!"

John turned and looked at Mike over the rim of his glasses. There was a brief moment of silence and Mike smiled back, waiting for a response.

John, solid as a rock, said nothing. He turned to Jack and said, "And *where* did you find him?"

Jack closed his eyes and shook his head, "Long story." He looked at Mike. "Now's quiet time, right? Lookie, no talkie."

Dirk came down the steps built into the inside of the hull. It was a posterior first entry and Mike was the only one watching him climb down. Dirk was a large man with a large waist who wore dark trousers high on his belly. The sky-blue shirt had perspiration spots. His outfit was pressed. Mike guessed his age at around fifty-five and that the ladder required more than a little effort. Jack noticed Mike smiling as Dirk climbed down. He tilted his head to get Mike's attention and gave him a warning glance.

Dirk stepped off the ladder and turned around. "Whew. Can't wait for you to launch this beast." He came over and shook hands. "Jack."

"Hey, Dirk." Phil called from the aft area and then came into the main space. "Yo, Phil."

"Dirk thanks for coming, this is Mike Ambrose. He's a friend of mine," Jack said to Dirk.

"Hello, Mike."

"Hi, Dirk. Nice to meet you."

Dirk put down the soft leather briefcase he had strapped around his shoulder and paused to catch his breath. He had graying brown hair and wore a full mustache with a long neatly trimmed goatee. "Okay, I think we have it nailed down." He pulled a CD out of his bag and handed it to John. Mike flirted with the world of make-believe. Here they were inside a twenty by thirty-foot room on a giant wooden boat that seemed to have a design that was hundreds of years old. He had thousands of questions he wanted to ask. And he was quite fascinated with this Dirk character and what was on the disc.

John took the disc and said, "Is this your new layer or the entire plan?"

"No, it's just my layer."

"Okay, good." John popped the disc into his computer and tapped his finger on the desk, waiting. "Hey Phil, can you grab a few bottles of water?" He flipped on a large fan.

"Are the new specs on the disc?" Jack asked.

"Yes. I also have a hard copy for you." Dirk pulled a folder from his briefcase and put it on the desk.

"Great. Thanks, Dirk," Jack said as he reached for the folder.

A set of small boxes of different sizes appeared on the screen. John zoomed into the drawing a bit more until the room they were in nearly filled the screen.

Dirk explained, "Okay, so now we have two five-way systems that are juxtaposed on either end of the room. This will sound quite rich anywhere you sit or stand. The modulation as you move around will be interesting, too." He pointed to different parts of the screen. "I've got the bass cabinets at opposite corners of the floor and the center speakers mounted to the overhead grid. John, can you turn the piano on?" John clicked the mouse and a piano appeared on the screen, just about where they were standing. "Yes, that's nice. This will be such a lovely space. I've made some changes to the utility grid. John, may I?" Dirk pointed to the mouse.

"Sure, by all means." John stepped to the side. No one else spoke.

Dirk stepped up to the keyboard and began typing. "Here's the new overhead grid." He clicked and a series of bold lines appeared over the area on the screen. "I've now got four overhead pipes running the full length of the room uninterrupted. I found a beautiful one-handed clamping system to attach the speakers, lights, microphones, and cameras. Two will do for each of the TV screens. The clamps run along a key on the piping, so they won't rotate. There's also shorter independent pipes running laterally. Athwart ships, that is." Dirk turned around with his eyebrows raised and said to Mike, "This is my first boat, but I catch on fast." He paused and laughed to himself. Mike could not place the accent, but it sounded possibly Northern or Eastern European. These characters, on the verge of caricature, swirled around Mike as he peered into the great face of this strange man.

Dirk carried on describing the changes. It was a custom designed audio and video system that could be easily configured for many specific uses onboard the boat. As the men got deeper into the design they spoke louder and often at the same time, nearly arguing.

Mike never saw the layer of the plans that showed where the kitchen cookware and stainless counters were going. He got lost in the details and began to wander around the boat. He eventually climbed out and explored the yard. He gravitated toward the woodshop, where a handful of men were drinking beer. The afternoon shadows were getting long, and Mike was thirsty. Phil caught up with him an hour later.

• • •

Mike had agreed to cook some rainbow trout one of them had caught on his lunch break. He eyeballed the grill on the dock by Phil's boat. "As long as you've got some olive oil and spices." This was not a problem. They all went to Phil's boat and Mike used his galley. Halfway through the preparation, he was calling to Phil for ingredients. A few more people arrived with wine. Jack called Phil's cell phone from across the yard and later showed up with John. They had loaves of crusty bread and a few more bottles of wine. Tomatoes, onions, a peach pie, and other items appeared mysteriously. By the time the seven fish were cleaned, there were thirteen people.

Mike grilled the vegetables first. After preparing a hearty garlic and rosemary-infused olive oil, he used it to dress the vegetables and then brushed it on the long slices of bread before grilling it as well. The meal ended up as large crostinis with grilled half-tomatoes, peppers, zucchini, scallions, and leaves from an entire basil plant. Mike was supremely impressed by the quality of the ingredients. The extra virgin olive oil in a plain bottle was obviously from the restaurant. Phil produced a heavy glass container that was filled with a flaky white sea salt from Cyprus. There was also some very fragrant ground fennel seed and a large hunk of hard cheese that Mike shaved on top of the crostinis.

When the vegetables were finished, Mike stoked the fire for the fish. As it got hot, he passed samples of the grilled vegetables on small pieces of bread. "I gotta keep everybody busy while they wait for the fish," he said.

All the while he was wiping the hot grill with a clean oily rag and Jack watched carefully. The fish remained whole and he cut diagonal slashes into the flesh. All the fins except the tail were trimmed off and the skin had been tamped dry. Mike rubbed the fish with the finely ground fennel seed, plenty of salt and pepper, and a touch of the garlic-flavored olive oil. The fish did not stick to the grill — Mike seemed to know they wouldn't — and they became a deep golden brown as he turned and basted them over the high heat. The whole fish were then allowed to rest. He carefully removed the bones while leaving fillets with the skin on. The steaming and moist meat with crispy skin was broken into pieces to garnish the top of the grilled vegetables, which sat on the grilled, oiled bread. The crostinis were delicious.

After cooking, Mike sat down and did not get up. He listened, talked, and thought about what was being said as he drank wine. Time became a blur that drifted into the past week. Driving home that night with Jack in the passenger seat, they rumbled along the dark roads. Jack occasionally pointed when Mike seemed unsure of a turn. Conversation was easy in the Cobra at low speeds. While shouting was de rigueur at top speeds, their spoken words echoed between the car's cockpit and the overhanging trees. Jack was doing most of the talking, tying numerous subjects together. He was in rare form and Mike assumed a Socratic attitude; questioning, doubting, and generally making Jack explain himself.

By the end of one conversation, Mike had Jack vehemently defending himself. Rare form indeed, but fascinating still. The topic was art and the importance of varied input and stimuli compared to sticking to a single discipline. Jack somehow connected this to local cuisines and went on, "If you travel around to the fishing villages of an area anywhere, Italy, Spain, France, you begin to see character. These are very old simple cooking methods that have been refined for generations. And they're very pure. Like a pure gene pool in Romania where most families haven't married outside the country. And so, the children are pure. But back to the cooks and their food. If you can get into that mindset of simple preparation, you just become a valve in the process of ingredients to table. At the same time, you need to have your eyes open because inspiration is everywhere. Then you're ready to allow it to happen. Potent expression. Or like Phil says, 'If it's not high resolution, why bother?' You agree with that right?" Jack paused. "Mike, what the hell? You're going ten miles an hour."

"Okay, go on." Mike was leaning close to the steering wheel so that he could hear. He took his eyes off the road and looked at the speedometer. He was indeed going nine miles an hour. He downshifted and gunned the engine. Mike asked another question and Jack started shouting again.

CHAPTER SIX

Invited

The following day, Mike made a point of getting to the kitchen early. He needed answers. When he arrived around nine-thirty, the bar, main dining area, and café tables up in the auditorium were empty. There were no sounds coming from the kitchen and the stillness of the space suddenly made him feel like an intruder. He walked to the bar and sat. Looking first at the surface of the bar, he then scanned the back area. It was worn and spotless, a well-kept busy workspace. He looked out at the auditorium and thought about Jack's table, trying to imagine what it was like in the early days of building the kitchen and the restaurant. His mind drifted to visions of John's grandfather and family here in the Roaring Twenties when suddenly he was startled nearly out of his seat.

"Boo!" Sarah was behind him. As she shouted, she grabbed his shoulders tightly and held on as he raised both arms and shouted back. Her cheek and hair brushed his ear and her spirit drifted over him as she laughed. Mike turned and took her hand as it slid down his back.

"Sarah! *Dog Gonnit!*" He held her hand as their eyes met and they smiled wildly. He brought her hand gently up to his mouth and kissed it. "Don't you ever do that again!" He let her hand down and she looked at him squarely. Mike didn't resist as she put her hand under his chin, turning his head slightly, and kissed his cheek.

"It's nice to see you, Mike." She stepped back, with one foot still forward and gave him a full body gaze. "You look great."

"Thanks, Sarah, so do you." She did look great. Wearing long sweatpants, her posture was lovely, and her character was pure beauty to him. "I have a book for you. Hopefully we can get together sometime soon." He shifted in his seat, once again aware of their surroundings.

Sarah straightened her pose. "I'm free next Sunday. Are you going to be around?"

Mike slowly blinked and smiled at her again. "Yes, I'll be around. In and out this week, though." He got up and looked toward the kitchen. He remembered Jack dropping him off at his place late last night. "It's so quiet. Is anyone else here?"

"Is anyone here? Of course there's people here. Remus and Paulo live here, and Jack stays here too. Phil comes in some mornings to work in the studio."

Mike looked away from Sarah's face as the door opened, and Phil came in from outside. He walked across the stage. "Hey, Mike. You're here early. Jack drive you back last night?" Phil laughed and looked a bit rough, like he'd slept on a couch.

"No, I drove. That's quite a place where you live, the boatyard." Mike looked at Phil proudly.

"Yeah, that was a good night. That trout you fixed was great. And the story about the *pirogue* — I'm going to look into that."

Sarah had her hands on her hips and looked from Phil to Mike conspiratorially. "Another late night at the boatyard, eh?"

Phil and Mike looked at each other. "Wasn't that late, was it?" Phil said.

"Don't think so," replied Mike.

"Right," said Sarah. "At least someone knows how to take a shower." She looked back at the clean-shaven Mike whose clothes were pressed. "Okay, boys, cappuccino machine's on." Sarah walked off to the kitchen. Mike watched her go and Phil rubbed his chin as he walked around to the cappuccino machine, wishing he'd shaved.

Remus came up the stairs. Wearing a white button-down shirt and black pants, he seemed particularly well-dressed this morning. Mike noticed the shoes.

"Morning, you all," Remus glanced over in Sarah's direction. "Hey, Mike, welcome back."

"Hey, Remus." Mike looked at Remus' outfit. He looked like Saturday night with a million bucks. "Wow, the shoes are great." He smiled as they shook hands.

"Thanks." Remus tipped back slightly on his heels and flexed his toes. The simple black loafers were beautiful. Well-worn and smartly polished. "When'd you get back?"

"I'm not sure. Yesterday, I guess. Things have been sort of non-stop lately. Actually, I've been here the whole time just in different places." Mike smiled, knowing Remus caught his play on time-space theory. "What about you? Where you off to?"

"I'm going up to Chicago for a few. . ."

At that moment, Jack walked in and crossed the stage. "Hey, Remus. Looks like you're all ready to go. Here's the keys. The goggles are in the glove box."

"Okay, Jack. Thanks." Remus winked at Mike. "A June bug hit him in the eye once. He won't let me drive the highway without 'em."

The spotlight above the bar came on and Phil was drenched in bright light. He dropped a spoon that clanged and echoed. The other three turned to look at him.

Jack stepped up behind a barstool and inspected Phil with an exaggerated air. "Phil, where's the camera? Man, you look like shit!"

As Mike and Remus laughed, the lights dimmed, and then came back on even brighter. Mike saw Sarah at the controls. "Ah-ha. Sarah!" He pointed. She was laughing at Phil in the spotlight.

Phil couldn't deny his predicament. He was always well-dressed in the evenings, but this morning he was wearing yesterday's dirty work clothes, and his hair was a nest. Sarah stepped into the circle of light and Phil said, "Okay, well, I'll just be going to the GYM. Then I'll be at YOGA. And then on the way back I'm going to have some yogurt and birdseed. I'll be fresh as a gardenia." Phil tilted his head from side to side as he spoke. Then he changed to a Darth Vader voice. "Then I return as Dominatrix. To rule the micro universe!"

Everyone laughed louder as Sarah twisted and curved her backbone sideways. She stuck out her hip and tongue at Phil, flipped her hair and went back to the kitchen. The moment passed and Jack turned back to Remus as Phil went downstairs to the studio.

"I have some coffee going. I'll be just a few minutes." Remus turned and headed for the stairs. As he reached the banister, he called over his shoulder, "You boys want a cup?" Mike looked at Jack and they both followed Remus.

In Remus' suite, Jack sat at the round table and Mike took a seat on the settee by the koa table. Remus went behind the curtain for the coffee.

He came out with the three coffee cups on a small tray. He served Mike, then Jack, and sat down at the piano.

"Thanks, Remus," Mike said. "Hey, that piano is really a beauty. Where's it from?"

"Yes sir, it is a very special piano. I've played it for years. So have a lot of other people." He lifted his cup and took a sip. "It's been at The Theatre since it opened."

Mike looked down at his cup and realized Remus had remembered how he liked it. Black with two lumps. He picked up the first cube of sugar and unwrapped the Italian label. He looked up, smiling, and said, "So this piano's had a bit of Chicago blues played on it?"

"St. Louis blues. Most of the good stuff, at least." Jack said after a big gulp.

Mike noticed Remus grinning at the piano he was sitting at and said, "So what's the gig, Remus? You playing up in Chicago?"

Remus hit a few high notes. "It's a regular thing I do with some guys I know up at The Drake. But this weekend's special." He looked at Jack.

Mike sat up and said, "The Drake Hotel. Cool, if the walls had ears. American history's gone down there. What a beautiful property!"

Jack sat back, returning Remus' glance and let him reply. Remus said, "Yeah, a lot's gone down there. Nearly as much as at this theater. You ever been there?" Mike was being scrutinized.

"Once or twice. How long you been playing piano there?" Mike giggled under his breath as if it were a juicy intrigue.

Remus hit a few more keys with his left hand, letting out a short phrase on the bass notes. He held the last bottom note as he spoke. "I've been playing piano up in Chicago for some twenty years."

"The piano is so loud. I can hear it resonating our voices."

"This baby is happy down here. Stays in tune real good." Remus put his hand on the top of the piano. "That piano out on stage's another story. It gets hot, damp, and there's always people walking nearby. Doggone thing's gotta be tuned every other week," he said, looking at the keys as he hit a few.

"Remus' been complaining about this since we started." Jack sat back with his eyebrows high, knowing Remus would continue.

Remus stopped playing and held up his arms. "What d'you expect? Here's this beautiful piano, somewhere in Italy for decades, never moved, stable environment. And then this guy decides to ship it how many thousand miles here to The Theatre and put it up on the stage and abuse it for seven or eight years. And now, he wants to put it in a boat and send it back across the ocean. I mean what are we gonna do? Bolt it to the deck? Really." Remus stood up. "Mike, help me out here."

Mike picked up his cup and looked around the room. "Sounds like another one of Jack's crazy ideas."

"Yeah. Another one of Jack's crazy ideas." Said Remus. Jack rolled his eyes as Remus went behind the curtain. He returned with a garment bag and suitcase and said, "Okay, I'm off." They all went into the corridor and toward the stairs.

On the way up through the kitchen, Jack stopped at the fridge to talk to Sarah. Remus continued out to the stage. Mike wasn't sure where to go, so he followed Remus.

He sat down at the bar and waved to Remus. "Okay, Remus. Have a good trip. How long you gone?"

Remus turned around, a bag in each hand. He looked at the bags. "Oh, I'd say three days. Be back Tuesday the latest. You know if you're not busy, why don't you come on along? There's plenty of space. It's gonna be a special date, too."

Mike didn't have to think twice. "Okay. My bag's still in my car. I haven't unpacked."

"All right then." Remus nodded and turned, continuing toward the door.

Mike got up, watching Remus go out the door. He looked over toward the curtain, didn't see anyone and called out, "See you all in a few days." And hurried out after Remus.

Remus' gentle manner set a new tone for riding in the Cobra. He stowed the bags in the small trunk and they settled into their seats. Mike marveled at the amount of room in the passenger seat. "I didn't think it was so big."

"What do you mean?"

"I sat on Phil's lap yesterday on the way out to John's place."

"You're kidding. And Jack drove?" Remus laughed out loud as he started the engine.

"Yeah, man. Never again." Mike put the seat belt on.

"Good Lord, that's insane! I hope the seat belt fit."

"I wish I'd had a helmet."

"Yeah, no doubt." They both laughed.

Remus eased the car out of the space and onto the road. It was definitely going to be a different type of drive than the one he'd experienced yesterday.

Mike looked around the interior. "The seats are very comfortable. And it's amazing how much room there is."

"It's a 1960s Roadster. Built for comfortable touring." Remus turned to Mike and made a mocking, dignified face. The goggles, his teeth, and the outfit made

Mike blink. Remus downshifted and pushed the Cobra up a long grade to the highway. He pointed to Mike's seat.

"We had the seats covered with the cordovan. And re-stuffed."

Mike put his hand on the corner of the cushion. "It's such a heavy leather. Horse, right?"

"Yes, sir. Inside and out."

"Oh, so it's got horsehair stuffing, too?"

"That's the way it was done in the old days."

"Hah. I never thought about that. What about the settee in your sitting room?"

"That, too. Actually, the car seats were done at the same plant up in Chicago where that settee was made, Cabani Leathers. It's the oldest commercial tannery in the country. It still produces shell cordovan. My cousin's been working there for almost thirty years."

They entered the highway and Remus continued louder once they were under way. "It took a lot of cordovan to cover that settee down in my room. These days it would cost a fortune. You only get two pairs of shoes from each animal. There's only a few tanneries in the country that produce it now. Back when they were building The Theatre, that was the only place to go for proper shell cordovan leather. It's from the rump, and burnishing the muscle by hand takes months."

Remus stopped talking as they passed a large tractor trailer that was exiting. The road stretched out and he continued. "John's grandfather spent a lot of time sourcing the woodwork in the VIP where I stay and the settee was sort of built into the room. He sent drawings up to Chicago for them to prepare the cushioning. It's in the journals. Istatore Cabani, the founder himself, came down to install it personally. There's some great stories in the journals. He's in the photos, too. Evidently, he and the Tenyons got on real well and Cabani stayed over at The Tavern for a week or so after the cushions were finished. He was fascinated by the construction of The Theatre and made a few more trips down over the years. He also did the chairs and booths that are in Heidle's Tavern. But those are just heavy cowhide. His trademark was this pinch he did on the corners and edging. I'll show you."

"Jack told me a little bit about when The Tavern was built and what went on there. I have to read the journals."

"Yes, you do. Wouldn't take much imagination to make a movie about it." A slight pause. "So anyway, a while back, Phil, Jimmy, Sarah, and I pitched in and had these seats done up in cordovan. It was Jack's birthday. My cousin works in the cutting room and so we had them measured one time I was up there with the car. I went back a few weeks later and had them fitted and installed."

"They really are beautiful seats." Mike spread his legs and looked down at the leather. "I didn't notice yesterday."

"I bet you had your eyes closed the whole time," Remus remarked with a smile.

"Shit we were yelling the whole way," said Mike and they both laughed.

"Give these seats a few more years. I treat 'em every now and again. This leather really gets better with time," Remus added.

"Like a good bottle of wine." Mike smiled.

"Or a beautiful woman, if you're lucky," Remus replied.

After a moment Mike said to Remus, "You know Remus I wanted to mention something when you were talking about the Stradivarius instruments and how they got their tone. I read the reason they sound so good was simply because they traveled so much. You know, like they were played in Vienna in December for the holidays and then in the spring they would be in London and so on. They would go from cold and dry to warm and damp for years and years and the wood became aged or fatigued by this. There's a guy who's taken this theory and created a process where he humidifies and dries an instrument. Yo-Yo Ma endorsed it. Seriously. Have you heard about this?"

Remus looked at Mike and smiled big. "Mike you are too much. And why didn't you mention this?"

"Well, we all had to split," Mike shrugged and looked away.

Remus laughed. "I have heard that theory, first thing I thought of when the boat came up. But damned if I'll tell it to Jack. I just like seeing him squirm."

Mike looked over at the passing countryside and said, "You're all players."

"What?" Remus couldn't hear.

"Nothing." Mike smiled. "Sarah told me everybody's so into their game they don't know how awesome the big picture is."

They rode on in silence and after a while Remus got off the highway. The scenery was beautiful and for Mike, it was now a pleasure riding in the Cobra. Remus drove as gently as he played piano. They continued with small talk, Mike asking about the towns they passed and Remus clearly happy to talk about this part of the country. After a while, they pulled off in a small Illinois town and had lunch at a roadside stop called Jerry James'. The owner recognized Remus as they sat at the counter.

Remus introduced Mike, and Jerry asked if Remus would like his regular. He handed a menu to Mike, who said, "I'll have what Remus is having."

Later, they chatted with Jerry, who eventually asked about what was up with the boat, and Remus laughed.

"Jerry, that's supposed to be a secret, and Jack asked me not to let Mike here in on the game. Especially since he plans to ask him to come along." Not looking at Mike, Remus took a bite out of his burger.

"Sounds to me like it'll get even more famous after you all take it over to Italy. With or without a writer on board," Jerry said.

Upon hearing this, Mike inhaled a piece of his burger and nearly choking, reached for his glass of milk. He took a sip and said to Jerry, who was looking at him, "Jerry, this is the best burger I've ever had." He took another sip and cleared his throat.

Jerry nodded his head. "Why, thank you, Mike. I'm glad you like it. I mix a little pork sausage in with the ground beef. Southern style. But Mother Nature does most of the work around here. You know there's no shortage of good beef in these parts," he laughed. "Or carnivores for that matter. But I also got a real special grill and that helps a lot." The phone rang and he excused himself.

Mike took another sip of milk and put it down. He spun his stool to face Remus, who was eating a French fry. Remus didn't look up. He knew what Mike was going to say.

"Okay, Remus, game's up. Tell me about the boat. Jack took me there yesterday, so he's not keeping it that much of a secret. I never got the story because I ended up cooking dinner."

Remus picked up his napkin and looked at Mike quizzically. He wiped his mouth and sat back from the counter. "Well, Mike, you see John's been building that boat forever. They were out there at the boatyard looking at the bar that's in The Theatre now. It came from a steamboat called Lady Prospect, of all things."

Mike shook his head. "Interesting." He thought about grabbing his audio recorder but let Remus continue.

He nodded and took another sip of his milk before he went on. "Right. Well, Jack saw the boat up there in John's building and fell in love with it. He eventually made a deal to trade him the theatre for it with the plan that he would finish the boat to Jack's specs." Remus raised his eyebrows.

"And what might those specs be?" Mike rolled his eyes and picked up his hamburger.

Remus waited, smiling as Mike frowned and tilted his head. He knew Mike didn't really have a clue and so he let the bomb drop. "Jack and John are going to dismantle The Theatre and use all the old wood paneling for the interior of the boat." Remus paused to let this sink in, and Mike seemed to be looking straight through him. "Then they're going to ship it across the Atlantic and make it available for exclusive dinner cruises and meetings in the Mediterranean."

Mike gazed over Remus' shoulder in recollection. "You've got to be kidding! And the guy there last night, Dirk, he's designing a video system so they can do the same thing they have downstairs at The Theatre."

Remus laughed. "Yeah, that's it, only times ten. He calls it 'executive video conferencing with a deluxe catering facility. Multi-use.'"

"Phil plans to film all the cooking and music and everything else that goes on and broadcast it from the boat." He laughed again as he put down the glass. "Jimmy and Sarah are going."

"I just can't imagine." Mike was amazed at the idea.

Remus assumed a more serious air. "I never heard of such a thing myself. Or if it's been done before. But they have a lot of people interested and a few solid bookings. Pamela's been working on all that. Her brother's been in this business for years. They call it 'charter yachting' or 'yacht charter something.' Anyway, they're making deals with hotels and working the corporate angle with folks Jack knows. Talking about video conferencing, dinners, music… The Monaco Grand Prix is booked, ten days next May. It's the first trip — a bunch of Jack's friends. The plan is to park the boat at a nearby port and show the races on the big screens inside the boat. They'll serve food and drinks all day. I think it's an investment bank company. Ten guys. They'll all be staying at a big hotel in town there."

"That is unbelievable, Remus."

"I know, isn't it?" He looked at Mike with open eyes.

"But, how did… I mean, was this Jack's original idea?"

"You know, Mike, I'm not sure. Was it all his idea? I don't think so. I watched it progress. See, what it's come to be now is a combination of a group of people working on it. It's like everything else. Phil's had an awful lot of input with the audio/video angle. Jack couldn't have come up with that himself. I heard Jack say, 'Hey, John. What if we took apart The Theatre and built the interior of the boat with it?' And 'Phil, how about if we designed a video system that could be set up a bunch of different ways?' He makes people scratch their heads and to tell you the truth I don't think he's serious half the time. He's just an abstract thinker with an imagination who gives resources to people. Then he just lets it grow and fit into some master plan. I don't think he even knows where it will go. What I think is that he's really just an artist whose medium is people and ideas."

Mike pondered this as he motioned to Jerry for the check. He handed the money to Jerry and said, "Jerry, that was a great burger."

Walking out to the car he looked forward to Chicago, returning to see Sarah, and once again considered himself a very lucky man.

Back in the Cobra, Mike put on his seatbelt. "So, Remus, what about you? What are you going to do?"

"Me? Why, I'm going with them. Are you kidding? I wouldn't miss it for the world. Besides, that piano on stage is going into the boat. I'll be entertaining in the salon." He struck a regal pose and started the car. Mike tried to imagine a more perfectly crafted plan.

• • •

Mike returned Thursday from Chicago and was anxious to document more of the operations of the kitchen. He knew the restaurant would be closing soon and the time was now.

He spent the next three nights in the kitchen and by Saturday confirmed dinner with Sarah at her place Sunday afternoon.

"Come on in," Sarah called from the kitchen. She was wearing a t-shirt, shorts, and a small apron when she greeted him at the door. "You're early." She kissed him on the cheek.

"I know. You wouldn't tell me what you were making, so I couldn't wait." Mike looked her in the eye.

"Okay. But I have to change. There's some wine in the fridge. And keep an eye on the stove."

Mike pulled a book from his satchel and handed it to her. "Here, take this with you."

"Oh, Mike. You were serious." She looked down at the bound volume. It was nearly one hundred years old and only slightly worn. The leather cover was tanned blue. The pages were a fine parchment, almost like rice paper. "These have the original Paget illustrations." She looked up at him and gently thumbed through a few pages. The book was printed in two columns per page, the type pressed into the paper.

"Actually, they're the second generation of the illustrations. These are the original weekly magazines from *The Strand* but they're toward the final stages of the Sherlock Holmes series. The additions were released twice a month. This volume is the first half of 1899, probably bound in the 20s. But see here, the later engravings include more of the settings and surroundings in the scenes." Mike flipped to an illustrated page. "Paget really worked on this final series. In the beginning, the original illustrations were just the characters on a blank background." He was moving his hands as he explained and touched her forearm before running his finger down the book's spine. "This one's in particularly good shape."

"You bet." She looked at him again. "I'll be right back." Sarah left him in the kitchen.

Mike went to the stove. There was spätzle browned in butter and simmering in a light cream with whole grain mustard flavoring the sauce. It had just been turned off. On a small sheet pan with clean tinfoil were some grilled sausages, most likely from Heidel's. There was very little else taking up the compact counter space. A bottle of olive oil, a small edge-grain cutting board, and some jars. She obviously liked lentils and rice; there were three or four of each. Smaller jars held spices, salt, and a few different chili peppers. The clean old knives were on a folded towel next to the cutting board. He looked in the fridge and found a bottle of Riesling. It was the same one he'd had at Heidle's. He poured a glass and looked at the sausages and spätzle. Was he lucky or did she know exactly what he liked? He went out to her sitting room and after half a glass of wine got up to look at the bookshelf.

A moment later, Sarah came out looking ravishing. And he was famished. It was the best meal he'd had in what seemed like years.

After dinner, they were sitting on her couch where they had dessert. Sarah had made a goat's milk, chocolate, and chipotle crème brûlée with a cardamom Florentine cookie stuck in the top. Mike got the last bit with his index finger, crunching the vanilla seeds collected in the corner of the ramekin. She'd served him a brandy, and her feet were in his lap as he massaged her heel and calf. He'd just finished telling a story about when he was living in France and the silence was comfortable.

"Remus told me about the boat. I can't believe it," Mike said, looking at her foot.

"I know. I think it's stupid. Why on earth would someone tear down a perfectly good café?" She started to sit up, the foot in his hand remaining in his lap. She bent forward with wonderful agility and put her arms around his shoulders and neck, kissing him on the lips for three, four, five seconds. Her lips were sweet, moist, and full.

Mike wanted every inch of her.

"Mmm..." She pulled back, looking at his face and running her hand over his forehead and through his hair. "You feel really good." She squeezed the hand that was on her foot before getting up off the couch. "Thanks for that."

"I'm not finished." He finished his brandy.

"I'm not either. I'm getting myself a drink. Would you like a refill?"

"Sure."

She came back with another glass and the bottle of Hennessey and poured generously for them both. Sitting next to Mike, she pulled both feet up onto the couch, her knee resting on his thigh. She laid one arm along the back of the couch and put her hand on the back of his neck.

"There's something weird about the boat." Sarah sniffed her glass and took a drink.

"What? I think it sounds awesome. Private charter yachting." Mike smiled as if he liked the way it sounded. "Sounds like he's got work. I'm not really familiar with the business, but it sounds interesting. What, you don't want to go yachting?" Mike added ruefully as he looked at her. Their eyes were a foot and a half apart.

"I don't know. Why, are you going?" She looked at him over the rim of the glass before taking another sip.

"Me? I just heard about it from Remus the other day. Jack hasn't said a word to me about it. Seems like it's some kind of secret." He took a drink. "Besides what would I do? Sign on as biographer?" He laughed.

"Maybe. I can't believe he hasn't said anything to you. I think he's counting on you being a part of it." She put her glass down. "He asked me, you know. He gave me an idea what it would be like, but I don't think he really knows what it'll be like. The money sounds great. But, Mike, I have a cat, an apartment. I do other things, you know? My life isn't just Jack's Café. Lord knows I spend enough time there."

"You run the place."

"Whatever." She put down her glass.

"Sarah, I can't believe you're not thinking about it. Sounds like the trip of a lifetime."

"I didn't say I'm not thinking about it. I'm thinking about it a lot. It's a lot to think about. You're probably more of a seasoned traveler than I am. Leaving home is a pretty big deal for me." She put her hand back on his shoulder.

Mike looked into his glass and on to Sarah's legs. It was difficult to contain himself. He put the glass down. "It's probably easier than you think, once you decide to do it." He put his hand lightly on her knee and gave a gentle shake. At that moment the cat jumped up and curled into the space in between their legs and the back of the couch. "What a pretty kitty." Mike began to pet the cat.

"Jack said he can come," she said shyly.

"Well, there you go!" Mike laughed out loud and tapped her knee.

The cat startled and looked at Mike. Wide-eyed with its ears straight up, it tensed and nearly got up on all fours. Sarah laughed and put her hand on top of Mike's. The cat settled back into its spot and Mike gave Sarah a kiss that ended in a laugh. And then another longer kiss.

• • •

After a late breakfast, Mike left Sarah's apartment. He checked his phone messages and had a call from his agent saying it was imperative that he come to the office in St. Louis at 7:00 p.m. and that he should bring his passport for a two-day job. Mike went back to his room at the motel and took a shower. He hadn't gotten much sleep the last few nights, so he took a long nap. He packed a small bag and got a cab into the city. At the office, he was met by a driver who took him to a hangar at St. Louis Lambert International. There was a large private jet and for some reason all he could think of was the Bugs Bunny cartoon where Bugs flew from *O'Hare!* Airport. The situation seemed a bit more serious when he mentioned this to the driver and was met by a cold stare. As he walked up the jetway, a woman greeted

162

him inside the jet's doorway. "Mr. Ambrose, welcome. We'll be taking an overseas flight. I understand this may have been short notice for you, but be assured we have anything you may need for a comfortable trip." She was Italian, brunette, with dark eyes wearing a navy pantsuit and white blouse. "You have your passport?"

"Okay, I have my passport. Where are we going?" Mike was impressed by the entire situation but still a bit baffled.

"Our final destination is Rome with a stop in Buenos Aires. Please, have a seat. We'll be taking off shortly. And if you wouldn't mind, leave your shoes here." She motioned toward a small basket inside the door.

"Rome." This was it. Mike looked at her. "When are we coming back?'

"I'm sorry, I don't know. Right this way." She ushered him into the main cabin where a well-dressed gentleman stood and greeted him.

He was wearing a light grey suit with a silk scarf draped over his jacket.

"Mr. Ambrose, thank you for joining me. My name is Lorenzo. It's very nice to meet you," He held out his hand.

Mike looked at the aristocratic face, well-groomed Van Dyke beard and elegant suit. He noticed a fine cologne. Mike guessed he was in his late sixties. Healthy with good posture.

It was all overwhelming, and Mike gave him his hand. "Nice to meet you, Lorenzo."

"Please, have a seat. Would you like something to drink?" They sat by a low table.

Mike looked around. What he would never know was how similar this seat was to the very seat Jack had sat on during his first trip to Rome nearly thirty years ago. Mike scanned the bar and noticed the Scotch. "Sure. Some of the Macallan. Neat please."

Lorenzo turned toward the woman as she was pouring. "Dalia, some Trebbiano for me."

"Sí." She did not turn around.

"Is it Michael or do you go by Mike?" Lorenzo looked at him with open eyes.

The stewardess brought the drinks and then shifted Mike's bag behind his seat. Mike looked closely at Lorenzo and recalled his talk with Jack about Rome. At that point things started to fall into place and Mike felt like he was at the center of a hurricane Jack only alluded to.

"Mike is fine." Mike could shorten Lorenzo's name. Lo, Lori, Renzo, Zo.

"We have a mutual friend." Lorenzo tilted his head and held out his hands as a sign of mutual understanding. "My colleagues and I are interested in where your work on the project with Jack Stanley stands." The jet's engines started up, and Lorenzo reached for his glass. Mike didn't move. This was it; big as it gets. He held Lorenzo's eyes, wondering what was next. The stewardess walked toward them, looking at their laps and Mike fastened his seat belt. Lorenzo waited for her to turn around, and Mike watched her go forward.

"Have you come across anything else besides the restaurant, that has to do with his past? Men he's worked for?" Mike detected the slightest stumble in the delivery. The jet started to move, and Mike picked up his Scotch. Lorenzo was indeed a sly cat.

"Lorenzo, was I hired to do this story for you and your *colleagues?*" He took a big drink, trying to hold his breath as he exhaled. He considered stonewalling but decided to play it safe. "Jack's got a nice restaurant going there in Samson, Missouri. Great food, great crew." He wanted another sip, but held Lorenzo's gaze and let him go next.

"Michael, it may be of great benefit to you to work with me." Lorenzo sat back and his demeanor changed. He was hard as a rock. The grace subsided and Mike knew he was in no man's land. He was on their jet, going to Rome, and Jack had told him how to handle it.

There was no way out and Jack had told him this. "No fuckin around now Mike. You won't be able to get out once you're in.

It wasn't just because he liked Jack and Phil and Jimmy and Remus or the whole thing about the boat. It was Sarah. She rocked his world and he wanted her more than anything.

"I'm in Jack," he'd said.

The plane quickly accelerated, tilted, and they were airborne. They both picked up their glasses and Mike was gently pushed back into his seat. Lorenzo fought gravity as Mike spoke.

"Jack mentioned some of the dinners he'd prepared for people he'd worked for. But he didn't go into much detail and it didn't really make much sense. He said he recorded the conversations to hear what they were saying about the food." They leveled out and Lorenzo ordered another round of drinks. He asked Mike to tell him everything he knew about Jack as they had hors d'oeuvres. Two hours later, Mike was shown to an aft cabin with a queen-size bed. He slept through the stop in Buenos Aires and woke up forty minutes outside Rome. He had coffee in his cabin and did not see Lorenzo until they deplaned. Not much was said on the drive into Rome. He was going to a private restaurant to tell the story to three gentlemen.

CHAPTER SEVEN

Closing

Mike's flight back from Rome brought him to St. Louis and he had asked if Lorenzo could get him a room for the evening of his return. The driver brought him to the Chase Park Plaza Hotel where Lorenzo had booked him an executive apartment. He was handed a card that listed Suite 7, and an account number, REV13:18. Mike took particular notice of this. Everything was on account.

The hotel had been built in the 1920s. The bar is beautiful, and the food is great. Mike stayed two nights without leaving the property. The morning of his departure he called Jack and arranged to meet at Heidle's for a late lunch.

They sat at the same table in the back and Mike went over his trip in detail. He was particularly happy to describe the nun who accompanied him to the villa. Jack was more interested in descriptions of the men at the dinner in Rome. He couldn't place the old man in the black suit.

"If I'd only given you a miniature camera to put in your coat," Jack said.

"No way. They went over me with a metal detector. I think they were checking for a recording device." Mike laughed. Jack didn't.

He asked Mike to describe the room where they ate, and how the man in black entered the room.

"Now that you mention it, I remember him coming into the room through a side door. I had entered from the opposite side, after walking down a wide corridor. Yeah, it was definitely a small elevator."

Jack pictured the old room and the elevator that brought people up from two stories below the street; people who couldn't afford to be seen together. "Anything else you can tell me about the guy who came in last?"

"You know, he had this beautiful ring. I've never seen anything like it. It looked like it was from the middle ages. It was big and gold."

Jack felt a cold shudder. "Can you draw me a picture of it?" Jack asked quietly.

"Sure. Here." Mike pulled out a pen and drew the ring on the back of an envelope.

Jack stared at it. It couldn't be. "And you were told to address him as Papa?"

"Yeah, but he sure didn't look like Hemingway."

"Did he look like a pope?" Jack had a strange expression on his face.

"What do you mean by that? Are you kidding? He was wearing shades and this really nice suit."

"Mike, can I see your phone? You can get online with it, right?"

"Yeah, why?" Mike reached into his bag and pulled it out.

"Here, hold on." Jack started tapping on the screen. "Is this the guy?" He handed the phone back to Mike.

"You know, yeah, that's him, maybe a little younger without the mustache. But the clothes… Wait…" Mike looked back at Jack's search. "Are you fucking kidding me? This is Pope John Paul I. He's been dead for nine years."

"Maybe not. You know they never found his ring. Some said Vilotti kept it. They always smash the pope's ring when he dies."

"Hold on, Jack. So, I just met Pope John Paul who supposedly died in the first month of his papacy. How many people know about this?"

"Probably three, and now five. Did you mention the ring or anything about Papa?"

"No, but when we shook hands, I looked at it closely and he pulled his hand away. I really didn't think anything of it."

"Well, I'm sure they'll be keeping a close eye on you now. Listen, you definitely cannot tell anyone about this. I've got the recordings, and I'll let them know there are a few complete copies."

Mike thought about Sarah. He wanted all of her. But he didn't want her in danger. "Fuck, Jack. I didn't want this." Suddenly Mike felt his simple life drifting out of reach.

"Sorry, Mike. Sorry for you, but I didn't write *this* book." Neither of them had moved in five minutes. Jack filled their glasses and called to Heidle for the check and a cork for the Riesling. Mike remained silent.

"Don't worry, Mike. You're cool. I got a few cards left to play and I'll make sure they don't mess with you."

"Sure. Whatever you say Jack." Mike didn't feel sure.

For Jack this twisted his plans a bit, but the more he thought about it, the more it made sense. Luciani, or Pope John Paul I, had radical ideas. Known as

"The Smiling Pope," "Gianpaulo," and "Papa." Members of the Roman Curia were discomforted by his conduct and his plans to "clean up the nefarious activities tarnishing his beloved Church." It had been leaked to the press that many high-ranking Vatican officials were not only Freemasons but also members of P2. This included Secretary of State Vilotti, Lorenzo and the president of the Vatican Bank. Not to mention a number of politicians from Europe and South America. Since the Catholic Church does not recognize Freemasonry, having members of P2 working for the Church was totally out of the question. Pope John Paul made it public he was going to relieve every mason on the list of his position. But this was impossible. Not only would the Vatican cease to function, but one of the fiercest battles against Communism would be defused. When Gianpaulo died the entire scandal was swept into the corners. Jack imagined that only Vilotti could craft such a solution and smiled to himself. He couldn't wait to sit and talk with him over dinner and wine. Jack mused that *this* was the person Mike should be writing about.

As they walked back to The Theatre, neither of them said a word. Jack thought it amusing that Mike kept looking over his shoulder.

"Mike, you're okay right? I don't want you getting weird on me. Really, every-thing's fine. Nothing is going to happen to you. They need you as much as I do." This seemed to make him feel better and Mike loosened up as they walked in.

Phil was looking sharp wearing a tailored black pinstripe suit and Remus was in the tuxedo he wore on weekends. This evening was a special party of Jack's clos-est friends. Whatever was cooking smelled especially good tonight. Pamela was behind the bar and Mike went toward the kitchen to see if anyone needed help. Peeking in, he'd never seen the kitchen in such a state at 5:00 p.m. Jimmy and Sarah were arguing about the use of the oven.

"You been in this oven for three friggin' hours!" shouted Sarah. Mike turned right around and went out. They continued arguing and Mike could hear it from the bar.

"Yeah, maybe if you came in a little earlier you wouldn't be in the weeds."

"Dammit, Jimmy! I was here all day yesterday prepping. What were you doing, watching funny car races? Butthead! Just because you want to do all your work in one day doesn't mean you can take over all the ovens."

Jack came out to the bar after Mike. "Fuck you!" Sarah yelled.

Jack winced. "I wouldn't go in there if I were you."

"Oh no! What's happening?" Mike whispered to Jack. "I'll come back later."

"No, no. Don't go anywhere. They'll make up. Do you have a few minutes? I'd like to talk to you about something else." Pamela was making a cappuccino, facing away from them.

"Sure." Mike looked at the open back of Pamela's dress. Wow. He'd never seen that much of her skin before.

"Come on downstairs." Jack headed down to the office. Mike had never been in there before and as he entered he was immediately struck by the austere milieu.

"Here, have a seat." Jack held out a hand toward the green leather wing chair and then sat at his desk. The antique cosmetics table against the wall was claw-footed, a fine example of nineteenth century carved American furniture. The coarsely grained white oak top and two turned posts had a dark satin finish.

"I'm sure you've heard about the boat and our plans. I'm sorry I couldn't let you know more in the beginning."

"I'm glad you didn't."

Pamela's voice came over an intercom. "Anybody want a cappuccino?"

Jack looked at Mike, who shook his head. "How 'bout some wine?" Jack said. Mike nodded and Jack pressed a button. "Can you bring us two glasses please, Pamela?"

Jack stood up, reached into one of four wooden crates next to his desk, and pulled out a large bottle of wine. He handed it to Mike. "Here, check this out." He turned the bottle so the label faced up at Mike.

"Oh, wow! I love Barolo. Nice. Eighty-one was a legendary year in Piedmont." The bottle was slightly cool and Mike looked at the label. "Borgogno, that's an old house."

Jack handed him a corkscrew and added, "Pamela and I were there on my birthday last year. They made jeroboams in '81. Special occasion that year. I got sixteen."

"Beautiful. Jeroboams are four-liter bottles right?" Mike opened up the blade on the corkscrew and put it to the neck of the bottle.

"Three-liter. That makes four bottles." Jack watched Mike's hands.

"Oh yea, a bottle's seven-fifty." With three cranks he cleanly removed the tip of the lead sheath, exposing the cork. Pamela came in with the glasses and an oversize decanter. She winked at Mike.

"How they doin' up there?" Jack looked up at Pamela as Mike popped the cork.

"They're fine. I've never seen so much prep."

Pamela was wearing a powder blue baby doll dress. Her hair was pulled close with a small spit curl, and she wore a narrow ivory headband.

"I know. They're really putting a lot into this dinner." Jack took the bottle and, using two hands, slowly poured the wine into the decanter. Mike watched the tawny colored liquid roll down the inside of the crystal vessel.

"Yes, they are. It's not every day Jack's Café closes, and the boss has his friends over for dinner," Pamela said.

"Yeah, yeah. Thanks, Pamela." Jack made it sound like a burden.

"Okay, boys." Pamela smiled and went out, quietly closing the door.

Jack finished filling, pouring all but the last inch into the decanter and put down the bottle. "How's that?" He picked up the decanter with one hand and giving it a gentle swirl poured a bit into one of the glasses. Mike guessed the weight at about twelve pounds and considered this a smooth move. Jack gave the glass a swirl and a sniff. "Well, it's still good." He took a taste and exhaled through his nose. "There's a note of licorice. You'll get it. Give it a minute. I noticed it the first time I tasted this harvest and it's in every bottle. I don't know how they did it, but my guess is that they didn't do much." He poured two glasses.

"The wine makers at Borgogno?" Mike said.

Jack nodded. "I bet you that year when summer set in, a few of the old men knew it would be a good year. But still, they never really know. So, they go about their work tending to everything like they usually do and then later that year they realize '*Holy fuck this only happens every eight or ten years.*' That's when they decide to produce the jeroboams. It's like falling for a woman. Everything goes well in the beginning. Maybe you're lucky once or twice and pull off some noble deed. But you never really know *how* she's gonna age. So, you look at her mother, right? It's the same with the harvests. The gardener where I worked, Geraldo, had been growing vegetables there for years. I also knew winemakers who had been doing it all their lives. These guys could always tell how things were gonna go. They could just see the signs in the weather and how everything was growing."

Mike thought about this and also Pamela's words about managing with minimal intervention. "Jesus, Jack. I've never seen a Jeroboam of '81 Barolo decanted. Here's to that. And your restaurant. Again." Mike picked up his glass. "It's an honor."

"Yeah. Here's to my restaurant. And here's to them." He looked up to the ceiling and they both drank. After a quiet moment, Jack started. "Okay you know just about everything that's going on here. We're closing, and I'm taking the boat to Europe," he said plainly.

"Remus finally told me. I had to pry it out of him." Mike took a sip. "I'm glad you didn't tell me before I started. Kept me open-minded. I'd have had a nostalgic feel if I'd known in the beginning."

"Yeah, naiveté really is a virtue. And your timing is impeccable."

"It all helps. Now tell me the big picture."

Jack opened a drawer and pulled out a cigar. He broke it in half and lit one.

"Jack, you gotta tell me about the cigars. What the hell? It looks like a twig."

"It's a *cheroot*. They're Tuscan." Jack spoke between puffs. "Break it in half before you smoke it." He put the unlit half in the ashtray. "You want a try?"

"Sure."

"Here." Jack pushed the ashtray toward him and handed him the lighter. He watched closely as Mike lit it and inhaled the first drag.

"Holy fuck!" Mike sputtered through the thick smoke, coughing.

"Sorry. I should've mentioned. You need to get it lit and then let it sit. The first drag can be harsh." Jack smiled.

"I'll say." Mike caught his breath and felt a strong rush. "Whew."

"You'll get over it. It's like the first shot of grappa." Jack picked up his cigar and took a drag.

"Or tequila." Mike coughed again. "You know I read tequila effects women differently than men, makes them… uninhibited."

"You watch too many reality shows."

"No, it was in a men's magazine."

"Exactly." He looked at Mike's face.

• • •

Over three glasses of wine Jack told Mike everything about the boat and then explained the events leading up to one of Europe's worst financial and political disasters to date. He also explained the gap between what the press and prosecution knew and the truth. The Vatican Bank stood to lose more than $1 billion and the real question was who was going to fry. The Vatican may be a sovereign state, but they still had to answer for all of it. Jack ended by saying, "You should look into it. It would make a great book."

They both drank the wine and a quiet moment passed. "So, we're going over with the boat to do private dinners. I'm going to propose to Lorenzo I continue with the surveillance and record the dinner conversations. I imagine he'll like the idea of easing off the political maneuvering and get into corporate espionage. In any case I figure he's into me for a couple hundred million for the sculpture scam. I don't need the money, but it should be fun goofing around the Med on a boat. You will all be busy, but you'll do really well. Mike, I gotta go. Big night. Listen, tomorrow night we're all going into the city for dinner. You join us. You can hear more about the boat and the plan."

Mike was thoroughly intrigued. "You got it. Tomorrow night?"

"Yeah, we're closed. It'll be Pamela, Remus, Jimmy, Phil, and Sarah." Jack picked up his glass. The tension left the room.

"And Mike, there's room if you want to go to Europe with us. They're all doing it. If you're interested, I'd like you to come along. You can write about it. There'll be some other things you can do to help out around the boat. Think about it. You'll be on the payroll like everybody else." Jack figured it would be best to keep him nearby.

"I'd also like you to do some research on The Theatre and John's family. I'll get you the journals and photo albums to look at."

"I'm totally up for that." Mike drank the wine and tasted the old country. He could not believe his ears.

"Good." Jack drank as well. "How was lunch with Pamela?"

"I love Heidle's place, and Pamela is an absolute gem. You have a Camelot here. Why on earth would you want to leave?" Mike was trying to make a point that didn't really hit the mark.

"Don't worry. It's not going anywhere. We're just sort of taking it somewhere. I was getting bored anyway. Let's talk tomorrow night. We'll go into the city and have something to eat."

"That sounds great." He picked up his glass. "Okay, I'm going to go see if Jimmy or Sarah need any help tonight." Mike finished his wine.

"No, you know what? Stay on the other side of the line and let them do their thing. Just observe. Here, have another glass. Review your notes." Jack stood up. "Do you have that little audio recorder with you?"

"Yeah, you want me to record them?"

"Yeah, Switch it on and give it to me. I'll stash it up there. It should be an interesting night, as you can imagine. Do you have enough tape to just let it record all night?"

Mike laughed at the idea. "Sure, I'd be happy to. But Jack, it's not tape anymore." He looked at the recorder and smiled.

Jack appreciated the humor. "Okay, okay. I want all the details, but right now I gotta jump in the shower." Jack walked out.

"Don't bang your *head!*" Mike said.

"Hah." Jack wondered if Mike knew how much he hated the tiny shower.

• • •

Once the paneling was removed from the sides of the auditorium, the only thing left was the stage planking and the kitchen equipment. At that point, there would be no more meals served. Jack had made many close friends who came in to eat over the years and so toward the end there were a few special events. The final week was fully booked with private parties on Monday, Wednesday, Friday, and Sunday. The restaurant had been closed to the public the week before.

For Sunday, Jack put together his own guest list. Vic Sindano, the governor's brother, Gene Nogara, Bern Calvi, and a few more of Jack's closest friends and guys he played cards with. There were eleven guests in total. The evening started with plates of hors d'oeuvres sent out to the bar as cocktails were served and guests trickled in. Then the men sat at one table the whole evening.

On Monday, Jack had asked Sarah and Jimmy each to make a list of what they'd like to prepare for the final party using what was on hand. Altogether there were thirty-nine items, Jack was glad he didn't ask them to arbitrate themselves. The items were richly detailed and everything sounded dynamite. He saved these original proposals to remember the evening and how hard it was to narrow down. It was clear to Jack that Sarah and Jimmy had put a lot of energy toward designing these special items, and there was no doubt the rivalry was fierce. In all the years and all the meals served here, he was sure this would be one of the greatest nights. Best of all, he would be able to sit and enjoy it all.

Jimmy's asparagus was one of his favorite starters. He'd taken bunches of thick, raw asparagus and roasting them slowly, basted them with a thyme-infused demi-

173

glace over a period of two and a half hours. The outside had a finish of thickly varnished weathered bronze with the inside soft as butter.

After preparing a gallon of fresh brown veal stock, he strained it and clarified it further by adding ground fresh veal, finely minced raw carrot, and egg whites. This was slowly heated while stirring the mixture with a wooden spatula. After about ten minutes of constant gentle stirring, a raft formed on top of the simmering consommé. This floating mass of coagulated albumin and cooked veal was bound by the minced carrot. It acted as a fine filter, clarifying the liquid as it percolated through a crack in its center. Once it cooled completely, the raft was removed and the resulting product had crystal clarity the tone of deep amber.

Finally, it was made into demi-glace. In a heavy, medium rondeau he placed a quarter cup each of white peppercorn and coriander seed that had been quickly rinsed and dried to remove any dust or grit. The pan was heated slowly until the spices became shiny and began to release their oils. Then the consommé was added one ladle at a time, tilting the pan to coat the bottom. Each ladleful reduced to half in an instant with another ladleful added immediately after. This generational, comprehensive technique of reduction produced a rich velvety body that turned to gelatin when cooled.

The three-inch tips of the asparagus were laid out in even rows on parchment. Using a one-inch brush, they were coated every few minutes. Reducing even further, the coating became dark and shiny like chestnut-colored ceramic glaze. The flavor of the asparagus remained strong and was complimented by the spicy, nutty character of the glaze. The finished spears were carefully transferred to clean parchment and chilled in the walk-in. Just before service, Jimmy made a lemon zest-infused hollandaise that was thickened with a buttery smooth roasted tomato purée. This sauce was spooned onto large porcelain serving platters and then lightly browned with a blowtorch. The asparagus spears were allowed to come up to room temperature and then delicately placed on top of the *gratinée* of sauce Choron. There were four of these platters sent out to the table.

Gene Nogara stood up at one point and insisted that Jack reassemble the restaurant so that it could remain open. "You can't close this restaurant, Jack. It's cruel and unusual punishment! Where are we going to eat when you go? Do we have to follow you to Italy?"

Some of the others laughed and Jack leaned back, looking up at Gene, who was next to him. "Yeah, Gene. You all got to come to Italy now for more of this." A few men shrugged as if to say that was fine with them. "At the very least I'll win back some of my damn poker money!"

Nogara raised his wine higher. "To Jack, and to his boat!" The table responded in unison, and everyone was standing. Few things can cause a group of wealthy friends in their fifties and sixties to shout with glasses in the air. It was a toast to Jack and his work, reciprocation for the pleasures he'd given them and to his future work in Europe.

Plates from the previous course had been cleared and Phil was at the bar ready to reset. Sarah stood by the curtain holding a large platter and everyone sat down. She nodded to Phil who started around the table placing a fresh plate, fork and knife for each setting. As Sarah came to Jack's side holding the garnished platter low so that everyone could see, she said, "Jack, this is the pheasant strudel."

Jack leaned in and inhaled as he got close to the food. "Mmm." He turned to face her with his arm on the back of the chair and said, "This looks beautiful, Sarah. Tell us what you've done."

The strudel was sliced and arranged in a graceful wave on a large silver platter. Sauce had been striped across the platter before the pieces were placed. At one end of the platter, five long feathers and two claws dramatically stated the filling.

The table was quiet and Phil came with a small pan and spooned sauce onto the plates before Sarah served each guest. She talked as she worked her way around.

"It's made with three wild pheasants from Joe Staniel's ranch in Tennessee. To start, I skinned the birds and then removed the meat from the bones. The meat has been flavored with fresh rosemary and ground Guajillo. This is a lightly smoked chili from Mexico."

She pointed with her spatula to the platter's garnish. At the base of the claws and feathers were a few of the long leathery chilis, a porcini, some herbs, lentils, and whole spices. "There's also a pinch of cinnamon and nutmeg for seasoning and some extra virgin olive oil. The character of the dish is a marriage of Western Europe and Central America." She placed the first piece on Jack's plate. "The meat was seasoned the night before. I seared it dark and then braised it. I coated the bones lightly with flour and roasted them with leeks and tomatoes to make the stock."

She was a third of the way around the table. Everyone was watching and listening, and some were looking at the plates on the table. "Jack, *please*, before it gets cold." She motioned with the spatula that he was to eat. He and the others who were served started in silently as she continued.

"I've also prepared some small green lentils from France. They're flavored with a base of Heidle's smoked bacon, garlic, and porcinis. I par cooked the lentils, strained them, and tossed them in the base to toast them for a few minutes. Bit by bit I added about a half bottle of Barolo and then some of the stock to finish cooking the lentils." She occasionally paused and looked up as she talked and served. "The strudel has a layer of the lentils along the bottom of the pastry and on top of that, the braised pheasant and vegetables from the stock. The pastry is made with our butter from Verona and on top are some chopped cracklins' from the birds' skin." There were two more plates to go. Everyone else was eating and the room was silent. Remus had stopped playing.

"And for the sauce, which Phil has so nicely put on the bottom of the plate… Thank you, Phil"—she gave him a beautiful smile, "The braising liquid and stock were reduced and finished with a bit of cream, sour cream, butter, and Heidle's whole grain mustard." The last plate was served. Holding out the empty platter on her arm, she raised the spatula. "Pheasant strudel." She looked around. Everyone was looking at her, and she bowed slightly.

Jack had finished his plate and pushed it back. He reached for his glass and seeing it empty, he picked up the decanter of the '81 Barolo Reserva. Raising it high, he said, "Brava, Sarah!"

Jack filled his glass and everyone at the table held up theirs, calling out, "Brava, Sarah!"

Bowing once more, she and Phil turned and went back to the kitchen.

"I've never seen him like this," Sarah said once they were back in the kitchen.

"Yeah. Wild shit." Phil laughed.

• • •

Closing a fully operational, world-class restaurant is not easy. With all the sweat and elegance and energy splattered across the walls, nobody really wants it to go away.

All the same, everyone was excited about the future. Toward the end there were a few particularly memorable evenings, parties for some of the local folks, and soon after that, Jack's Café became nostalgia. A moment in time fondly remembered.

176

It had been decided early on that the restaurant would stay open during the deconstruction. "It'll be an obscure form of live entertainment," Jack had said.

"Great, and we can turn up the piano. I wonder how it'll sound without all the paneling." Phil had always wanted to turn up the piano.

Over a period of seventeen days, all the interior paneling and finally the stage planking were removed. Phil took hundreds of photos during the last month using the same large format view camera John's great-uncle had used to start the photo journals of The Theatre's construction. For the last three years, the camera had been at John's boatyard, where Phil had been photographing the boatbuilding. He'd also taken approximately three hundred photos during the restaurant construction. He was putting together an evolutionary slideshow of the life of The Theatre: being built in the '20s, being transformed into and operating as a restaurant, and then finally being stripped apart.

The piano was finally delivered to the boatyard, where it was to be craned up into the boat. A large portable dehumidification and cooling system was set up outside to climate-control the interior of the boat.

At this point, all the major systems and equipment had been installed, uninstalled, taken apart, and finally reinstalled inside the boat. The drive train and engine had been fitted and assembled. The struts, shaft, and stuffing box were bedded in, and the engine mounts and stabilizers were set. What awaited was splashdown, shakedown, and final adjustments. Fire hoses and a large pump brought river water to and from the boat to start the engines and raw water intakes, and also to test the air conditioning and plumbing systems.

The master bath was located centrally in the large aft stateroom where Jack planned to stay. This included a a large cast iton and portable tub. Jack had found the tub a year ago at an estate sale in Georgia. The tub had a large shower that was fed by a one-inch pipe. Two water heaters provided more than ninety gallons of hot water on demand throughout the boat. The luxurious tub alone required more than fifty gallons. This was one of Jack's only indulgences.

Wiring for the lighting, video system, and appliances was carefully laid, tied, and mounted. The deck and cabin top was fabricated of wood and fiberglass in six sections. The forward and aft areas of the deck were now closed off.

The yard team was finessing the cabinetry and paneling. The stainless shelving and counters from the kitchen were slightly modified and reinstalled around the heavy equipment. Finally, the piano went in, and the central parts of the decking and cabin superstructure were positioned overhead and permanently installed. This effectively sealed off the boat, making it ready for launch.

Closing Jack's Café created an urgency with many facets. Jack had been on a personal timeline for a while. As word about the closing got out to the public, feelings twisted even further. Rumors and conjecture made it seem almost more romantic than it actually was. Almost.

Two days later, the "Med crew plus Mike," as Phil called it, met for dinner. Pamela had arranged for a private room at the Clayton Club in St. Louis and Jack hired a large van to drive them in and out of the city. It was rare that this core group met outside the restaurant, let alone dressed up and going out to dinner. Sarah was wearing a simple black dress and Mike could barely keep his eyes off her legs. She was a knockout.

After a few bottles of wine in the kitchen they left through the side door. It was around seven thirty and the sun was just getting ready to set. The long rays lit up a light rain coming from a lone cloud. Jack locked the door and turned around to see everyone looking at him. His eyes were wide, and he made a few strange movements with his mouth. No one would ever admit that it seemed his eyes were watering. "Shit." He looked at his keys. "You all remember standing out here that first night."

Phil interrupted. "I was thinking the same thing."

"Like it was yesterday," said Remus.

"I remember," said Pamela. "You were talking about hanging out in Paris with your friend the fishmonger. Delivering seafood in the rain to all the top restaurants in Rome. You were eating live sea urchin roe with caviar and having champagne at each stop."

Pamela was a sparkling joy, if only for her wonderful memory. Jack smiled at her and then looked at the others. "Well, it was just an idea I had, but you all really made it happen. I never could've imagined how great it would be."

"Hell, I'd probably be in jail if it weren't for this place," Jimmy said as he lit a cigarette.

"Or worse," Sarah chimed in.

"I just hope the damn thing floats," Jack added. He turned and started walking down the sidewalk to the van waiting at the corner.

"Gonna be some weird shit go down in France, I'll tell you that," Jimmy laughed as they started walking.

"Shut up, Jimmy," Sarah said as she elbowed him off the sidewalk.

Jack reached the van first and opened the door for Remus. "Thanks. Hey Martin. What up?" he said to the driver, clapping him on the shoulder on the way in.

"All good, man. All good. Big night tonight." Martin had a great big smile and teeth like Remus'. "This the new guy I heard about?"

Mike laughed as he climbed in behind Remus. "Brothers?" he mouthed to Sarah, who sat next to him. She nodded.

The van was roomy inside with one large black leather seat along the left side and rear. The interior was comfortable and plush. Jazz piped in softly through unseen speakers and the tiny bright pin spots elegantly lit their faces, clothing, and seating. Martin wore a simple black wool suit with grey pinstripes.

"Martin, this is Mike Ambrose. Mike, this is my brother, Martin."

"Hey, Martin. How did I know you two were brothers?" Mike waved from the back of the van.

"Couldn't be the clothes," added Remus.

Martin spun around in the driver's seat to face them. The fabric of their suits was indeed identical, though the cut differed slightly. "Hah," said Mike. "Look at that. But I was thinking more of your teeth."

"Our cousin's a tailor. It's cheaper this way." Martin adjusted his cuff.

"We don't go out much together, so it's easy to plan," Remus added. They laughed.

Jack stooped on his way in, turning his head sideways to look forward. "Hey, Martin. You two dressing up the same again?" He held out his hand for a light high-five. Jimmy followed Jack into the van.

Remus rolled his eyes and said, "Least we ain't twins."

"Thank the Lord for that." Martin turned and started the big diesel engine. The lights dimmed slightly as the door shut like a vapor lock. Phil was carrying a duffel bag that contained packages for each of the crew. He sat in the big front passenger seat and had spun the chair around to face the others. Pamela sat between Jack and Remus, with Jimmy in the corner next to Sarah and Mike in the rear forward-facing seat. It was quite comfortable, and Jack suggested that they should sit around the dining table the same way. This was silently agreed to as Martin eased the big limo onto the street

The private club leased the top three floors of one of St. Louis's tallest building. The private dining rooms were on the top floor. The two floors below housed a handful of luxurious private residences, a spa and gym, corporate business services, the bar and the club's management offices. Pamela had taken care of the arrangements, the table settings, and the menu. Jack had ordered the wine.

Pamela managed to secure use of the large oval boardroom table. It was twelve feet long with a polished cherry top and solid maple bull nose around the edge. The tabletop alone weighed more than seven hundred pounds. All the chairs were high backed with wheels and armrests. The carpeting was thin dark green wool with firm padding.

This room was named VIP west. It was a corner space with two sides of twelve-foot floor-to-ceiling windows. The sunset was in full glory, and the curtains were pulled back. They stood on the thirty-ninth floor. The table was laid diagonally with the head setting in the corner of the windows. Jack made his place there and the others filed in on either side. The view and the light were fantastic, and the table was beautiful.

Phil opened his duffel bag and handed a thin leather valise to everyone at the table. Each case was unique in style with a personalized ID tag. Inside each case were a handful of folders and a cell phone.

A waiter came into the room and began pouring water. Another man in a tuxedo came in pushing a large butcher-block cart on wheels. A small wine rack, sommelier's tools, and a complete set of stemware son top. Below was a large ice bin with chilled bottles of white wine. There was also a silver ice bucket holding a magnum of champagne. He placed a matching tray on a side table, covered it with a linen cloth, and hefted the silver bucket onto it.

Behind him followed an older gentleman in an elegant slate grey suit. He came to Jack's side and put his hand on the back of his chair.

"Good evening, Jack. And welcome everyone. My name is Michael." His gracious smile and glance to each of the guests did not require a response. They sat back comfortably, though everyone was interested in the folders. Jimmy spun his chair gently back and forth. They looked up and gave him their full attention.

"Jack has selected some of the wines for tonight and Raymondo will be here to pour for you." He waved an open hand toward the sommelier, who was preparing to cork a bottle of champagne. "He'll give you a short description of each wine."

After removing the wire and foil from around the cork, the sommelier pulled the bottle from the ice and neatly wrapped a white linen cloth around the bottom. He handed it to Michael. "But first the House would like to propose a toast." He presented the bottle to Jack, who put on his glasses to inspect the label. "Jack, this is from our private collection. It's a semi-dry rosé from Epernay, 1974."

"Michael, that's wonderful. Thank you." Jack looked up as Michael handed him the cork. Holding the large bottle with two hands, he gingerly filled the eight glasses on a tray held by Raymondo.

When all the glasses were poured, Michael had half a glass in one hand and held out both arms. "Jack, to you and the great work you've done with your restaurant. We'll miss you, but now that you're closed, I'm sure we'll see our own food and beverage sales increase dramatically."

"Well, you can't sail a ship without a crew." Jack held out his glass to the table, and everyone drank.

"Bravo, Jack." Michael finished his champagne and placed the glass on the side table. "Charles will bring out some hors d'oeuvres and I'll be back later to tell you about the dinner selections. Please use this to ring me if there's anything you need." He pulled a small device from his jacket pocket and placed it next to Jack's setting. About the size of a pack of gum, it was ivory in color with a single button. "I'll be standing by."

Michael and the waiter left, closing the door gently behind them. At that point, Raymondo began the presentation of the wines. Jack took the small device and handed it to Phil, telling him to put it inside the duffel bag.

After closing the door, Michael walked down the emergency stairs one flight to his office. He closed the door behind him and pressed two buttons on his cell phone. He began speaking rapidly in Italian.

"What do you mean there's no signal? I've just put it on the table. You tested it!" He was getting upset but kept his voice low. "You heard him say what? Put it in the bag?" Michael got up and poured a Scotch from the wet bar. "Shit. Switch to Line Two." He knocked back the drink. "I know the damned pickup is in the center of the room. Turn up the bloody gain then!" A pause. "And he's asked for the music to be turned up. Well, that's just fine, Angelo. I suggest you get a video feed on him and find me a damn lip reader." He was about to hang up the phone when he listened closer. "He's dimmed the lights as well?" With nothing else to say, he shut the phone and tossed it on his desk. The slightest hint of a grin crossed his face. He would simply tell the men he'd done what he could. But what could Jack possibly be running out of a boat and a restaurant that was so important? He smiled to himself. This man certainly was smooth.

Angelo sat at the controls of the high-tech audio equipment. The club's security office routinely made surreptitious audio and video recordings of all meetings in the private dining rooms as well as the residence spaces, sauna, and office service areas. They also monitored web traffic and communications through the club's WiFi network. He didn't know what was so important about this dinner party, but he was told to check and recheck all equipment and to make sure that there were no mistakes. Upstairs the wine service began.

• • •

"Well, this a pleasure Jack. You've put together a wonderful selection tonight." Raymondo began his presentation of the wines from the end of the table opposite Jack. The door opened and Charles the waiter rolled in with a table draped to the floor in off-white linen. On it were two three-tiered hors d'oeuvre trays. He placed them on the table and left without a word, taking the cart with him. Raymondo continued as they began the hors d'oeuvres.

"There will be fish and vegetable courses to start and some meats toward the end of the meal. We have two whites and two reds and of course cordials and cigars can be found in the piano bar after dinner." As he spoke, he placed an ice bucket on the table. Everyone was impressed by the selection and realized it was to be quite a meal. Jack had mentioned very little about tonight's meeting.

"First, we have a Sauvignon Blanc from Sancerre. It's a rosé from the town of Bué. This town is known for having a 'white soil' of clay and shells rather than the typical limestone of the region. This gives us a fruitier wine that's best young. We had only a few of last year's bottling and that's what Jack has chosen. I would recommend this with the hors d'oeuvres." He looked around at the table. Mike and Jimmy were digging into the hors d'oeuvres. Pamela and Sarah had eaten two each. Jack, Phil, and Remus had none. Phil was arranging some paperwork.

Jack nodded to Raymondo. "Thanks, Raymondo. We'd love to start with the Sancerre. And please, tell us about the Gaya as you pour. We can continue with the reds later."

Raymondo nodded, thinking, *That was pretty classy — cut the shit and leave us alone. Whatever. This guy knows how to tip, and he's got good taste in wine.*

"And make sure you taste everything," Jack said to Raymondo as he uncorked the bottle.

"No problem, Jack. Thanks." He tasted the wine, poured Jack's glass first and began talking about the Gaya as he poured for the rest of the table.

"The other white selection is a chardonnay, Gaia & Rey. The vintage is 1982. It's from the Langhe in Northern Italy and is one of the only whites Gaja produces. It's a very rare wine and 1982 was a particularly good year there. Nice choice, Jack."

"All right, Raymondo, that was great. Tell Charles I'll buzz him when we're ready for the food."

Raymondo closed the door behind himself. He'd worked much harder for cheap wine. *Fine, serve yourselves for the next hour*, he thought. *But Gerard's not going to be happy holding the first of seven courses that long. I'll tell Michael and let him deal with it.* He went down to the crew lounge for a cigarette and the start of the Nascar race.

Everyone was enjoying the first glass of wine, nibbling and chatting. Jack reached into his briefcase for the phone and dialed Mike's number. He stood up and went close to the window with the phone, and no one took any notice. As it rang Mike looked around and then at his case. Befuddled, he reached inside and pulled it out. He looked at it as it rang again. Everyone was looking at him as he answered it.

"Hello?" he said.

"She's got nice legs, eh?" Jack spoke softly into the phone so no one could hear.

"I beg your…" Mike looked over at Jack.

Jack turned around and held out the phone. "I'm sorry, Mike. Was that you?" Jack was grinning.

Everyone laughed and began pulling out their phones and pressing buttons. Pamela was first to get a call through, and it was Remus' phone that rang. He picked it up with a smile as he looked around the table. Jimmy's rang and he couldn't figure out how to answer it.

Jack remained standing. "Okay, we all have a new cell phone."

Jimmy's phone kept ringing, but he put it down and reached for his cigarettes. Phil reached over and shut it off.

Jack laughed, "Jimmy, this is a non-smoking room."

"So, arrest me," he said as he lit up.

"Okay." Jack pressed a few buttons on his phone and Jimmy's rang again.

Jimmy picked up the phone and tossed it into his valise. He sat back and smoked. It kept ringing until Mike pulled it out and shut it off.

"Okay, the phones work." Jack put his down. "Pamela's done a nice job setting them up and she's put together most of the info in the brief." Jack turned to Pamela with a warm smile. "She also picked out the leather bags for everyone and chose the phone colors."

She replied with the dazzling sparkle of a sophomore. "I tried to match personalities."

Jack picked up the first folder. Each one had a heavy plastic cover. The pages inside were coated stock held together at the side by a long flat clamp. It was all very durable.

"Pamela will tell you all you need to know about the phone. Basically, it's the family plan. You're all covered for unlimited text, data, and Internet in Europe. Thanks to Pamela, there's a lot of numbers already in the phone — all of our numbers, and other useful contacts for places we're going." Jack opened the dossier and looked at the first page for a moment.

"Okay, let me go through some of my contacts and then Pamela can give you some more details. Phil's also got some interesting info on the boat." He drank some of his water and began.

"I have a banker in Italy — Milan actually. It's Vic's other brother, Michele Sindano. Everyone will be paid by direct deposit, and you each have an account set up with a debit card. Of course, if you want to take care of your own finances, that's fine, too. We'll all meet him once we're in San Remo. Hopefully in June."

A drink of wine. "I'll say he's a sharp financier. He's been managing my family's estate for years. If anyone's interested in investments, he'd be an excellent guide. We can also think about investing in something jointly between all of us, if anyone's interested. In any case, he's a fascinating character and I'm sure it'll be fun to have him over for dinner. He's also got some interesting friends.

"There's some information on him in the back of this folder and his number's in your phone. I also have a lawyer in Italy who can take care of anything in Europe.

His name is Paul Marzincus. Let me say one thing clearly. If anything serious ever happens to any of you, you call me first. If you can't get me, it's Phil. And if you can't get either of us, you call Mr. Marzincus. If you're traveling and have passport problems, lose your ID, car accident, mugging, hospital, arrested, whatever. We'll keep it in-house and he'll deal with it."

No one moved. It was all very compelling, and everyone was listening closely. No one really had any idea what the trip would be like. Up until now everything had been vague and romantic at best. The table was silent, and Jack went on.

"Good. There's also a few shipping agents listed. Each one is a specialist in his own game. If you need to send something stateside or have something sent over to Europe — anything big or special that needs to cross borders — I'm sure one of these will be your best bet." Jack picked up his wine and drank before sitting down. "That's about it for me. Pamela's got some interesting local color."

Pamela had both of her hands on her dossier. When Jack finished, she stood up slowly with a lovely movement.

She smiled and her lipstick was perfect. It was a rich, glossy fire engine red. Her lips were beautifully proportioned to her facial features and suited to this dramatic style of makeup. A statement of their own, her lips could not outshine the shade of her bright green eyes, deep and dark. They contrasted the hue of her lips with similar temperature. The neckline of the crème-colored silk blouse was cut just wide enough to feature her shoulders. The skirt was a Wedgewood blue silk that reached her mid-thigh. A dramatic beauty, she was not only gorgeous and sexy, but also very smart.

"I've made a list of the port cities where we'll be staying. There's also a list of suppliers and a calendar of market days. As Jack mentioned, your phone is loaded with all the contacts. Names, numbers, email, websites, and physical addresses." She paused and sipped her wine. Everyone at the table was looking at this dossier, the thickest of the three, with a curious air. Jimmy was beginning to play with his phone.

"For each port city, as well as some interesting nearby towns, I've included restaurants, bars, museums, and some history of the area. There's train schedules, airport, and taxi info, and addresses of the marinas where we'll be staying. All of this in in your phones as well. There'll be a small van or some kind of vehicle at the dock everywhere we go. The taxi drivers I've listed speak English and have been very helpful to me. If anyone needs a rental or a driver for something, I can take care of it. I'll also be able to help with things like banking, insurance, and accounting. The laundry and dry cleaning, linens, uniforms, and personal clothing, will be handled locally, off the boat. It's a big boat but with all of us living there it's bound to get cozy, so we won't be doing any laundry on board. Oh, and we're all going to be fitted for new work outfits by Jack's tailor. Jack, what was the man's name? I forget and I don't have my glasses." Mike wondered what she looked like in reading glasses. Remus and Jack both knew.

"Gamaretti. He's in Rome," Jack said to everyone. He was eating some bread.

"Yes, Gamaretti. He's a wonderful man and his shop is amazing." She looked at Jack.

"Third generation Roman," Jack would offer no more information as he reached for an olive. Jack had been to this very shop more than thirty years ago.

"There's a few styles we can choose from, and the fabrics are to die for." Pamela was pleased with this. She went on.

"As we all know, Remus has done the final finish on all the interior woodwork, and this will require some regular upkeep. Mike, Jack thought you might be able to help with this and some of the maintenance." She paused and Mike looked up. Unsure if he should answer, he said, "Sure. I always wanted to learn French polish. And I love how Italians do their laundry. Just hang it out from your windows."

"Most of it's done by hand," Jack was looking at his phone and then looked up. "But we won't be hanging our laundry out on the boat."

"Literally or figuratively?" Mike said. There was no response to this comment.

"Mike is also going to be journaling the trip. It will be uploaded to the website once a week." No one, least of all Mike, had considered this. A website?

"Mike will also be handling public relations. This includes press releases for the web and print as well as radio and television contacts for local cable and satellite broadcast." Pamela stopped. It was quite a delivery, and everyone was captivated. She drank some water. It still sounded incredible. "There's also business cards. Everyone has their own. One thing about this boat is that this whole concept is for sale. If anyone manages to make an initial contact that ends up in a sale, there's a finder's fee. This would be a percentage of something like twenty million for the boat. You can talk to Jack about that." Pamela looked at Jack; she was on fire but still poised.

Jack got up and grabbed the next bottle of Sancerre. "Thanks, Pamela, that was beautiful." He filled her glass. "And the dossiers are dynamite. Great job."

Most everyone had at least two of the files out of their valise and all were deeply engrossed. Sarah responded first. "Pamela, this is quite a project. You must've been working on it for months." Sarah drank some wine and watched Pamela closely. The others nodded and agreed. "You've been working on a lot of things without anyone knowing. You've been to all these places, haven't you?" Sarah held a slight frown with a sly grin. Looking straight at Pamela, and then to Jack.

"Yessss, we have," said Pamela. To see a gorgeous woman like Pamela blush and look out of the corner of her eye (at Jack) is worth a million words.

"I thought so! You two went to Europe the last two vacations! I knew it!" Sarah sat back and looked up at Jack, who was filling her wine. "Thank you, sir — dog."

"Phil, you're up." Jack didn't waste a moment. "Let's get the rest of this out of the way before the food starts." Jack reached for an hors d'oeuvre.

"Right." Phil stayed in his seat as the humorous air dissipated.

"The last folder is the ship's information. The boat's a hundred twenty-nine feet long and has a gross displacement of sixteen hundred tons. It's named, or will be christened at launch, Motor Yacht *Prospect Due*. Designed and built by Tenyon Shipbuilders, DeSoto, Missouri. It's registered to Prospect Due Ltd. in Naples. We all work for an Italian company now. As Pamela mentioned, we'd love to sell it and build another one so the ship's info here will help familiarize everyone with the details. The first three pages include all the physical and mechanical specs: the ship's dimensions, range, tankage, and the materials used in the build. There's also a complete list of the plumbing and electrical components as well as the entertainment system and galley equipment."

Very little had been said about the boat. In fact, it wasn't until nearly five years after Jack made the deal with John that anyone, other than Remus and Phil, knew about it. It was now becoming clear that this was a very big project. Jack sat back and listened, and the table was quiet.

"The second item is the promotional brochure." Phil picked up one off the table and leafed through. Everyone at the table had his or hers out, looking at them. It was eight by ten inches of heavy gloss stock. The six pages of drawings, photographs, and layout were elegantly styled and detailed.

"What we're selling first is the services available. It's fine dining at its core and our target market is executive corporate service. We're featuring the video conferencing for meetings and communications. The following pages describe the boat as a catering and private dining facility for special events. We'll have cooking events available and performances by Remus. The audio/visual system is unique and will probably raise some eyebrows on the tech network." Accentuating this last statement, he proudly arched his eyebrows in mock dignity.

"The arrangement of the three cameras, and the three screens can be configured many different ways. We plan to assemble an archive of the food content filmed in the cooking and prep areas. This can be displayed in real time on the two large screens and will also be recorded and uploaded to our server. I'll also be audio and video recording Remus' performances. All of this material, the cooking and the music, will be available for broadcast. The series will be called *Live at Jack's*. The goal is to start generating as much content, income, and interest as possible, as soon as possible."

Silence. Most of them didn't know anything about these things. Jack had been very careful in the beginning to keep the projects compartmentalized and the effect was impressive. Phil got up to fill his wine and noticed a few other glasses in need. He poured as he talked, working his way around the table.

"We have about a thousand of the printed copies of the brochure to give out and there's also a pdf version on your phone that you can send. The other thing we're selling is the boat itself."

He put the empty wine back in the bucket and sat down. "Basically, the boat is for sale now. If it were to sell, it would be sold as a business, and we would all stay on as independents while we build another. And as Pamela mentioned, any contact that results in a sale will generate a finder's fee. Whether it's a facility gig, media sale, or sale of the boat, the finder gets a cut. The idea is if we can make this work here in the Mediterranean, it should also work in New York, San Francisco, Amsterdam…" Phil shrugged.

"Woohoo, Amsterdam! Jack why don't we go to Amsterdam first?" Jimmy finished his glass and got up to get more.

"Because Jimmy, we're not going to Amsterdam first. You can go to Amsterdam as often as you like," Jack replied calmly.

Sarah rolled her eyes and sat back. "How big *is* this boat we're all going to be living on?"

Phil blinked and nodded. "Okay. The first thing to keep in mind is that we're going to be in some of the greatest port cities in France, Spain, and Italy. There will be down time when there's nothing happening on the boat, and I'm sure there's going to be lots to do on shore. Yes, we'll all be living on the boat, but we have connections to find pretty much anything we need on shore. Including a gym, yoga, cat food…" Phil bent forward toward Sarah for the benefit of the last sentence. She stuck out her tongue and folded her arms.

"To answer your question, if you look at the overhead plan of the boat, we're all up forward. We each have our own cabin, and each has a large portlight and deck prisms. They're nice."

Mike held up a finger and Phil gave him an upward nod. "Mike, what's up?"

"What's a deck prism?" Mike asked.

"It's a big piece of cut glass mounted into the deck that lets light into the cabin below. It's like an eight-sided pyramid with the bottom flush with the deck. These are one of John's early specs. It's a traditional feature of old wooden boats. If you look at it from above, on deck, it looks like an octagon set flush into the deck. John had these custom-ground and they're a bit oversized. But the light it lets in is incredible. See, on the inside looking up at it, the octagon comes down to a point. They're about eighteen inches in diameter and the point of the octagon, like an eight-sided pyramid, comes down nine inches. They're clear glass and each one weighs about twenty-five pounds. The cabins have nice paneling, reading lights above the bunks, which are all queen-sized, and a small desk. They're cozy. Trust me, you'll be pleased. We'll all go out next week and see it."

This satisfied Sarah for the moment. She looked like a twelve-year-old as her mind wandered out the window trying to imagine her cabin on a big wooden boat with her cat there was an excited air of travel in the room.

"Sarah, you and Remus each have your own shower, and Jimmy, Mike, and I will share another one in the forepeak. One thing that makes the design of this boat unique is that yachts of this size usually have crew quarters for five or six, plus guest cabins for six or eight. But there are no guest cabins on this boat. This means the lower level and main salon are combined into one large space with a very high ceiling. All of the interior paneling is from The Theatre. It's really pretty dramatic and there's certainly no other boat like it. So, we'll be showing it fairly regularly. We plan to have it featured in a few of the boat shows and yachting magazines." Phil looked at Jack, who nodded slightly.

"The last thing is The Theatre. Everyone's been wondering what's going to happen to the space when we leave. And of course, there have been lots of rumors. But like the boat, Jack's keeping things…" Phil stopped, Jack was making circles with his hand, gesturing for him to come out with it.

Phil carried on dutifully. "Right, so Jack traded John the Theatre for the boat minus all the interior paneling and the stage. John is going to travel with us and drive the boat during the first season or so. Then he's going to rebuild the interior and put another restaurant in it." Phil laughed and everyone was silent. He paused and continued, "Anyway we're planning on shipping the boat from Miami in about six weeks, around the middle of March. We'll meet in San Remo a few weeks later, and the boat should arrive in another week or so after us."

Jimmy reached for his cigarettes. "Bullshit. How come you never mentioned any of this?"

Mike put his hand behind Sarah's shoulder stealthily and dug in with his thumb. She responded by sitting up straight and putting her hand on Mike's thigh.

Remus let out an uncharacteristic laugh, pulled out a thin cigar, and stood up. "I'll be in the bar."

"I'm with you, Remus." Jimmy stood up as well. "I need something more than this rosé wine. They gotta have whiskey here."

"Rosé is what you drink in the south of France in the summer," Jack said to Jimmy as he walked to the door.

"Whatever, man." Jimmy went out the door.

"Mike, you ever work a grill?" Jack pulled out a cigar.

"Sure, boss. Whatever you need. Just give me some back-up." He put his arm on the back of his chair facing Sarah from the side.

She ran her hand up his arm to his shoulder and stood. "I've got to use the ladies."

Pamela got up to join her and the door closed behind them.

Jack blew a sputtering laugh from his lips. Phil put his folders back in the valise and tossed it on top of the duffel. Mike poured himself another glass of wine.

"So much for surprises." Jack said. He stood up.

"I think it's great," Mike said enthusiastically.

Phil stood up and went to the window. "It'll work. With or without Jimmy."

"If we got the right people, we can do anything. Come on. Let's go down to the bar." Jack looked over as Charles came into the room with a strange look on his face. Raymondo followed him in and went to the wine cart.

Jack spoke to Charles. "Listen, Charles, let's do the first few courses set up family-style, say two big platters with everything on each, okay? Open two of the cold Gaja y Rey now, and bring us some new glasses for the Barolo. In fact, you can open two of the Barolos now as well. Then if Gerard's not too upset, he can plate the beef and lamb dishes, each on separate platters, and bring them out when the first round is done." Jack had a questioning tone. "Are we okay with that?" He looked at Charles clearing the glasses and straightening the place settings.

"No problem Jack." He didn't look up. He would tell Michael, who would inform Gerard of the changes. The chef would most certainly throw a fit, and Charles would do his best to stay out of the kitchen.

"Good. We'll be in the bar. When we come back up you can start with the fish." Jack nodded sideways for Mike and Phil to follow him out. They walked into the corridor and Jack looked around. Phil pointed to the right. "This way."

They got into the elevator and Jack had the unlit cigar in his mouth. Phil pressed the button, and they were all looking at their shoes on the blue carpeting.

Jack took the cigar out of his mouth and said, "Well?"

"If anybody knows how to piss off the chef at the Clayton Club, it's you Jack." Mike was enjoying the ride. Phil laughed.

"Nah. It's easier for them this way." Jack pulled out his lighter as the elevator door opened. The atmosphere that greeted them was subdued with dark lighting and chatter. There was a piano player and vocalist duet on a small stage in the corner. A few people were smoking, but the air was clear. They spotted Jimmy, Remus, and the girls.

Jimmy watched them come over with an irritated air. Jack noticed the glass in his hand and the empty next to his ashtray. Bad barman.

"So, Jack. What's with all the secrecy? How come you gotta wait 'til now to let us all in on the whole game?" There was a bit of ambient noise, but Jimmy was being loud. He was pointing with his glass.

Jack stepped close to Jimmy but spoke so the others could hear. "What's that?

Old Grand Dad or Dickel bourbon?" Jack picked up the empty and hailed the bartender for two more.

The double whiskeys came and Jack took one. It was getting louder at the bar and Jack had to shout. "Would you rather I'd told you all my personal thoughts along the way while I figured it all out and made changes? Well guess what, that's not the way it's going. This is how I did it and that's how it is. If you don't like it, you can go back to running craps out back of The Seven's Top." Jack drank the shot. The others busied themselves with the surroundings, but the tension was apparent.

"Thanks, Jack."

"Jimmy. Listen, I also need somebody to look after a pair of Cat C3512s." Jack watched this slowly sunk in.

Jimmy had his glass to his lips and blinked in mid-sip. "Where'd you get those?"

"John Tenyon found them in New Orleans. Came out of a brand-new tugboat that had a fire and never launched. There's like three hundred hours on each."

"What? They're friggin' barely burned in. I know that engine. It's a workhorse." Jimmy answered without moving. "How…"

"I know you know that engine. Same as the one in a lot of the rigs you've been working on all these years. And now we got a complete set of new spares for each. Injectors, oil coolers, raw water pumps, and more. And a nice set of tools," Phil added.

"I prolly rebuilt three of those. Now I know you're full of it." Jimmy finished his whiskey. "You fuck, you knew about this too and didn't say anything?" He laughed and held up his glass.

Phil shrugged. "We'll go out and see 'em tomorrow. And the tools. You'll freak." Phil was serious. He knew Jimmy had a penchant for big diesel engines and Jack thought it might be just the thing to keep him in line and out of the whorehouses and bars. Maybe.

Remus was talking to a woman next to him, whom he seemed to know. Mike and Sarah drifted off into an unrelated conversation.

• • •

Upstairs at that moment, Charles walked into the crew lounge, unable to find Michael. Two of the cooks were there smoking. One had a glass of wine, the other a Budweiser. They both looked at him expectantly.

192

"What's up with VIP west? Can we start with the first course?" The one with the wine asked.

"In a minute. But he wants everything plated family-style on platters. Served in two courses."

"What?" Budweiser stubbed out his butt. "We been working on this menu for three days! What about the garnishes!"

Wineglass finished his drink and laughed. "You go tell Gerard. He wants to go home now. It'll be easier this way."

"No. Where's Michael? He can tell Gerard."

The cooks shook their heads. No one had seen Michael recently.

"Shit. I've got to find him." Charles left the lounge.

Michael was presently in the security office berating Angelo the audio tech. "What do you mean you've got nothing from the past hour!" He was spitting. "Get another recording device up there and put it in the fucking peppermill if you have to!"

Angelo was sure he was going to lose his job. The dark, grainy video from the "smoke detector" had shown that most of the business had been discussed, and the paperwork had been put away. His experience told him they'd been foiled tonight and there was nothing more to be gained from the meeting. Angelo took a further step.

"This guy is obviously covering his tracks. I don't think we'll get any more tonight. But let me try the bar. They might go down for a smoke. I might be able to get you something from there."

"It's a little late for that Angelo. For your sake, I hope you come up with something."

Michael picked up his phone and left the office. Rome had called twice during the day and was waiting for transcripts of the dinner conversations. In a few hours, he would have to make a call saying he had nothing.

• • •

Pamela knew the singer and had gone over to talk to her and the pianist during their break. Sarah and Mike were in close conversation with Sarah doing most of the talking. Remus had motioned to Jack and was introducing him to a very attractive younger woman. Jimmy and Phil were still at the bar and had each ordered another round.

Sarah excused herself and Mike moved over to speak to Jimmy. "Come on, man. This is a trip of a lifetime. Hey, if you got something better to do, let me know!"

"No, I got nothing better to do. I just want to know what I'm getting into." Jimmy considered his drink but didn't raise it.

Phil lifted his glass to Jimmy. "Listen, Jack's right. You put something like this together and you gotta go slow. One piece at a time. And that's what he did. And now it's happening and we're all in. Right?" Phil took a drink.

"Yeah. But I feel like there's something we don't know about this trip. He's like a master of intrigue. What is this, a spy novel? I wonder what else he's not telling us?"

"Jimmy. It's a boat. That's all. Same thing as the restaurant, just a different place. Simple as that. If there was any more to it, I'd tell you." Phil was lying and Mike knew it. "Plus, it's in Europe. Duh!"

"Yeah, I guess you're right." Jimmy finished his whiskey and turned a new leaf. "Come on, let's eat." Jimmy was loud again. Mike looked at Jimmy and then Phil, who looked away.

Sarah returned and they were all reunited at the bar. Jack and Remus put down their cigars and the music started up. Jack leaned over to the bartender. "Johnny, can you tell Charles we're headed back up?"

The bartender nodded. "I got you Jack."

Mike looked at Phil's empty glass. "Hey man, can we hang out for a minute?"

Phil met his gaze as Mike picked up his glass with a bit left. Phil didn't drink much but he enjoyed it. He considered the importance of the dinner upstairs and the fact that he didn't know when, if ever, he'd be back at this bar with a ride home, "You bet."

"Hey Jack, Mike and I are gonna finish our drinks. Okay if we come up in a few?"

"Sure, no rush."

Mike looked over to the bartender who was conveniently near and watching them. He looked at their glasses with a slight upward nod. Mike waved at their glasses. Without a word he returned, put down the drinks and walked away.

"Phil, tell me, what is Europe all about? I mean, I'm in. It all sounds great. I'm going to write about it, we're going to travel. And Sarah... But what's it all about?"

Phil spun in the comfortable high back barstool with armrests and took a good draft of his Scotch. There was a fair amount of ambient noise and after a few drinks they were probably talking a bit louder than they should.

"She's a hot babe." Phil said. Mike nodded, not what he wanted to talk about.

Jack not only trusted Phil, but he also knew that at this point whatever Phil knew was okay to share with Mike. What none of them knew was that Johnny the bartender had $500 in his pocket for placing the small bar top lamp with a tiny microphone directly in front of them. And that Michael would finally have something to send to Salvi's team in Rome. It wouldn't matter. Salvi would be dead in a few days. The end of his own road.

Phil nodded. "Jack tell you about the sculpture scam?"

Mike nodded. "Yeah."

"Cool. Mike, whatever *Europe* is, it's different for everybody. For me, it's a dream come true. I get to produce and hopefully broadcast an incredible audio/video project. Jack's given me free reign; equipment, contacts, and an unlimited source of talent. That's what it is to me." He shrugged. "For you it's different but kind of the same. You're a writer and you got an unlimited new world of source material. What else do you need to know?" He finished his drink.

Mike looked down at his drink. "Yeah, I guess." He took an extra big gulp and coughed. Phil glanced at Johnny who came over and silently refilled the glasses.

"Listen Mike, whatever it is to Jack is his business. He knows what he's doing and you gotta trust him. If you don't, then man, that's your problem. We're all gonna find out more about Jack, and each other and what it's all about. It's like Jimmy getting pissed off about not being told about everything from the start. It's a work in progress and the plan is nobody's business but Jack's. Hey, I know how he operates. It's gonna morph and develop and change. He doesn't plan the end in the beginning. And by the way, don't be like Jimmy coming on to Jack like he did. There's no calling him out and if you want to try, you better have your fucking ducks in a row. Jimmy may be on his way out if you ask me."

"Fuck no. How would that be that possible?"

"Nobody's irreplaceable."

"But who would cook with Sarah?"

Phil laughed. "I don't know man, probably you."

"Me?! Uh uh, no way, I could never..." Mike now had much more than he cared to think about. His notions of living with Sarah on the boat was vague at best with its own share of unknown dark corners. Not to mention doing espionage for a political terrorist who probably operates on the dark side of history.

Phil pulled out a twenty and put it on the bar. "Let's go."

They didn't speak on the way up to the dining room.

• • •

The remaining five had crowded into the elevator and as the doors closed, the sounds of the bar disappeared. Those nine seconds going up were as quiet as they'd ever been together.

Jack was impishly content as he looked at the group in the mirror. He was back in the saddle, barreling along in a locomotive, somewhere between the edge of control and chaos. In ten weeks, they'd all be in Italy.

Mike and Phil entered the private dining room and Jimmy roared, "Where the fuck you guys been! Fuckin' food is great!" He was drunk. Jack made an uncharacteristic *I don't know* face, drank some wine and continued with his Dover sole. He was enjoying everything.

Mike sat down next to Sarah. She and Pamela were talking about something on their plates and pointing at one of the platters. Sarah gracefully picked up her napkin and with her free hand, gave a tight squeeze to Mike's upper thigh.

Mike sat up straight and said, "Ooh everything smells good."

Jack motioned with his fork, "Have some sole while it's warm."

Michael had followed the boys in and was busying himself at the side table.

"Michael, what's next? Was it lamb?" Jack called over to Michael.

"Yes, Jack. We have the lamb loin. The medallions are Francese style, warm with juniper, lemon and mint. We also have the duck legs confit."

"Great! Bring 'em on. And let's have the decanter of Gaya Barolo. Jimmy, how 'bout some red wine?"

"Fuck yeah!"

The meal was truly spectacular. For the finale Chef Gerard himself came up and prepared the flambe' of cherries in crêpes with vanilla bean ice cream. There was plenty of *Beaumes de Venise,* some Spanish brandy and coffees all around. The evening gently wound down, Jimmy calmed down, and it was a great night. One of many to come.

Jack and Pamela stayed at the club and Martin drove Remus, Jimmy, and Phil back to Samson. Mike arranged for a limo and he and Sarah made love twice on the ride back to her place. He thought about throwing the cat off her bed, but played it safe. They didn't fall asleep until well after sunrise.

• • •

The boat was loaded onto the freighter in Miami and John insisted on traveling with it. At the last minute it was decided that one of the engineers who installed the stabilizers would come for the shakedown cruise and also join John on the delivery to Genoa. There were some minor mechanical projects to be finished, and John wanted to add another coat of bottom paint.

Jimmy had always wanted to visit Amsterdam, and he spent two weeks there before he was scheduled to meet everyone in Genoa. He'd never been outside the state of Missouri, and it was an eye-opening experience for him, on many levels.

Jack and Phil met in Nice a few days early and were there to help John when the boat was launched from the freighter and docked in Genoa. From the moment it went into the water it leaked like hell. Jack and Phil nearly freaked out. For more than twelve hours they sat in the boat with all the floorboards up watching water pour in through every seam below the water line. John reassured them this was normal as they drank nearly four bottles of wine. It was past midnight when the seams finally swelled back up, and the torrent dwindled to a trickle. The pumps began to cycle and eventually pumped for just a few seconds every ten minutes or so.

Jimmy arrived two days later and the following morning they delivered the boat to their first home port of Imperia. It was a ten-hour trip, their first in open sea, and to everyone's relief, uneventful. It was a beautiful day, and the boat handled nicely.

Mike and Sarah flew to Barcelona and took a leisurely fifteen-day drive to Imperia in Italy. They rented three different farmhouses, shopping, cooking, and drinking their way through the Pyrenees Mountains, Provence France, and into Piedmont in Northern Italy.

Pamela and Remus arrived a week after the others. Once they were all there, Jack set about organizing his rendezvous with Lorenzo.

They all settled comfortably into their cabins on the boat. Fortunately, they'd been practically living together back in the states and knew each other well enough. Jimmy and Sarah checked out the markets, butchers, and fishmongers. Pamela hired a driver who was happy to take the two of them around, translate, and give them plenty of local information. Sarah had gotten an Italian/English dictionary and a few phrase books and was not afraid of trying to speak to locals in town. She was impressed by Mike's fluency in Italian and his ability to engage strangers and make them smile and laugh. Jimmy made no effort to learn Italian and spent most of his free time at an American sports bar that had a large TV.

Remus was acclimating by playing the piano on the boat every day and also in the evenings. The setting and the sound of the piano was quite different from The Theatre. But the main cabin had a warmth all its own. Phil was tuning the sound system for the piano and everyone agreed he was finding the sweet spot. A local piano tuner came in after Remus arrived, but it wasn't the same as having old Helmut there. Jack understood this and suggested they try a few more until Remus found a guy he liked. Vivien, their agent in San Remo, found a small cabaret in the old town with a piano and arranged for Remus and Pamela to play and sing there twice a week.

The first trip with guests wasn't for another five weeks and Jack wanted to spend at least a week outside Rome with the boat. Mike had been in contact with Lorenzo at least once a week since he returned from his trip to Rome. He kept Lorenzo up to date with plenty of details about the boat, and as always, told him exactly what Jack had instructed him to say.

Jack had not seen or spoken to Lorenzo in over nine years and wanted to meet with him first on neutral ground. He chose the island of Elba, he'd spent lots of time there during his years in Italy and always enjoyed the old port and rugged coastline. Pamela arranged for a car to take him down to the airport in Florence. The three-hour drive brought Jack back in time thru the countryside and the helicopter ride from Florence out to Elba was spectacular. He'd forgotten how blue the Mediterranean could be. After a short walk to Porto Ferrario, he took a seat inside a small café. The gentleman behind the bar recognized him immediately and came around to his table with open arms.

"Licio, so good to see you! It's been too long! Everything good?"

Speaking the Italian language came back in an instant as he stood and accepted the customary kiss on both cheeks.

"Davio. Yes, things are good. You haven't changed a bit." Jack held his belt, smiling at Davio's, which had indeed changed.

"Ahh, Licio, if anyone knows we're blessed by the food here, it's you. We need to eat like there's no tomorrow!" He smiled warmly, looking Jack in the eye.

It was around 11:30 a.m. and a few of the dishwashers and cooks were eating at a corner table. "You must be hungry. Sit, let me get you something."

Jack had a lot on his mind and wasn't really hungry. But he wasn't about to insult Davio by not eating. "Thank you, Davio. Anything. Whatever you're having." He motioned toward the crew table.

Davio brought out a small carafe of red wine, a piece of bread, and a bowl of the soup. "Here. Buon appetito. We'll talk in a minute."

The classic tomato broth stew was made with various pieces of different sized fish, fennel, garlic, and herbs. Jack had forgotten how good this kind of simple food was and how hard it was to find. All you had to do was visit the place where it had originated. It was eaten with a spoon and also your fingers. And there was always a pile of clean bones and shells left on the side of the plate.

After clearing the food, Davio sat and joined him, pouring himself a glass of wine from the carafe. "Licio, what happened to you? We missed you. Nobody could tell us a thing. What have you been doing?"

Jack didn't want to talk much and carefully changed the subject to food. He remembered how the soup was made, like he'd made it yesterday. The strange flat shrimp didn't have much meat, but they were always getting caught in the nets. They were sliced in half lengthwise and then simmered in fresh water with tomatoes and fennel. After an hour or so, the whole thing was strained and pressed through a sieve, leaving a beautiful red broth with a delicate body and a hint of the ocean and fennel. It was a staple in these coastal area kitchens. After Jack explained how much of his heart was still in Italy, he asked Davio for a favor.

"Davio, I need to rent a house here on the island for a few days. I need to meet with someone, and I'd like some privacy, and a kitchen. Two bedrooms are all I need. Do you know anyone who might have something like this?" The island was only eighty-four square miles, and Davio was an established businessman who'd grown up there. If anyone knew, he would. Davio imagined a romantic getaway with one of the many elegant women, Jack used to travel with. He couldn't be more wrong.

Davio understood what Jack meant by private — away from the port. "Would you like to be able to see the water?" This would undoubtedly be a premium residence.

"Yes, I would." Jack sat back and finished his water. He was hoping Davio could take care of it today, and he did.

Davio pulled out his phone and after a burst of short sentences over three calls said to Jack, "No problem. It's not cheap, but there's a car and the kitchen is very nice."

Jack shrugged. "Is there a bathtub?"

"Of course, and from it you can look west toward the sunset and the sea."

Over the years, Jack had visited Elba regularly, alone and with his parents or a guest, when he had time off. He usually stayed in town by the port, renting an apartment with a kitchen. Davio had always arranged this for Jack and remembered his penchant for top floors, lots of windows, and a large bathtub.

Jack pulled out some cash and motioned toward the table. He wondered how much Davio would make for organizing the rental.

Davio frowned and shook his head. "Licio, please. Put that away. You don't pay me for food."

Jack fingered the bills and looked toward the boy who'd gotten up to plate his stew.

"Whatever you want to do," said Davio.

Jack went over to the crew table and handed the bills to the cook. "Il brodo e squisito."

The boy nodded. "Grazie."

Davio cleared the table, and Jack went to the bar.

"Café?" asked Davio.

"Please."

"Whenever you're ready, I'll have someone pick you up."

Jack said, "Yes."

Davio nodded and made another call as he prepared the espresso.

The ride across the island took about twenty-five minutes. The car was a tiny beat-up old Ford Fiesta. The driver smelled like horses and there was a rifle on the back seat. Jack hoped the house was a bit more refined.

The small villa was spectacular, facing the sea to the west as Davio had described. He got out and grabbed his bag. There was a woman working in the garden and Jack asked, "Who's she?"

"She's the gardener. She lives here," said the driver.

"Tell her to go home," Jack said.

"I can't tell her to go home."

"Okay, I will." Jack walked over to the woman and after a brief conversation and hand movements she smiled and took off her apron. A few more words and they shook hands. She was saying thank you. She walked over to a table to gather her tools, and Jack came back to the car.

"How'd you do that?" The driver was laughing.

"I told her Davio sent me up here to tell her she could have the week off." They laughed.

"Listen, Marco. You're Marco, right?" Jack knew how to say it.

"Yes, sir."

"Good. And listen, Call me Jack."

Marko nodded.

"Ok. I need some things from the market. Can you go down to the port and get them for me?"

"The market is closed now. It's siesta. Everything is closed."

"I know. When you can." Jack handed him some cash. "Tell you what. I'll phone Davio and have him put it together. He'll call you when it's ready. Take this. Whatever's left you can have. Here, give me your number." Jack pulled out the cellphone he got last week. This was the fifth time he'd ever used it. "Here, put it in for me. You know how?"

"Sí."

Jack watched Marco navigate the phone. "Okay. No problem." Marco said. There was plenty of money for the food and ample left over.

The gardener and Marco left at the same time. Jack walked around the house and onto the veranda looking out over the sea. He wanted to forget everything and stay here. He went inside and found the tub. It was perfect.

He called Davio to thank him and give him the grocery list. He also loved the place and wanted to know how much it would sell. A few hours later, Marco dropped off the provisions: a case of water, a few bottles of wine, a bottle of olive oil, cheese, bread, salamis, olives, a basket of plums, lemons, onions, garlic, parsley, a peppermill, some sea salt, a tin of coffee, and a bottle of cream. In a plastic tub were two small sea bass. They were still stiffly bent from rigor mortis. The eyes were clear and the gills were bright red. Jack was sure they'd been brought in after lunch.

His next call was to Mike.

"Get a hold of Lorenzo and tell him I'm on Elba and want to meet him tomorrow, alone. Tell him I'm alone and there's accommodation for him. I'll make dinner."

After hanging up, Jack walked down the narrow stone steps to the water. The afternoon was calm, and he jumped off a rock into the cold water. An hour later, he walked back up to the house and took a bath. When he got out, the sun was low and he opened a bottle of wine. After two glasses, Jack was asleep in a lounge chair on the veranda. The sounds of the surf and a deep purple sunset remained in his subconscious.

CHAPTER EIGHT

Reparations

Later that evening, Mike tried to call Jack, who never heard the phone. He called back in the morning to say Lorenzo would arrive that afternoon around four thirty. Jack knew where the helicopter would land, and he had a driver in mind. Marco's Ford Fiesta would be perfect.

Jack ate one of the fish for lunch, finished the open bottle of wine, and went for a swim. By four o'clock, he'd showered and was sitting on the veranda, waiting for Marco's call.

At four forty-five, Marco called to say Lorenzo had just gotten into the car and they were driving to the villa. Jack had told Marco to take the longer route and to drive fast. Thirty minutes later, the tiny Ford rumbled up the drive and came to a hard stop.

Jack went out to greet Lorenzo and took his bag from the back of the Fiesta. There were no rear seats and the bag had been tossed on top of some gardening tools; it was now very dirty.

Lorenzo got out of the car and stood up brushing off his clothes. It was way too hot for the suit and Jack knew he had the advantage.

"Lorenzo," Jack said. He held out his hand.

"Licio. It's nice to see you." There was no kiss. The handshake alone between these two men, with such a past, was strange to both of them.

Jack thanked Marco and pulled out some money. "Marco, can you bring me two nice fish for dinner? Whatever Dario has."

"Yes, sir. I'll be back soon." Marco accepted the money and got into the car. He liked this guy.

They walked into the villa and Jack put down the bag. Lorenzo looked exhausted. As they stood in front of a side bar, Lorenzo looked through to the veranda.

"What can I get you?"

"Scotch please, Licio. Thank you. Can we have a seat? Outside?"

It seemed to Jack that Lorenzo was slightly out of breath. Jack thought about how rough the ride must have been, but didn't regret it a bit. He had Lorenzo right where he wanted him; he just didn't want him to have a heart attack here at the villa.

"Yes, of course. Let me show you to your room. . ."

"No, Licio. Let's just sit."

"Absolutely." Jack left the bag on the table and carried two glasses and the bottle of Scotch out to the veranda. The sun was on their faces as they both took in the view.

"Licio, you're well?" Lorenzo poured himself some water.

"Yes, I'm fine, thank you, and you?"

"You know some things begin to fail over time. We're all old men at some point."

Jack looked at Lorenzo. He *was* getting old, but Jack had no pity for the man.

Lorenzo sank into the large chair. He was indeed worried about the recordings, but what was even worse was that Jack knew about the sculpture rip off. It was all very personal. The power Jack wielded with the information he had was incalculable. More than he himself had ever had.

"Licio, what do you want? I understand your feelings, but we both need to go forward." Lorenzo pulled himself up in the chair. He knew Jack was not stupid, but neither was he. "Tell me where we stand."

It was both interesting and good that Lorenzo didn't apologize. Jack had no tolerance for apologies. Beneath the hatred there were things Jack respected in Lorenzo. Not the least was his diligence in the battle against communism.

Jack stood up and lit a cigar. He walked to the thick stone railing of the veranda. The sky was changing colors by the minute, and he changed the subject.

"How's the fight? And how is Gianpaulo?" He let the statement hang low and wasn't surprised by Lorenzo's mildly shocked expression. Lorenzo was unable to respond in real-time, so Jack continued. "How lazy you've gotten. Bringing your mole back to Rome and letting him see his ring." Jack laughed. "But thanks for that. I thought I had a hornet's nest, but now I have a hurricane. How utterly crafty. You know the more I thought about it the more I knew it was only you who could've come up with such an idea. It *was* your idea wasn't it?"

Lorenzo tried to suppress a waggish grin. "You know I wasn't exactly serious when I brought it up…"

"Well, it's pure genius." Jack tipped his ash over the veranda and crossed his arms. "Luciani becomes Pope amidst horrific scandal within the Vatican and vows to restore the reputation of his beloved church by 'cleaning house.' But a month into his pontificate he dies, and everything is swept under the rug. Really, Lorenzo…" Jack tossed his cigar and refilled the glasses of Scotch. "Then the Pole comes in with Solidarity and you're all in the clear. Really, it's beautiful."

"Licio, the weather is a complicated system. We're achieving great things. You must understand." Lorenzo wanted to explain that Jack's coming to Italy in the beginning was also his idea and in fact was meant to be a form of reparation. That they'd all felt guilty after the sculpture scam took off. But Lorenzo knew now was not the time to bring this up; it would seem as if he were pleading. Later, after they came to an agreement, would be a more noble time to bring it up.

"Sure. Ask my mother. She died a few months after my father. I'm with you in your war, but I will not forget what you've done to my family." Jack had thought about these words for years and the simplicity of his statement said so.

"I don't care about Gianpaulo, honestly." Jack held out his arms. "But I would like to see him. So, you can arrange it, among other things. I hope he's well."

Lorenzo knew he had a duty to Jack, and that reparations would have to be made. "He is, and we are doing great things. He will want to see you, I'm certain. Believe me, I understand your feelings," he paused. "Licio, I'm asking you, what do you want?"

"I've no need for money. You know that. I have a small crew of cooks and a boat where people can come and eat. No overnight accommodation. I want you to employ us. Indefinitely. Perhaps I can continue the recordings at table. And you can continue to keep tabs on those you wish to." Jack got up, brought the bottle of Scotch to the table, and sat down.

Relief seemed to come over Lorenzo. And also, a moment of deep thought. He'd never considered this, and it was brilliant. He finished his Scotch and regarded Jack in a new light. "I may be able to arrange this." This was interesting, he thought. He waited for Jack to say more.

"Good. Here's how it will work. I'll need at least ten to fifteen bookings a month, dinners for no more than eight. Just like what we did in Rome. You'll pay for the full-time dockage and maintenance of the boat and all the food. You'll also pay my crew. They each get a thousand dollars U.S. for each dinner. There are seven crew members right now, including me. And by the way, none of them know anything about you or what we've talked about."

"And Michael?"

"Mike knows nothing other than what he's told you. And of course, what he's seen. You're welcome to keep an eye on him, but you do not touch him. Do we have an understanding?" Jack was beginning to relax. He'd won.

Lorenzo nodded and held up his glass. "Licio, please."

Jack stood and looked down at the frail figure in the silk suit. "Lorenzo, here, come inside. I'll start a fire." He took the glass from him and held his arm as he stood.

• • •

After Marco dropped off the fish, Jack started cooking and the topic of conversation changed. They talked about their travels together and meals he'd prepared. Jack was both pleased with and surprised by Lorenzo's memory. They both knew there would be great nights to come in the near future. He also made a point of thanking Lorenzo for giving him such an opportunity and experience when he was young. He knew this had been Lorenzo's idea and it was something Jack had always wanted to thank him for.

They talked for hours until Lorenzo could barely stay awake. Jack had opened his laptop and showed Lorenzo the directory for the recordings and let him listen to a few. He was impressed and told Jack he should have used him for more than his cooking. He asked if he could have a copy and Jack declined, making it clear there were three more encrypted copies of the journal, each with explicit instructions should anything happen to him or any of his crew.

Lorenzo was resigned to all of this and they hammered out details on how the bookings would be arranged and who would be likely to use the boat. There was to be nothing less than forty-eight hours of advance notice. Jack described the video system available and made it clear that any day or night cruising with the boat would need to be arranged far in advance and could be canceled for any reason, at any time. Lorenzo was impressed with the brochure and wanted to see the boat as soon as possible.

Lorenzo asked if Jack was still playing the lute. Jack nodded and told him about Remus, Pamela, and the piano but stopped short of telling the story of the encyclical in the leg of the piano; that would come later. "What would we ever have done without Vilotti?" Lorenzo asked.

They were silent, and then Jack said, "You and he will visit the boat. I'll arrange it." Lorenzo nodded. "Yes."

"I'll be in Rome in a week or so. I'd like to have dinner with him."

"Certainly. I will arrange it."

"At the restaurant."

"Of course." Lorenzo paused and finished his drink and chuckled. "The walls do have ears there. You know this all started because we wanted you to come back and cook for us."

"No, this all started because I wanted to know what my lute sounded like in the dining room."

• • •

After Lorenzo went to bed, Jack had another drink and called Davio. It was around nine-thirty and Jack figured Davio was just about to close. "Davio, I hope it's not too late."

"No, Licio, no. I was just counting the money. How's the villa?" Davio had done well on the deal.

"It's very nice. How much?" Jack pictured Davio's face.

"Licio, anything is for sale, at the right price. You know that." Davio perked up.

"Yes, I do. The woman has done a lovely job with the grounds."

"She takes care of the inside, too. She grew up there. Her parents died when she was a child. Tragic, her mother died young after a long illness and shortly after, her father drowned. He was a fisherman. There's a small outbuilding fixed up as an apartment. The family who bought it took her in when she was seven. She's been there ever since. The owners rarely visit."

"She's beautiful," Jack said quietly.

"Yes, she is. And a very interesting woman. She also speaks English, French, Spanish, and Latin, I hear. There must be a thousand books up there at the villa's library and I'm told she's read everything. And she plays the cello to make your heart sing." Davio was practically singing.

Jack could not wait to see her again. "Davio, whatever you can do, do it. I want the house, and the woman can stay. I'll be here for a few more days."

207

Davio looked at his watch. It was not too late to make a few calls. "Licio, I'm at your service. I'll let you know."

"Ciao, e grazie, Davio. Ciao."

"Prego, Licio. Ciao, ciao."

Jack felt flushed and decided on one more drink. He pictured the remarkable woman with the unkempt brown hair and dark brown eyes. He was sure he hadn't felt like this in a long time.

That night, both men slept the deep sleep of relief and resolution. For Jack, there were dreams of restitution mixed with lust and the chance to finally live. Finally free from the shadow of anger that had consumed him for years just as his mother said. Bounty is so much sweeter when it's shared.

There was much more in store for them that coming summer. They were going to travel around the Mediterranean, the crew would make plenty of money, and it wouldn't cost him a penny. He'd never been sure if it would really come together, but it had become more than he'd imagined. His last thought before falling asleep was his mother's voice telling him he could do anything he set his mind to.

• • •

Jack and the crew will return in Yacht Prospect Due
detailing their further adventures in the Mediterranean...